Bad Dreams

BAD DREAMS

KIM NEWMAN

Carroll & Graf Publishers, Inc.
New York

Copyright © 1990 by Kim Newman

Published by arrangement with the author.

First published by Simon & Schuster, London.

First Carroll & Graf edition 1991

Carroll & Graf Publishers, Inc.
260 Fifth Avenue
New York, NY 10001

Library of Congress Cataloging-in-Publication Data

Newman, Kim.
    Bad dreams / by Kim Newman. — 1st Carroll & Graf ed.
      p,   cm.
    ISBN: 0-88184-781-X : $18.95
    I. Title.
    PS3564.E91626B3   1991
    813'.54—dc20   91-27044
                                                          CIP

Manufactured in the United States of America

For The Peace and Love Corporation, Plc.

'First you dream, then you die.'
Cornell Woolrich

The Morning Before

one

JUDI DREAMED she was waking up. Without moving, she got out of the double bed, pulled a rough towel robe over the things she was still wearing, and searched the mess on the carpeted floor for her Camels. She found most of her clothes, relatively unspoiled, mixed up with Coral's. Also three empty Dom Perignon bottles, a shredded Iris Murdoch paperback, some studded leather fripperies and a multi-coloured scattering of pills. Her head was an open wound, leaking steadily, and she had either vomited recently or would do so soon. She hauled her heavy black jacket out of the heap and patted its zippered pockets. No luck. She walked across the room, knees and ankles threatening to fail her, and became acutely aware of the sticky ache between her legs.

Sweet Jesus, did we get raped again?

Most of one wall was mirrored. On this side only, of course. The room beyond was dark. Even if she put her face close to the glass she couldn't see through. It was probably empty this early in the morning. The show was over. She sat at the dressing table and scratched her scalp. The spiky perm was well into its decay. She pulled her handbag open and went through it. The Camels were there, but someone had snapped her disposable lighter in half. Her money, credit cards, diary, hankies and address book were soaked. She stuck the least wet cigarette in her mouth, hoping she would not burn half her face off.

No matches. She would have to wake Coral.

The other girl was still in bed, comatose. She had been twisting and turning as if buried alive. A nylon sheet wound around her like a soiled blue boa constrictor. The bare mattress was missing several buttons, and patterned with old pee, blood and come stains. In the bruising on Coral's back, bottom and legs, Judi could see designs. The yellow and blue smudges were handsome faces with red welts for eyes. The faces coalesced, making a Japanese dragon with heaving shoulderblades for wings and penny-sized scales of ragged flesh.

The little green scorpion tattooed on Coral's wrist scuttled out from under her digital watch and took refuge in her armpit. Judi was back in the bed now, sinking into the mattress, soothing the ruffled dragon with practised massage. She had given up on Coral's matches, and spat the Camel out onto the pillow. The bed hugged her. The duvet slithered up over her bare legs. Judi's eyes turned inward, focusing on a white hot point three inches behind the bridge of her nose. The pain went away.

She was not dreaming she was awake any more. She opened her eyes and saw the skylight. The dingy grey looked about ready to fall. She had always thought Chicken Licken had a better grasp of cosmology than Galileo.

Really awake, she sat up in bed, wearily ready to go through it all again.

That was when she realised she was handcuffed to a severed arm.

two

THE OLD, OLD MAN watched, his own reflection faintly superimposed on the dusty one-way glass. In his current condition, he was glad not to be looking at the silvered side of the mirror. He had lost a lot of weight recently. He did not like to be reminded of his flesh. It was turning into greasy lumps that shifted and shrank beneath his slackening skin. The fabric of his quilted dressing gown hung heavily on his arm as he raised a hand to the cold glass. His fingers were dead, the knuckles swollen with ersatz arthritis.

He was unaroused by the spectacle. Judi was thrashing around the room, unsuccessfully trying to rid herself of the dead weight hanging from her wrist. She was screaming, but he had chosen to switch off the intercom. He could still just hear the racket, but these Victorian walls had been built for privacy. Already, the girl was beginning to wear herself down. Already, he was beginning to feel the warmth.

He knew his face was filling out, settling comfortably again onto his skull. His hands grew fatter. The skin crept back over the half-moons of his fingernails. His fingers bent, knuckles cracking, he made a comfortable vice-grip fist. He felt himself expanding to fit his clothes. His dry mouth filled again with water. His teeth swelled, and sharpened, changing the shape of his jaw, making him grin.

Now, he was ready for Judi.

He used the connecting door. It had never been locked, but there was no handle on her side. Judi had finished with her hysterics, and was back in the bed. She was coiled in a foetal ball, with Coral's arm sticking out in place of an umbilical cord. The little green scorpion was resting. It had been neatly done. There was almost no blood. The room smelled musty. He caught the residues of spent lusts in his nostrils, and drew them into himself, tasting them as they went down.

The things he had watched last night were replayed inside his head. He smiled, new skin tight over his cheekbones. Judi, he remembered. And Coral. The clients. Pain and pleasure, locked together. And the almost pathetic pettiness of it all. It had barely been an appetiser for what he would do now. Coral, a pretty but dull girl, would have been a less substantial delight than Judi. Barely a morsel. But still, it was a shame she had been wasted. Her death had given him little sustenance.

He climbed into bed and cuddled Judi. He touched her fractured mind, feeling for the spots that would give first, sinking black fingers into her confusion. She was delicious. He stroked her side, his nails turned to bony scalpels. He opened her at the hip, and scraped the bone. She convulsed like an electro-shock patient. He clamped a passionless kiss over her shriek. He swallowed air, and her cries echoed inside him.

He fed off her for hours, until her heart burst.

Daytime

one

A NNE WAS waiting for The Call.
Every couple of days, she would telephone the old family home, and talk with Dad's nurse. She had never met the woman, and at the echoing end of the transatlantic line, she sounded like a little girl a long way away. Her father had had his second stroke back in September, and all the doctors were expecting the third soon. If not before the end of the year, then early in January. The first heart attack, three years earlier, had just slowed him down and slurred his words. The second had put him in a chair and made talking a supreme effort. The third would kill him.

She had the Radio 4 early morning current affairs show on in the tiny kitchen, and the Channel 4 breakfast television service on in her front room, and was dividing her attention between them, following several stories as they broke. It was mostly international activity, in Central America and Eastern Europe, but there were a few local, London-based, items she was keeping an ear to. She had already done her two days in the newsroom this week, but she was scheduled to turn in a couple of pieces by Friday, to meet the deadline for the Christmas double issue. The Aziz inquest would be turning in a verdict in the next few days, and, depending on the degree of officially admitted police involvement in the youth's death, that would affect the conclusions she would draw in the last of her articles on racist attacks.

The old boiler rattled, and Anne checked the heating. The flame was going full inside, but the flat was not getting any warmer. She really ought to start looking for a new place in the New Year. When her father died, there would be some

money from the estate. She shivered with the thought, and
tried to unthink it, forcing it back into the blacks of her mind.
She shivered again, only with the cold, and pulled her robe
tighter over her nightie. It would be warmer when she had
her clothes on.

There were tanks moving through rubble-strewn streets
on television, and a foreign correspondent on the radio was
making a report with the whoosh of anti-tank rockets in the
background. Anne was not sure whether the coverages were
of the same crisis. Usually, news wound down for Christmas;
this year, events were speeding up as the holiday approached.
Some governments were probably planning to spring nasty
surprises over the Christmas break, purely to avoid publicity.
TV programmers had already overloaded the airwaves with
blockbuster movies, light entertainment specials and quiz-
of-the-year features, and there was no room at the inn for
states of emergency, covert activities or the odd execution.

She had a morning at home due, and the notes for her pieces
were neatly piled by the word processor in the front room.
That meant, since she did not have to struggle through the
rush hour to get to Clerkenwell, she could take some care
over breakfast. 'The most important meal of the day,' her
British friends would tell her as her stomach somersaulted
at the sight of grease-grilled bacon, runny eggs and a horror
they called fried bread. In the kitchen, a cheerful vicar on
'Thought for the Day' was trying to draw some Biblical
parallel between current events and those in Nazareth at
the time of the Nativity. While her old-fashioned percolator
dripped thick coffee, she mixed St Michael's 'Thick and
Creamy' strawberry and mango yoghurt with Neal's Yard
muesli, and added just a little milk. Two croissants were
gently warming in the depths of the oven.

At eight o'clock, the radio and the TV hit news bulletins at
the same time, and told the same stories in slightly varying
ways. Anne did the remains of last night's washing-up. Two
teacups, two wine-glasses, and the dug-out-from-somewhere
ashtray. For a moment, she wondered if Mark had expected
to stay the night with her. She thought that was not going to

happen, but recently, he had been a bit broody around her at the office. He went all quiet and British when she was talking to anyone else, and was hearty with her in that slightly hollow way of his. She put the dripping cups and glasses up on the rack to dry. She was getting the impression that Mark was capable of a species of desperate devotion she would find stifling. For her, this year, turning thirty without having been married or had children had not been the stereotypical shock. The only thing she wished she had done was write a book, and there was plenty of time for that. Maybe she could fix up the racist attack series. It was an important subject.

She took the croissants out, welcoming the outrush of warm air from the oven. Outside the fire escape window, she could see frost-furred ironwork. It was cold, and the forecasters were saying it would get colder. She carried her breakfast tray through to the front room. The television was warning of a traffic snarl-up in North London. The trains were running intermittently because of the cold. Every year, winter caught London Regional Transport by surprise, as if they expected a dingy summer to stretch on until the year's end. Anne's fingers felt the chill, and she warmed them on the croissants. Sitting at the folding table she had pulled out for Mark and not put away, she ate the croissants and watched the television.

Usually, with her breakfast, she opened her mail and set aside letters that needed immediate replies, listed cheques in her account books and paid bills. She liked to get that out of the way before she started anything. Her father's lawyers were sending her a packet of legal documents federal express. But, thanks to the Christmas post, the mail was not arriving until late in the morning this week. She already had too many cards for her limited mantelpiece and shelf space, and was beginning to regret her decision not to bother this year. She took her first caffeine hit of the day, and considered the museli and yoghurt.

At first, the expectation of The Call had been constant. Every time she heard a telephone ring, even if she was not in her flat or an office where she could be traced, she had been instantly certain that this was it, and felt her heart squeeze. Then, the dread had turned to a dull resignation, although she realised that, when it came, it would still surprise her.

Fathers died, she knew. Hers had written an entire play about the fact. And when the third seizure came, the film of the play would undoubtedly be pulled out of the vaults and shown on late-night television as a tribute. She had videoed *On the Graveyard Shift at Sam's Bar-B-Q and Grill* the last time it was on, but had not got around to watching it again. Produced on Broadway in 1954 and filmed in 1955, the property had been cited by the Nobel Prize Committee as a great achievement, but it had also dwarfed everything else Cameron Nielson ever did, including raise children. Anne still found it hard to associate the play, written before she was born, with the distant, kindly, disappointed man she had known all her life. In the big, last-act speech, where Maish Johnson – the role that proved Brando's Stanley Kowalski was not a one-off achievement – angrily expressed his grief at the death of Sam, the fatherly-wise owner of the all-night Bar-B-Q and Grill, and denounced everyone else's numbed reaction to the bad news, Anne knew that her father had written the cornerstone of his own obituary. He had been a young man when he wrote Maish's speech, fiercely identifying with his hero; how would he feel now that he had been pushed, presumably kicking and screaming inside his chairbound bone-and-flesh prison, into the Lee J. Cobb role of Sam?

She took a spoon to the muesli and yoghurt, and mixed them up more thoroughly. The news was starting to repeat, so she zapped from channel to channel, getting an early morning educational show about claw-feed grinding, a high-tech commercial for a bank, and three presenters on a pastel couch swapping mild innuendoes with a teenage pop star. The coffee was getting into her system, waking her up. She laced her cold fingers, and rubbed her palms together, generating some warmth. Back at the news, there was a thirty second blip on the Aziz incident: a black and white photograph, grainily enlarged, of the smiling Pakistani at his wedding; another, post-mortem, of his swollen face on a pillow; a brief, live, snippet of Constable Erskine, in uniform, being hustled out of the inquest, dodging microphones.

At the sight of Erskine's face, Anne felt a flash of cold anger. She had never met the policeman, but she had read the doctor's reports on Charlie Aziz, arrested for 'driving without due care and attention', breathalysed and proved not under the influence of alcohol, then battered to death by 'person or persons unknown' in a South London cell. The official version was that Charlie suffered a claustrophobic spell and injured himself fatally, but Anne knew that was not consistent with his all-round injuries and with the police force's unexplained suspension of Erskine, the arresting officer. Erskine, a blandly handsome young man, did not look like a monster, but then they never did. In his off hours, according to Anne's investigation, Erskine was a member of the English Liberation Front, a far right splinter group who alleged that immigrants from the Indian sub-continent and the Caribbean constitute an army of occupation and should be resisted with *maquis* tactics.

Aziz's parents were glimpsed, but they did not get to say anything. Over the last few weeks, attending meetings of the Charlie Aziz Memorial Committee to Stop the Attacks, Anne had got quite close to the boy's mother. She admired the woman's quiet determination, and her ability to cope with family tragedy while doing something concrete about it. Mrs Aziz, Anne believed, was quite capable of forcing answers from the police where years of investigating journalists would only get nothingy press hand-outs. And if that happened, there would definitely be a book in it. Perhaps even a television docu-drama. Perhaps . . .

She picked up her spoon, and the telephone rang. She dropped the spoon, and found herself shaking. It was only partly the cold. Using the remote control, she turned off the television. The ringing was needlessly loud.

Nerving herself for The Call, she picked up the telephone, and said 'hello'.

The line did not crackle. It was not from America. This was not The Call.

'Anne . . .' It was Mark. Her whole body tensed. She did not need an '. . . about last night . . .' conversation. 'Anne, I'm ringing from the office . . .'

He sounded edgy, urgent, like a conspirator during a crisis.

'Mark, I . . .'

'The police have been checking up on you, Anne . . .'

The doorbell rang.

'Mark, excuse me, someone at the door . . .'

She put the receiver down, and stabbed the entryphone buzzer. It would be the postman, and she did not want to miss him and have to take the trip to the sorting office to pick up the Federal Express packet. She unlatched her door, and stepped out onto the landing.

It was not the postman. Anne shrank back, mentally kicking herself for her lack of caution. In New York, that sort of mistake could get you killed; and London these days was not exactly a paradise of non-violence either.

'Good morning,' said the visitor. 'Anne Nielson?'

It was a civil service type in a grey topcoat, but the dread did not lift.

'Yes?'

He showed her a card, with his photograph under plastic. She looked at it, but could not focus on the words.

'I'm Inspector Joseph Hollis, from the Holborn Police Station.'

The name did not mean anything to her. She looked backwards, at the still off-the-hook telephone. She adopted a neutral expression, and did not invite the policeman into her flat. Any business they had could be done on the landing. She was not paranoid, but she had friends who had been harassed for what they wrote. She had not expected any official feedback on her Aziz pieces, but she was not surprised.

'Miss Nielson?'

The face was unreadable but vaguely sympathetic, the voice professionally expressionless.

She took a breath. 'Yes.'

'Anne *Veronica* Nielson?'

She expected to be told her rights. 'Uh-huh.'

'And do you have a sister, *Judith* Nielson?'

Judi! She always came out of left field, but today . . .

'Yes. What is this about?'

This time, the policeman drew breath. Whatever it was, she knew, it would be bad. With Judi, it was always bad.

'I'm sorry, miss, but I have to tell you that your sister is dead.'

two

THE NIGHT BEFORE, Nina had been out with Rollo, one of her regulars. They had ended up at his maisonette in Hackney. She had tried her best, but just was not up to it. Afterwards, she had vomited biriani on his new duvet cover. It was decorated with ringlet-haired ancient Greeks kaleidoscopically demonstrating an assortment of lovemaking positions. It was supposed to be tasteful.

Rollo had kicked her off his futon and called for a minicab. He had given her less money than usual, and made her wait for the taxi outside his front door. She had got cold listening to him clatter about the house, tidying up, and had come even further down. Her toes were still frozen, without feeling, from the twenty minutes outside. She had had to pay the driver out of her earnings. Usually, Rollo would give the cabman ten pounds to cover it. He had not made a date to see her again. They had met in the first place through the 'Heartland' section of *City Limits*. He was 'in the music business', but did not have any records out at the moment. His sitting room was full of framed posters for concerts by bands she could barely remember.

Back in the flat, she hugged her Snoopy pyjama case, imagining a gentle and considerate lover. Someone like Jeremy Irons in *Brideshead Revisited*. A schoolfriend had once told her that all prostitutes were really lesbians. But, then again, Nina was not a real prostitute. She was . . . What was she? A party girl, she supposed. Like everyone else, she called herself a model on her tax returns.

Exhausted, she did not dream.

When she woke up, she felt ghastly. It was then that she

decided to quit using smack. But smack was not ready to
leave off using her.

Aware that she needed to build her strength again, she fixed
up as substantial a breakfast as was possible with what she
had left in the tiny fridge and the cupboard over the sink.
Branflakes, six cheddar thins, grapefruit juice and a cup of
jasmine tea.

She sat at the kitchen table, looking at the neatly laid
breakfast for a quarter of an hour. The hot water in the
teacup slowly darkened until she could no longer see the
sachet in the bottom. She took the paper tab and hauled
the teabag out on its length of cotton. She dangled it in
front of her face, and took the soggy lump into her mouth.
It was slightly scalding, but the flavour was good. She could
taste the perfume.

She spat the bag out into a saucer, and began to nibble one
of the biscuits. Her stomach contracted sharply. 'Soon,' she
said, 'it's coming soon.' She kept the cheesy pulp in her
mouth for minutes, squeezing it through her teeth. Finally,
she swallowed. It hurt going down, but it hurt a lot more
coming up.

She bent double, cracking the cereal bowl with her forehead. The spasms hit her again and again in the belly. She
twisted off the stool and dived for the kitchen mat, curling
up around her pain. Milk and bran dried on her face. She
managed to control herself before the kicking started.

This had happened before. She could live through it.

After a while, she calmed down. She unwound herself,
and lay face up on the floor, looking up at the Marvel
comic covers pasted to the ceiling by a previous tenant.
Silver Surfer and *Daredevil*, *Iron Man* and *The Avengers*. She
had had a guy around for a party once who was a comic
collector. He claimed that, unmutilated, several of the '60s
issues that had been cut up for wallpaper were worth around
fifty pounds. What a waste.

She sat up, and felt temporarily at peace with herself. It
would not last. There was no smack in the place. She had
hoped to be able to find the silver paper her last jab had

come in, but it was lost. She had got a hit off that kind of minute residue before, by licking it. It felt like sherbert on the tongue, and a carnival in her brain. At least, it had once. More recently, she had been treading water, using the shot to stay even, not to get ahead. That was dangerous, but she was a strong person, she told herself, she could deal with it.

It took her a full minute to dial Clive's seven figure number. Apart from her own, it was the only one she knew. She had forgotten her mother's, and had a little book for regulars and friends.

Clive. Charming Clive. Well-spoken Clive. Cunning Clive. He was the one who had found the song with her name in it. Nina Kenyon. He had suggested she find a partner called Ina Carver. It was the first line of 'My Darling Clementine'. Ina Carver, Nina Kenyon. Excavating for a mine. Clive would have smack. He always had smack.

Clive's telephone rang four times, then his answering machine cut in. It told her in the kind of voice she usually only heard on *University Challenge* that Clive Broome was out right now and that she could leave a message after the bleeps if she wanted to. She did not.

She could not quite get her phone back on the hook. The tangled cord got in the way.

In any case, she knew Clive would only come across if she paid him for her last shot. He was her friend and he loved her, but he was a businessman like any other and he could not make that kind of exception. She barely had enough cash left over from last night to get her through the day.

Even from the other side of the room, she could hear the phone. The dialing tone buzzed, annoyingly loud, like a persistent insect.

She squandered a fifty pence coin on the electricity meter and turned the fire on full strength. Standing up, she felt pins and needles in her knees. The gilt-edged invitation that had come in yesterday's post was on top of a pile of newspapers, magazines and bills on the coffee table. Under the copperplate request for the pleasure of her company and the address, Amelia had written 'bring a friend'.

So, if she could get herself together, there was the prospect of earning some good money. Not in a terribly comfortable way, but good money was good money. She had been to Amelia's 'entertainments' before and survived.

And Clive would be at Amelia's 'entertainment'. And wherever Clive went, he did business.

'Bring a friend.' Nina had not known if Amelia was being graciously hospitable, or issuing an order. 'A friend'?

Nina had thought that had to mean Coral. The last time she had met Amelia, she had been with the skinny blonde in the Club Des Esseintes. The hostess could easily have been quite taken with Coral. The girl had certainly been exciting attention for as long as Nina had known her.

They had come from the same school in North London originally. At first, Nina had been the one to show Coral how to get along. They had worked as a sister act for a while, but had got on each other's nerves. They went back too far to be comfortable together these days. Coral could be a moody cow when she wanted to, and was ungenerous with her gear. She had stopped crashing most nights on Nina's floor a few months before, and found a place with the American girl, Judi. Once Coral moved out, Nina found she got on better with her friend. There were plenty of relationships that worked best that way.

Judi? Maybe Amelia meant Judi. Nina had introduced her to the hostess as well. The more she had thought about it yesterday, the less she had known whether to call Judi or Coral. In the end, it had hit her that she did not have to make a choice. Judi and Coral were still together, at the same address. If she phoned them, one would answer the phone. Today, she could not remember which she had spoken to. But she had arranged to meet with one of the girls at the Club. Judi or Coral. She wondered which.

In the cramped bathroom, it took Nina a while to get dressed. She kept being distracted by her face in the mirror. Even before she washed the bran off, she did not look like the girl in the old smack adverts. The ones that said it screws you up. Just because she did smack did not mean she could not wash and comb her hair – although soapy water did make her feel squirmy sometimes – and put a little make-up over the blue-ish crescents under her eyes.

She dressed for the party, mainly in her best black. She favoured forties styles, with padded shoulders and deep pleats. She always wore long sleeves. Nina posed like a model in front of the tall mirror. She looked so much better since she started losing weight. She did not have to suck her cheeks in to appear glamorous any more, and she had completely lost her stomach.

She still thought she could get by doing modelling, but she never had the money to assemble a decent portfolio and that was what you needed if you wanted to get into the big money. She only had one nice photo of herself, and that was years out of date now. One of her regulars had wanted her to model for him, but he turned out to be interested only in private camera sessions. She did not want any of *those* photos.

She brushed the tangles out of her hair, feeling the scratch of the tines on her scalp. There was nothing wrong with parties, really. They were probably easier than modelling jobs.

More in control now, she got back to the telephone. After putting the receiver properly in its cradle, she picked it up and, flipping her book open to the number, called Coral and Judi. Knowing what they were like, they probably needed reminding about the meet. Their phone rang and rang until she gave up. She tried Clive again, but put the phone down before his machine could finish.

There were hours to go before Amelia's 'entertainment', so she would have time to set something up with Coral and/or Judi, and to pull herself together.

three

WHILE ANNE waited for the policeman to come back, she listened to the hospital piped music. They were playing something strangled by a million strings. Irritated, she recognised 'I Saw Her Standing There' under the Mantovani massacre. Messages from administrators to doctors chirruped in the background like signals gone astray in deep space. The Synthesised Celestial Choir segued into 'Do You Want to Know a Secret?'

Even under normal circumstances, she could not comfortably listen to The Beatles any more. They had been so much a part of her pre-adolescence. The four chord melancholies and ecstasies had turned scary. It had been 'Helter Skelter'. They had gutted Sharon Tate in Hollywood, and shot John Lennon in New York. All that was left was musak.

Judi had been into groups with more honestly horrific names. Paranoid Realities, Skullflower, Coil, Bad Dreamings, The Manson Family Reunion, Three More Bullets and a Shovel. She would have spat on 'Love Me Do' and 'Please Please Me'.

Still, The Beatles had been with her all her life. Anne's first memory was of her father letting her stay up past her bedtime to watch them on *The Ed Sullivan Show*. Not the first time, but a re-run. Judi had not been born yet. Later, the *Double White* was the first album she had bought with her own money. She had played it over and over on the old phonograph in the cellar rumpus room of the summer house in New Hampshire. Cam had taken personal offence at 'Revolution No. 9', and so it automatically became her favourite track. Even so, she would lift the needle over it when he was not there.

Judi was around then, making her presence felt everywhere, all the time. She had been reading almost before she could put a real sentence together in her mouth, and father had taught her long division before she ever saw the inside of the school. There had been no doubt about it: Judi had been the clever child, the pretty child, the promising child. Cam was the first-born, and thus beloved of God (and his mother, Dad's ex-wife). That left Anne as the nondescript one in the middle.

Now, Cam was as rich and famous as it was possible for a self-styled *avant garde* composer to be, Anne was working her way up the ladder as a journalist, and Judi was dead.

'I'm sorry, miss, but I have to tell you that your sister is dead,' Inspector Hollis had said. No tactful build-up, no euphemisms. The policeman had simply established that he was talking to Anne Nielson, and told her what he had to. She could not help but wonder whether he was familiar with her Aziz pieces. They had not been calculated to endear her to the Metropolitan Police. But she knew really that this was how everybody got treated.

There are a million stories in the naked city, and not enough words to go around. What with government cuts, a copper's vocabulary would have to be pared down to the absolute minimum. No surplus circumlocutions, synonyms hoarded like golden acorns.

Back in November, Anne had interviewed an ex-marine who had written a good book about Vietnam. He never used the words 'kill' or 'dead', just 'waste' and 'wasted'. That was bluntly the best way of putting it. Wasted.

Anne saw the doctor who was supposed to have looked at Judi when she was brought in. He was busy now, pulling apart the do-it-yourself mummy swathings wrapped around the head of a little West Indian boy. She glimpsed red cheeks, raw meat rather than blushes. This time, she was impressed by the doctor's performance as he kept up a non-stop stream of soothing chatter for the boy and his visibly anxious mother.

With Anne, he had been offhand, awkward. She wasn't his patient, just related to an inconvenient lump of deadness he could have nothing more to do with. Alive, you are a challenge; dead, you are an embarrassment.

There were uniformed soldiers, unarmed, in the corridor. With the ambulance drivers' dispute dragging on, many local authorities were calling in troops to man the emergency services. Two squaddies, berets folded and tucked into the epaulettes of their olive-drab jerseys, were sharing a cigarette and a joke in an alcove, trying to keep out of the way. Their presence in the hospital made the place not feel like mainland Britain. Anne assumed this was what combat zone first-aid centres were like, in Belfast or in Central America. Even this early in the day, the casualty reception was busy. With the holidays starting, it was a prime time for accidents. Anne had had to do the hospital ring-round when she was starting out as a journalist, fishing for stories. Now, that seemed a long time ago.

Anne had been at home that summer when Judi was fifteen. She was freshly graduated from journalism college, doing bits for the local paper and working on the novel she never did finish. She had been a witness to what their mother, in one of her infrequent bursts of British understatement, called 'Judi's turn for the worse'. It was as much her fault as father's, or Cam's, or anyone's. 'There are some days,' Judi had told her in a rare communicative mood, 'when I think that life is an unending Hell of misery and desolation, and others when it seems merely to be a purposeless punishment, unending in its monotony.' It was hard to come back with something like 'yes, but what will you be wearing to the junior prom, sis?'

That summer, Judi had realised that being clever was not getting her what she wanted out of life, and so she had decided to be stupid instead. She had stolen money from Cam's wallet and bought a Greyhound ticket to New York. In the city, it had not taken her long to find 42nd Street. On 42nd Street, it had taken her an absurdly, and probably mercifully, short time to find the undercover vice cop.

Father, the Great Man, had shrugged into a fit of inertia when the NYPD called, and so Anne had had to deal with it. Cameron Nielson Sr came up with the bail, his agent kept it out of the papers, and Anne went to town to pull her little sister out of the pussy posse's holding cells.

The next time, Judi had used her one telephone call to get in touch with a stringer for a paper so yellow that a dog could piss on it without making a difference. He had to be told who Cameron Nielson was, but he came up with the headlines anyway. NOBEL PRIZE-WINNER'S DOPER DAUGHTER IN B'WAY BUST. BAR-B-Q MAN'S GIRL IN SEX FOR DRUGS RACKET. Shit, that had been bad for all of them.

Anne thought again about The Call. Father could not talk any more. He had not written anything much since the late '60s. But he had been the only Nobel laureate ever to write for Rock Hudson and Doris Day, and then have his script redone by a kid fresh from two episodes of *The Mod Squad* and some quickies for *Laugh-In*. Anne thought that humiliation had done more to Cameron Nielson than any of Judi's exploits. More even than Hugh Farnham and his Committee. His only substantial work in the last ten years was *The Rat Jacket*, an intensely personal one-acter about an informer committing suicide. Widely interpreted as autobiographical, the piece – Anne suspected – would eventually be seen as one of his most important. There was talk of Robert Altman doing it as a television play with Harry Dean Stanton.

'Miss Nielson,' said Hollis, not unkindly, 'we're ready for you now.'

The policeman escorted her to the lift. He took a gentle hold of her upper arm and steered her. She was too drained to be annoyed by the imposition. The lift was large enough to accommodate several six-foot stretchers, and smelled like a dentist's office.

'We've contacted your brother. He was at the Grafton, like you said.'

'That's where he usually stays when he's in London.'

'Cameron Nielson? That's a famous name.' He was trying to make conversation, keep her mind busy. 'Any relation?'

'We're his children. It's Cameron Nielson *Junior*.'

'*On the Graveyard Shift at Sam's Bar-B-Q and Grill*. It's a 20th century classic.'

'That's what they say.'

'I saw it at the National when Albert Finney did the revival. With Donald Pleasence as Sam. Of course, I've seen the film. . .'

'Elia Kazan directed that.'

'. . . with Marlon Brando, Lee J. Cobb, Therese Colt and Eli Wallach and . . . who was the girl? The English actress?'

'Victoria Page. My mother. And Judi's. Not Cam's. That was another actress, a woman who divorced Dad in the fifties.'

They were there.

It was not like morgues in the movies. They did not have walls with long drawers. The bodies were on gurneys like elongated tea trolleys, with green sheets over them. The air conditioning was breathing low, cooling the place even in December. The place could as easily have been a school kitchen.

Movie morgues were always antiseptic, as clean and dignified as chapels. This was dirty. The waste bins overflowed with plastic cups and used paper towels. Someone had left an oily car battery recharging on a wash stand, and the only attendant was a kid with an unstarched mohican. He wore a Cramps T-shirt under his soiled hospital whites and he was reading the Arts pages of *The Independent*.

'Of course,' said Hollis, 'we've already identified her from fingerprints. . .'

'Yes, this is just a formality, but it has to be done. Right? You have forms to fill in before you can forget her.'

She was immediately sorry for snapping at him. After all, he was not P.C. Erskine. Hollis continued without taking notice. He must be used to dealing with irrational people.

'You knew that your sister had a criminal record?'

'Oh yes.' Here and in New York. Possession, soliciting, resisting arrest, carrying a concealed weapon, whatever. Judi's Interpol file was probably more substantial than anything Anne had written.

Hollis lifted the sheet himself.

There had been a mistake. It was not Judi.

This woman was old. All the substance beneath her mottled skin had drained away. She looked like a life-size shrunken head. The hair was dyed a blotchy black, but the roots were the white-yellow colour of drought-killed grass.

'It's a mistake,' said Anne, disorientated. 'It's not her. She was . . .'

'Twenty-five. We know.'

'But . . .'

'Look again.'

The eyes were open, rolled up into the skull, whites red-veined. The dead old woman's mouth was shrunken, but still firm. She had all her teeth.

Not wanting to, Anne touched the face. There was a spot on the upper lip, where Bogart had a scar, where Judi had a mole.

'It can't be. How . . .?' She looked at Hollis, and answered her own question. 'Drugs. Heroin?'

Hollis gently eased the left arm out from under the sheet. He ran a finger over the extensive abrasions. Amid the bruises, Anne could see fresh and ancient pinpricks. And there was Judi's crescent scar over the inoculation marks. A childhood scrape with an electric lamp.

Anne wanted to cry, to break down, to give up.

Hollis was talking, almost lecturing.

'She was an addict. We know that. Recently, there have been some quantum leaps in the drugs industry. They don't need to import as much opium-derived heroin as they used to. The stuff can be synthesised in laboratories. Designer drugs, they're called. From California, originally. The stuff is cheaper, purer, more debilitating. Strictly, it's not even illegal yet. I've seen senile teenagers. It affects the metabolic rate. The processes that make you grow old . . . I don't really understand this . . . they get speeded up . . .'

Poor Judi. Wasted. Her whole life literally used up. Anne looked at the old woman's face and saw the child her sister had been. Judi had not died easily.

Hollis covered Judi again, tucking her in.

'Did she do this to herself?' Anne asked.

Hollis looked at the floor, not quite shrugging.

Anne did not say any more. She was too good a judge of her own character. She knew what she wanted. It was the same when their mother had left, and when the novel had not worked out, when she had first heard of Charlie Aziz, and when father had wound up mute in a chair. For her, it was only natural.

She wanted someone to blame.

four

*. . . EVEN THE Kind dreamed. But with the passing of so many
years, the old man had outlived his imagination. All his mind had
left was the almost unbearable weight of memory. There was so much
he could no longer consciously recollect. Yet all of it existed, untapped
by his waking self, in his night thoughts . . .*

By the standards of centuries he would live to see, it had
hardly been a battle at all. A routine patrol of six or seven
horsemen with maybe two lances between them had come
upon the enemy encamped in a shallow valley and, against
his orders, engaged them. The din had carried in the strong
winds, and his own camp had been roused to the combat. His
hand thus forced, he had committed his men to the skirmish.
It had turned into a minor massacre.

Taking both armies into account, there were perhaps one
hundred dead. But he was well pleased. The English captain
had been taken, and he had spent a long, rewarding afternoon
with him. The man had been a genuine soldier, not some
royal cousin assigned a command to keep him out of treason
and plotting at home. He was much more resilient than the
children who were his frequent guests between wars, but, in
the end, he had yielded as completely as the scrawniest peasant
brat.

He was satisfied, glutted, complete. Beneath his helmet,
the tangle of his hair, grey-streaked at dawn, was a match
now for the purest sable. His lieutenants no longer remarked
upon the changes in him. By now, they were used to his cycles
and simply put his occasional youthful appearance down to
sorcery. A few of them were given to boasting about their
master's skill in the Black Arts, and that could be useful from

time to time. Poor Sieur Barbe-Bleue, meticulously obsessive
as ever, was even trying through atrocity and alchemy to ape
him, searching in the ruined and abused flesh of small boys
for an elusive immortality. But some of his other officers, an
unfortunate number who would soon learn better, had almost
forgotten to fear him. For them, the English captain should
have been saved for a ransom, not wasted on pleasure.

He had his ragged cloth-of-gold pitched on the bloody
grass, about where the fighting had been most concentrated.
He looked forward to stretching out on the insanguinated
ground and luxuriating in the residues as others would in a
heated and perfumed bath.

After the Englishman was exhausted, and consigned to the
bonfires with his followers and the dead horses, he paid a visit
to the girl.

She was squatting between the fires, her face still streaked
with blood, her hands clasped in prayer. Sometimes he
wondered what she said to her saints. Did she apologise for
the extra load of souls that were lining up outside the Gates
of Heaven as a result of her conversations with dead divines?

He knelt before her, and took her young head in his hands.
His fingers slid into her cropped, coarse hair. He picked out
a hard-shelled parasite and popped it between thumb and
forefinger.

He, the Monster, kissed her, the Saint.

That year, he favoured little boys. But his congress with
the girl was different. Her skin was permanently marked with
the weave of chain mail. During the physical act of love, she
called him 'father' several times. Whether she meant her father
in the village, a father at the church, or the Father in Heaven,
he could not say.

The wind tore at the already tattered walls of the tent,
detaching wisps of golden thread that floated over the camp. A
detail was stripping the dead of their armour, and piling it up.
The fires burned fiercely, roasting and consuming carcasses
with much crackling and hissing. The soldiers sang, words
about intercourse with goats set to sacred tunes.

Every so often, there was a gurgling cry. He had ordered

the whores to comb the battlefield, cutting the throats of the wounded, no matter whose colours they wore.

Close to his already dwindling body, the girl slept, doubtless dreaming of the young king and the angelic voices that whispered inside her skull. He touched his head gently to hers and sadly tasted the emptiness within. Briefly, he thought there was something, but it was just a memory of the unending winds that forced this girl, and all like her, to and fro without regard.

Strangely, he did not feed off her.

<u>five</u>

THERE WERE Monsters, Anne knew. It was a secret she shared with Judi. Their father had met a Monster, and lost, before they were born. Anne knew all about it. She had seen the kinescopes. She knew the face of the Monster, and that their family bogeyman had once had a name, Hugh Farnham, but that was the least of it. He went on forever, revealed only by a tone of voice, a strident attitude, an indestructible set of mind, a few whistled bars of an old film theme tune.

'You have to stop thinking in absolutes,' her journalism tutor had told her. 'Life isn't a movie, with good guys and bad guys, heroes and monsters.'

She knew there were no heroes, but she could see the Monsters everywhere. Hugh Farnham was long gone, but there were others. P.C. Barry 'The Batterer' Erskine, the hate-consumed Ulster clergyman, the calf-faced girl on Page Three of *The Sun*, the presidential advisor, the Soviet chess grand master, the old hippie rock musician, the Middle Eastern mullah, the television quiz show m.c., the political columnist in the downmarket Sunday paper, the science fiction writer hawking the fourth volume of his trilogy, and a thousand other, lesser, demons.

'Annie, did you know they had your old man on film in the archives?' Pat, her college roommate, had asked. 'They've got his appearance before McCarthy.'

Strictly speaking, it had not been McCarthy. He had gone down with the astonishing hearings in 1954, when he had been crucified in court for daring to graduate from the easy pickings of Hollywood to try to detect traces of Communist infiltration in President Eisenower's *Alma Mater*, the army.

Father had been up before Hugh Farnham three years later, at the tail-end of the blacklist.

She had resisted the temptation for weeks, but finally she gave in. She had to scratch the itch, even if it turned into an open sore. Frankly pleading her special interest to the head of the Modern American History department, she was given access. She had to thread the projector herself, and confront the Monster in a drafty basement screening room with uncomfortable seats and a strict no smoking rule. In those days, she had been a smoker. In those days, like everyone else, she had even played around with drugs.

The kinescopes were not properly catalogued, so she had to watch until she found what she was looking for. Her father did not show up until the fourteenth of twenty half-hour reels, covering nearly ten years of different sessions, but she was still fascinated. It was Hugh Farnham, the Monster. Joe McCarthy had got all the contemporary press coverage and had an -ism named after him, and Richard Nixon had used the hearings as a springboard into grown-up politics. Even Roy Cohn, the legal *éminence grise* who had died of AIDS a few years back, was comparatively well-remembered. But Farnham was Something Else. The others were in it for patriotism, self-advancement, megalomania, paranoid self-justification and financial gain. Half-way through his delicate dissection of Martin Ritt, Anne realised with a dizzying rush of vertigo that Farnham tormented people because it was his idea of fun. It met a need in him he could not slake any other way.

His eyes were nothing in particular in black and white, certainly not burning coals of melodramatic malevolence. And his voice was like a Broadway actor's in a Shakespeare play, unaccented but more British than American. He had always been something of a mystery man; in theory, Anne knew where he had come from and what he had done before the hearings, but, watching his smile, she found she had forgotten the precise details. His face was unforgettable, as if the skin of a pale cobra had been stretched over the bone structure of Montgomery Clift.

She wondered what had happened to him. Perhaps he had been badly burned in the War, and had had to be patched together by expensive teams of plastic surgeons intent on performing miracles. In the shadows of the courtroom, he looked older than Dracula, but, when he was firing questions at unfriendly witnesses like Kim Hunter or Zero Mostel, he was younger, more virile, more in control, than a matinée idol on a triumphant opening night.

'Are you now,' Farnham kept asking, always with the biting pause in the same place, 'or have you ever been, a member of the Communist Party?'

Unlike McCarthy, Farnham did not pronounce it 'commonest party'. The only thing her father had ever said about the Monster was that, at the height of the televised hearings, Hugh Farnham received more fan mail from women than Elvis.

Thirty-five years later, it was all clear. McCarthy was stupid – a blustering clown. It was incredible that he had got away with it for so long. The one indelible image of the period was of McCarthy whispering in Roy Cohn's ear like a school bully suddenly desperate for advice, and the lawyer looking shocked and shattered as he realises just how doomed his buffoon boss is among all the smart lawyers. Nixon was a glowering, unshaven crook, a sweaty Boris Karloff in *Arsenic and Old Lace*. Anne understood why he had been God's gift to the protest movement, an Establishment villain who always looked and acted like one. And the 'friendly' witnesses – Robert Taylor, Adolph Menjou, Therese Colt – embarrassed themselves and flushed lesser people down the toilet as they blurted out their hatred of anyone in Hollywood they thought might be communists even if they could not think of any actual proof of their left-leaning politics. But Congressman Hugh Farnham was John Wayne, Captain America, Parsifal and the young Jack Kennedy rolled into one.

Sweet Jesus, this man could have been *president*.

Waving a petition against the Committee signed by various Hollywood notables, Farnham even got chilling laughs with one speech. 'I want to read you some of these names,' he began, in a mildly sardonic manner, a brow arched. 'One of the names is June Havoc. We found out from the Motion Picture Almanac that her real name is June *Hovick*. Another one is Danny Kaye, and we find his real name is David Daniel *Kaminsky*. Then we have the case of Mr John Garfield, *né* Julius *Garfinkle*. Eddie Cantor, known to his mother as Eddie *Iskowitz*. The famous Edward G. Robinson, a.k.a Emmanuel *Goldenberg*. A fellow who signs his autograph Melvyn Douglas, but who is really not a Douglas at all but a *Hesselberg*. A promising Broadway gent called Cameron Nielson whose birth certificate reads Comrade . . . pardon me, *Conrad* Nastase. There are others too numerous to mention. They are attacking this house for doing its duty to protect this country and save the American people from the horrible fate the communists have meted out to the unfortunate Christian people of Europe.'

When her father showed up, late in the day, she did not recognise him. It was a fluke that his hearing, which was officially an 'enquiry into the misuse of a United States passport' although the criminal charge hanging over him was actually Contempt of Congress, had been televised. By the time his name came up, everyone but the witchfinders had lost interest. It must have been a ratings-slow period. It was hard to connect the young man with the dark hair, quick grin and self-confident way with words to the person she had grown up around. All that was there were the horn-rimmed glasses and unearned Ivy League tie.

In the film, Cameron Nielson was confident that he could defeat the Monster. His daughter knew that he had been destroyed by it.

In 1957, the days of the blacklist were supposedly over, but her father was unemployable in Hollywood, his TV play *The Crunch* had been bounced without comment by all three networks, and his 'historical pageant' *Cochise and Geronimo* had closed after three weeks and two days on Broadway.

But he did not care. He had secret weapons. He was rich, he did not have to work. He had the example of his friend Arthur Miller, who had stood up straight at his hearing a

year earlier and been treated leniently, his minimal sentence
rapidly overturned. He had the Nobel Prize for Literature.
That made it official: he was a national resource, like O'Neill,
Faulkner or Hemingway. He did not have to prove anything.
He had nothing to lose.

He did not even have to plead the fifth amendment. He
simply did not have to answer the Question.

'Are you now,' said Farnham, 'or have you ever been, a
member of the Communist Party?'

There was a long pause, long enough for the station to cut
to a Kraft commercial if they had wanted to.

Cameron Nielson smiled, and hooked his thumbs into his
vest pockets. If he had had a hat on, he would have tilted it to
the back of his head. Suddenly, Anne realised how much her
father had known about live television. He looked straight at
the camera which must have had the orange operational light
on, and answered the Question with another question.

'Well, Congressman Farnham, that depends . . .' His voice
was full of New York shrewdness. 'That depends on who the
fuck wants to know.'

There was commotion in the court. Someone – Sterling
Hayden? – applauded loudly. The camera swivelled, and
there was a brief shot of a director ripping off his earphones,
unable to believe what he had heard. The camera calmed,
and came to rest on the Congressman. Farnham did not
show a flicker of emotion, but Anne could see his killer's
smile.

'Mr Nielson,' he said, his eyes enlarging visibly, '*I* want to
know.'

Farnham simply looked at her father, and Cameron Nielson
began to crack. The Congressman asked the Question again,
calmly, and waited . . .

The camera held on her father, his smile twitching. He
was sweating now, his one shot spent and useless. Finally,
he made another move, shakily. 'Congressman, I believe the
Constitution enshrines the right to freedom of . . .'

'Freedom?' interrupted Farnham, his teeth sharp in his grin.
'That's an awfully large word.'

Anne was sitting forward in her seat, sweaty hands on her knees. She had never really understood what had happened next. None of the accounts she had heard or read agreed. Her father never spoke about it, except perhaps for a few veiled hints in *The Rat Jacket*, in which the informer protagonist is grilled by a chess-playing genius policeman with a sadistic streak.

The film did not explain anything. By the end of the reel, her father had turned into the middle-aged man Anne had grown up with. Farnham kept asking questions, asking *the* Question, and then interrupting Cameron Nielson if he did not answer to the point. Evidence was produced – the membership lists of various Hollywood charitable organisations later proved to be Communist fronts, signatures on petitions in support of unionisation, Sacco and Vanzetti, Soviet-American collaboration, supposedly propagandist passages in his plays. But the evidence was not important. This was a duel of character between Congressman Hugh Farnham and Nobel laureate Cameron Nielson, and, finally, her father caved in.

He did not go to prison like Hammett and the Hollywood Ten, he did not flee the country like Joseph Losey, Larry Adler or Carl Foreman, and he did not get away with it like Miller.

Cameron Nielson answered the Question. Of course, he named names. And, of course, careers were ruined, friendships broken, lives smashed . . .

She could not watch any more. It was the first and last time a movie made Anne cry.

six

ANNE'S RELATIONSHIP with her half-brother had always been, at best, considerably strained. They had not talked since she had described his *Orpheus to the Power of One Hundred* in print as 'music to cut your wrists by' and accused him of stealing most of his ideas from Karl-Heinz Stockhausen, John Cage and Spike Jones.

She knew he was in London for the première of his *Telemachus Symphony*, a piece he had been working on for eight years. He had not complained about the intrusion into his busy schedule of rehearsal, but Anne knew Cam well enough to realise how little he was interested in Judi's life and death.

As Cam talked on the in-house telephone, trying to get some breakfast sent up to his suite, Anne tried to remember how he had been with Judi. Cam had been away at school when Judi was born, and he had spent very few summers at their father's house. He was with his mother, or touring Europe with his octet.

To him, Judi was someone he saw once a year at Christmas and did not really like much in the first place. The last Christmas they were all together, seven years ago, Cam had given Judi a book about Beethoven, and she had given him three pairs of multi-coloured socks.

The only time Judi had ever affected him was when she was a news item. The reviews of his first New York concert, even in the heavy papers, gave as much space to his half-sister's criminal record as his father's Broadway career.

'Success at last,' he announced. 'They stopped serving breakfast at ten, but they have some tea and scones left over.'

Anne looked at the smooth stranger. She understood only too well how he could think of tea and scones half an hour after looking at Judi dead on a collapsible table. She remembered her own breakfast, abandoned back in Kentish Town.

A discreet maid wheeled in the breakfast. They ate without much conversation. Anne scalded her tongue by drinking too soon the too hot, too weak tea. Cam showed her the cover design for his concert programme; a broken Greek mask, with white space for eyeholes.

They were interrupted by a telephone call. Anne was sure it would be more bad news, and felt a chill as Cam listened intently to a woman's tiny voice.

'Lex,' he said, 'precisely 7:35. Insist on it.'

It was Alexia, Cam's assistant at the concert hall. Cam was insisting the performance commence at 7:35 to the second because he had written in two minutes of minimal music between 7:59 and 8:01, during which he hoped his background chords would interact with the scattered beeping of the digital watches spread throughout the auditorium. He liked to include random factors in his pieces.

Alexia explained something, and Cam whistled unconsciously, an old habit. The crisis dealt with, he hung up.

'How's Dad?' she asked, wondering if he had heard more recently from the nurse.

'The same,' he said.

It cannot be much longer now, she thought.

He nodded, as if agreeing with her unspoken sentiment.

'Should we tell him?' she asked.

'I'm not sure he'd understand,' he said. 'You can't tell whether he hears or not. It might be best to leave him in peace.'

A pause. They were vacuum-cleaning the hallways outside. It sounded like one of Cam's bass lines.

'Cam, I'm not letting it go.'

'I know. I knew as soon as I heard. Annie, I know you won't listen but . . . Fuck it, you do not need to understand all this.

It's not really anything to do with you or me. Judi is gone
now . . .'

Wasted.

'. . . it was suicide really, you have to admit that . . .'

'Crap, Cam. Crap. You saw her. She was a hundred years
old. And Hollis says it was not just drugs. She'd been beaten
up. Lots of times. And she was torn open . . .'

The body had been found by dustbinmen, under some
rubbish bags in a Soho alley. She had been dumped. The
police thought the wounds on her hips and thighs were from
rats.

'It was part of . . . part of the way she lived, Annie. She
must have been beaten up and cut open every night. You
know what kind of a whore she was. No wonder her heart
gave out. Face it, she had been killing herself for a long time.
This time, she finally managed to pull it off. Now, let's just
leave her alone, please . . .'

Give him credit, she thought, he has not said anything about
publicity, about his symphony, about his career.

He has not *said* anything.

He was whistling again, nervous and atonal. It was the
signature sound that always insinuated itself into his work.
Now, it struck a long-forgotten chord.

'Mr Whistle,' Anne said, startling Cam. Her brother
stopped in mid-whine and closed his lips.

'I'm not scared of the bogeyman any more, Annie.'

Cam had been a strange kid, Anne remembered. How
many other children had *scary* imaginary playmates? For a
while, she had had bad dreams about Mr Whistle too. Now,
she could not remember even what the nightmare child was
supposed to look like.

'There are no bogeymen,' Cam said.

'No, but there *are* Monsters. We all know that.'

Anne picked up her shoulderbag, and the lumpy clear
plastic carrier with Judi's personal effects.

'Monsters,' he shrugged. 'You shouldn't think like that. It's
not helpful. There are only people. Don't people scare you
enough?'

She walked to the door.

'Annie, where are you going?'

'Anywhere I have to.'

Five minutes after she was gone, Anne knew Cam would be on the telephone to the concert hall again, asking them to send a taxi over for him. He would be still worried about the two minutes' beeping.

She had tickets for tonight, but she doubted she would get to use them.

seven

THE IMMORTAL EMPIRE fell before it was born.

Even after so many years, he could still learn. In Shanghai, Tarr, Sniezawski and Baum had taught him to beware the complacency of the Kind. Life sometimes seems to slow like a river, almost coming to a comfortable rest. But there are always dangers. There are always dragonslayers, always Fearless Vampire Killers.

Although an orphan, he had always known he was not entirely alone. He had met his cousins at the sites of great plagues and disasters, and recognised in them the same unease he felt in himself. The Kind, he learned, were as old as humanity itself. Theirs was a secret history, never written in a living language, much of it concealed even from his questions. Comparatively young, he understood that the elders of the Kind had withdrawn entirely from the affairs of men and retreated to the shrinking white spaces on the map. He was impatient with such dainty cowardice, and, as if in the grip of a feeding frenzy, felt the zeal of a crusader as he set out to become King of the Cats.

There had been Kings before, Kings of the Kind, and Kind Kings who had ruled over the nations of humanity. The title, as he understood it, had been unused in centuries. Its last holders had abdicated or been overthrown. He had only to establish his Palace of Perpetuity and throw his court open to attract the others. The old ones, his uncles and aunts, maintained their loftiness and stayed in their seclusion, but their juniors, his cousins, were as eager as he to end the centuries of wandering. He was accepted as King by those to whom such things mattered. In Shanghai, he built his

Palace and waited. Soon, its fame spread among the Kind. A mating pair arrived from the Dark Continent, no longer able to retreat from the explorers and the empires of Europe. Giselle, the exquisite child, slipped out of the darkness one night, cocooned in silver furs. It was she, thinking of a fairy tale, who had invented his title, the King of the Cats. Almost as old as he, she was still capable of seeming a genuine child. With each new member of the circle, he was able to piece together more of the history.

With Giselle, he shared the Dream, an experience he had rarely been able to approach, even with the dearest of his prey. Shaping everything within their perceptions, they had fused until their personalities could no longer be distinguished. They would reign, as King and Queen of the Cats, for an eternity.

The circle grew, but not as rapidly as he had expected. He was surprised to learn how reduced the numbers of the Kind were. Every newcomer seemed to bring the story of the death of another of the ancients. With each loss, irretrievable stretches of the history sank into oblivion like water in sand. Short-lived mankind might be, but it had multiplied insanely in the last few centuries. It was learning many new things, and forgetting its old fears.

He had taken more wives, had children. His cousins followed suit. The densely populated port, with its refugees, sailors and unnoticed masses, was perfect for the Kind. The international confusion of administration and corruption left many gaps that could be exploited. With several fortunes, aggregated down through the centuries in the world's great banking houses, at his disposal, he played by the rules of humanity for years. Officials in the service of the Dowager Empress and of the many foreign interests in the city were properly bribed. There were many willing to serve the King of the Cats, out of fear or desire. His strength, and the strength of his circle, surpassed itself.

Among so many robed orientals, he affected Western dress, importing black frock coats from England, satin-lined opera cloaks from Paris, linens from Holland. Giselle he dressed up like a doll, amusing her with each extravagant wardrobe. Always attuned to the pleasures of feeding, he took the time to appreciate other luxuries. Music, wine, art, literature, philosophy. With a dilettante's delight, he followed the threads of human endeavour, intrigued by their irrelevant attempts to chart their world, to map their fragile Dreams. He read his Darwin with interest. He could well appreciate the mastery of that which was best fit to survive.

But there never was an Immortal Empire. After one of the court's masques, a silky courtesan, the gift of the Empress who had provided the company with a pleasurable evening in the labyrinth beneath the Palace, was seen cast used and lifeless into the streets as her reward. The girl had had three devoted lovers, and they set about avenging her.

Philip Tarr, the British merchant skipper, Niall Baum, the Irish Jew spice trader, and Stefan Sniezawski, the much-decorated Polish mercenary. Practicality, mysticism and endeavour incarnate. The Kind had grown careless, had remained in the city long enough for their longevity to be noticed. The would-be avengers had heard all the stories about the creatures in the Palace. They consulted wise men and fools, and they framed their plans against the court.

During the celebration of the Chinese New Year, while the bulk of the company were amusing themselves with some guests in the maze, the Palace of Perpetuity was dynamited. He had been on the lowest level, feeding with Giselle. Their prey was a brother and sister who should have lasted for days. Buried alive, he had to transform himself drastically in order to get free. He burrowed upwards, insinuating himself through the loose rubble like a manta ray negotiating the complex cross-currents of the deep. He erupted into a courtyard, and found what was left of those who had escaped the initial explosion. Apart from Giselle, who followed his wormhole to the surface, none of the Kind had survived.

The three had brought a righteous mob with them, and applied the traditional remedies. Using ink-stringed cat's cradles, each of the courtiers had been trapped. Then, hawthorne and rosewood stakes had been pounded through their chests, pinning them to the ground. Finally, their heads had been lopped off with silver-coated scythes. Afterwards, some morbid wit had jumbled up the heads, matching them to the wrong bodies. The Kind did not give up life easily. He found impaled corpses pouring out blood hours after the initial butchery. Cloves of garlic had been shoved into slack mouths, and there were religious symbols everywhere, crosses, statues of the Buddha, icons, a Star of David. His eldest daughter's head lay in a shallow pool, its eyes still moving, a yellow prayer parchment pasted to its forehead.

The rage, the sorrow, the tangible residue of the recent slaughter. All these things made him stronger. The skin he had scraped off as he struggled to the surface grew back.

He spread the fires, lighting up an entire quarter of the city. Paper dragons caught easily, and flimsy houses burned like children's lanterns. He laid the company's remains where the flames would consume them totally. His duties done to the dead, he turned to revenge. With no especial joy, he destroyed his enemies.

Amid the holocaust, he found the Britisher, supervising a chain of bucket-passing coolies on the docks. He had embraced bluff Philip from behind, reaching up under his ribs and squeezing his heart with talons of ice. Giselle joined him, inflating her throat like a toad's to accommodate the gush of blood. With seven-inch fingers, she tore chunks of flesh from the dead, and chewed them like sweetmeats. She had not spoken since the explosions, but he could feel the emotion pouring out of her. He had to shut his mind to her silent screeching, lest her newfound madness carry him off, divert him from his purpose.

When Tarr was found, the other two followed them, blinded by idiocies about herbs and crucifixes and boxes of native earth. He fled inland with Giselle, leaving human carcasses and nightmare memories at every resting place along the way. Then, they reached the shunned temple in the hills, and turned around to wait for the Pole and the Irish Jew.

The Pole came first, clad in a lancer's greatcoat and carrying a new Winchester rifle. The least superstitious and most competent of the three, he was surprisingly easy. Afflicted with the sentimental streak of his people, he had lost much of his purpose with the death of his yellow harlot.

He took Sniezawski and changed him, pulling his neck out of true and crushing the rest of him into an eggshape. He fashioned a bony shell, like that of a Galapagos turtle, and slipped the Pole into it. The creature, its moustached head bobbing on an elongated stalk, its booted feet useless as flippers, made a spectacle of itself. Giselle howled with empty-headed laughter. In a moment of compassion, he lopped Sniezawski's head off.

The Irish Jew was more cunning, and more dangerous. His red hair shaven and in the robes of a monk, he came to the temple and was admitted as a pilgrim to the shrine. With the wooden daggers concealed in his habit, he killed Giselle. He used a silver-edged hatchet on her corpse, quartering her beyond repair. Then he sat on a mat, surrounded by fragments of the blessed bread, and waited for the Monster.

He found the last of his three enemies surrounded by the dead but shrieking body of his wife. Baum held up a consecrated wafer.

He leaned forwards, opening wide his mouth. The hinges of his jaw dislocated, and his neck vertebrae arched. The throat gaped, and extra rows of teeth sprouted. The walls rippled with the force of the changes, as he sucked Baum into the Dream.

With his first bite, he took Baum's arm off up to the elbow. The host disintegrated like wet paper in his gullet. He swallowed, and fingers relaxed in his belly.

Baum shrank within himself, and tried to run. But he was caught. This was not feeding. This was killing.

Then, King of the Cats no longer, he bit the Irish Jew's head off. And was done with it.

eight

ANNE PHONED the offices from the Nellie Dean in Dean Street. She had to offload some of her responsibilities.

'Hello. Editorial,' said the voice she had hoped not to hear.

'Mark?'

'Anne. Hi,' a long pause. 'What happened to you? You never came back to the phone . . .'

She realised her receiver would be buzzing, still off the hook in the flat.

'The policeman? I was trying to tell you that that dopey Sharon gave out your home address.'

'It's all right.'

'You're not on the electoral roll? That's how they usually trace you.'

'No.' She had slipped through, three moves ago, and only now felt ashamed of it. She was committed, so she ought at least to be able to vote.

There was a fuss in the background.

'We've got a crisis right now,' Mark said before she could answer. 'We're trying to get the Central America thing into the Christmas issue. Can I call you back?'

'I'm on a pay phone. Listen, my sister has died. I need some time.'

'Lord . . .'

She could picture Mark not knowing what to say. She wished someone she knew less well had answered her call, someone who could take down her information like notes for a news item and tell everyone who needed to be told.

'What are you going to do?'

'Nothing stupid. Don't worry. But I need to ask some questions. I can't just let it drop, you know.'

'Okay. Well, I've got you down to write the Poll Tax vigil piece. Clare can do that. The homelessness feature is Nigel's baby, really. I'll do the sidebars myself.'

'My notes are on the computer. It's mostly done.'

'Fine. But there's the Aziz inquest. You've been on that story from the first.'

Anne had not thought of that. She felt she owed Mrs Aziz her continued support. And Erskine was still out there, waiting to get back on the beat.

'Don't worry,' Mark said, drawing in a breath, 'I was just thinking aloud. There's no blame involved. I'll deal with it.'

She imagined him juggling notes on his desk, trying to find room for what he wanted to say to her.

'Anne, about last night . . .'

'I know, Mark. Look, I'm sorry, but . . .'

She tried to picture his expression. It was hard to tell what he was thinking face to face. The telephone disguised him completely.

'Anne, I understand. This isn't a normal thing. Call in when you want to come out of the cold. Can I get you at the flat?'

'I don't know. Maybe not. I think I've got a week or so left over in holiday time. And it's Christmas the week after next, anyway.'

'Christ yes. I'm sure the collective can get its collective head around the concept of compassionate leave. I'll stamp it through the next magazine meeting.'

She thanked him, hearing the bustle of the newsroom in the background. Phones ringing, people laughing, typing, making tea. Life going on. She supposed she would not be at the office party this year. Just as well. It would only have meant another painfully circumspect hour or two with Mark. And she could do without the mistletoe and drunkenness jokes, or Clare trying to get everyone to dance to her old Abba records.

'Your sister?' he asked. 'The one who had the trouble?'

'Judi. Yes. Trouble.' The pips sounded. 'I don't have any more change. I'll be . . .'

Buzz.

She had lied; she did have two more twenty pence pieces. She dropped them in the slot, and punched the Aziz number. She owed Charlie's mother an explanation. She could talk to the woman. As she listened to the unanswered phone ringing, she wondered how alike she and Mrs Aziz were in their reactions to death. After a full minute, she assumed everyone was out, and gave up. She must call later. She did not want Mrs Aziz to hear from Mark that she was off the story for now.

Reclaiming her coins, she collected a perrier water and an egg salad sandwich from the bar, and sat down alone. It was not twelve yet and the pub was practically empty. A fat alternative comedian Anne had seen on television was insulting the barmaid, and she was pretending he was hilarious. The bland Christmas record she hated – 'Christmas Caroline' – was playing through the speakers over the bar.

The largest of Judi's effects was a leather handbag. Anne had put all the other stuff in it and thrown away the plastic carrier the police had given her. Hollis had said that Judi's clothes would be released later, before the funeral.

Shit, the funeral. Anne did not even know how to go about arranging that. She supposed she would just have to look up 'Undertakers' in Yellow Pages and go with the Acme Funeral Company or whoever was at the top of the list. The Nielsons were third generation agnostics. A critic had once said their father spent his whole life looking for God, but Anne could not see that. She knew she would go for the simplest, most secular ceremony available. She was tempted to collapse, and play on Mark's British protectiveness to have him take care of the arrangements. He would know what to do, and be supremely efficient at it, sparing her as much of the strain as possible. But she could not do that. Anne Nielson did not use men as crutches. These were the '90s. Besides, Mark would use it as a way of getting closer to her, and he was too close already. This was family.

Judi's lighter had cracked, and the inside of her bag smelled flammable. There was not much to pick through, but she sorted all the items out and laid them on the table. Some plain rings; a skull earring; a studded leather armlet; a plastic bottle of codeine; a package of paper tissues; three shades of lipstick, scarlet, crimson and black; American Express and Visa cards; fifty pounds in fives; a purseful of loose change; a cardboard tube with a rocketship in it that contained two 'Invader' brand prophylactics, 'Launched by Automach Peterborough'; an imitation leather-bound diary/address book; and a man's wallet.

Anne played with the wallet. It was stuffed with photographs and newspaper clippings. There was an old snapshot of the sisters, as children, with a pony, somewhere in New England; Anne was standing, smiling, holding the bridle while Judi, little more than a baby, perched fat and fed-up on the saddle, dress ridden up over her thighs. A photo booth strip of a young man Anne did not recognise. Judi grown up, with two other girls, caught in a flashbulb glare, trying to look deliriously abandoned in a nightclub. The last shot made Anne shiver.

The cuttings were an odd selection: a piece from *The Guardian* about father's stroke, a favourable review of one of Cam's concerts at the Pompidou Centre, a *Radio Times* listing for a late night screening of *On the Graveyard Shift at Sam's Bar-B-Q and Grill*, and samples of Anne's work from various papers and magazines. There was also an ancient anonymous letter Anne remembered arriving at the house and upsetting Dad. It called him a fink for informing on fellow travellers in '57. It had disappeared, and only now she realised Judi must have sent it herself, and that Dad must have known: over the years, there had been a steady trickle of abuse, but this one had really nettled their father. The only thing there that was about Judi was a report on a coroner's hearing she had given evidence at. Anne had not heard of the dead man, a stabbing victim, and could not work out what his connection with Judi had been.

'Checking the loot, eh, love?' said the comedian, laughing. 'Funny how the muggers get younger and prettier every day, innit?'

Anne looked up at the man. His chins were shaking, and he had a beerfoam moustache.

'Fuck off,' she said, her eyes fixed. His grin froze, and fell apart. He turned back to the barmaid, and made a remark Anne did not catch, laughing again.

Anne looked again at the items on the table, and tried in her mind to connect them with Judi.

As soon as Judi had arrived in London, she had telephoned her sister, but only to cadge some money. That had been two years ago. The sisters had not met since. Like Anne, Judi had right of residence thanks to their English mother. Two years was time enough to make a whole life. She picked up the armlet. The leather was cracked, and a few of the studs were missing, leaving tiny wounds. Not for the first time, Anne wondered how exactly her sister had lived.

And what was she looking for anyway? Keepsakes? Messages from the grave? Clues?

She had saved the book until last. It was such an obvious source of information. Under today's date was neatly printed 'N. Club D.E. 1.00'. N? A name? One o'clock? Morning or afternoon? Club D.E.? Going through the addresses at the back of the book, she found any number of people with N for a first or second initial, and addresses for several clubs, among them the Club Des Esseintes. That was in Brewer Street, just around the corner.

The Club Des Esseintes.

nine

H IS HAIRCUT cost more than the average suit, and his suits individually cost more than the average good-condition second-hand car. Clive Broome had the Business sussed, and the first thing he had learned was the importance of always being well turned-out. If transactions needed to be made in venues where his style would be suspicious, he could always buy some spiky-haired lout to handle it. He preferred not to get too close to the retail end of the trade anyway. He was moving up the pyramid, and he wanted everyone he dealt with to know it.

Most nights of the week, Clive liked to screw somebody. But he insisted on sleeping alone. He hated the thought of waking up with a pair of alien elbows in his ribs and the sheets in a mess. After they had done the business, he had shifted last night's cunt into the spare room. By the time he was ready to get up, she was long gone. He also liked to sleep late.

As far as he could tell, nothing was missing. Gretchen, from Barnet, with a butterfly tattoo. She should be not hard to find. If any of his things had taken a walk, he would have the Sergeant Major cut one of her boobs off. Or give her to Mr Skinner.

He went cold, fast-forwarding through yesterday's business. The call from Mr Skinner, the deliveries, the white faces of the girls, the disposal. That was not over yet. One down, he told himself, one to go. He should not really get involved in deals like that. But they were useful. The Games Master was such a strange customer. It was well worth the risk of the disposal job to have Mr Skinner wrapped up and tied in with something messy. The man was monied enough to have some pull somewhere, and Clive could always use someone with pull. After the disposal, Mr Skinner owed him plenty. Still, Judi's face had been a frightener.

After dressing, he sat down in his work-room to go through the post and deal with the morning's telephone messages. Most of the letters were Christmas cards, from Business contacts and sentimental cunts, but there was also a whingeing note from his mother and his subscription copies of *Viz* and *The Economist*. Most of the people who had called him up had not left any sort of message, but Mink said that he had received the shipment of Brussels sprouts he had been expecting.

Clive still thought the vegetable talk was fucking stupid. He was supposed to be a wholesale produce importer, supplying his own chain of fashionably overpriced health food shops. Through design-oriented marketing, he had ridden the Green wave and successfully negated the duffel-coated hippie image of health foods to target the high disposable income of yuppies in high-stress jobs who would follow any dietary plan as long as it was expensive and minimal. The food business was even quite lucrative, but actually his real trade was drugs. The code-names just made Mink feel like he was in a spy film. It was a typical dopehead way of justifying habitual paranoia. It also suggested he thought he was just playing a game, and Clive was serious about what he did for a living. He was not thirty yet, but already he had been in the Business twice as long as most of the people he worked with. It was all about being careful.

But Mink's message was good news. Clive could now go down to the Hackney wholefood store and pick up the heroin his people were waiting for. New drug-of-the-month crazes like Ecstasy and crack might come along, and Clive was conscious that he had to keep such items in stock, while cocaine was capturing a more exclusive portion of the market but heroin was the white bread of the Business. There was always a market for the old staple diet of junkies. After a night in the space behind his airing cupboard, the gear would go to the Sergeant Major and be repackaged for his men in the marketplace. And he would be able to meet Mr Skinner's standing order.

Mr Skinner would be very pleased. Clive sometimes wondered what the man was up to. Obviously, the skag he bought wound up in someone or other's arm. His version was that heroin was much more convenient than cash. He was right there. Surely, the Games Master wasn't stuck on the H himself. He was not anyone's idea of normal, but he was not stupid. Clive was well aware of his position in the Business, at precisely that cusp where men in smart suits with career structures deal with deadbeats in torn jeans with minimal life expectancies. Mr Skinner was higher up the pyramid. When you got to where he was, it stopped being Business and started getting Political. Right now, it was down to Clive to make himself indispensible.

Clive started doing sums on his expensive pocket calculator. He had an upper second in business studies from the University of East Anglia. Most of the people he had known up there were working in the City, for the media or unemployed these days. Several of them were customers, although they saw the Sergeant Major's lads rather than him. He liked to think he was making more money and paying less tax than any of them. His calculator played the first eight notes of 'Money Makes the World Go Around'. That always gave him a giggle.

He was proud of the fact that he had three times voted for the best government the country had had in his lifetime. There was a picture of him shaking hands with Margaret Thatcher at a Young Entrepreneur of the Year dinner on his desk next to his Sinclair micro. He really admired her for the way she had opened up the economy to individual enterprise. He was a practised and popular after dinner speaker at local affairs, and his favourite address was entitled 'The Strength of a Nation Lies in its Human Resources.' For him, the Business was a business, not an amusement or an adjunct to a personal need. The drug trade was a consumer-led market, and he had got into it at the right time, meeting an increased demand and offering a better service than his competitors. The '80s had been a growth period, but he knew that bull markets always eventually swelled and burst. He could foresee the point when he would get out of drugs – at the right time, of course – and step up the pyramid.

Although the very nature of the Business brought him into contact with a load of moaning minnies and smackhead losers, he had started to employ only men who had proved themselves possessed of a decent amount of backbone. The Sergeant Major had been in Northern Ireland for a couple of years before they sent him to Pentonville, and he had brought some good new lads into the operation. One or two of the carriers had served in the Falklands. Clive did not employ users, and the Sergeant Major had standing orders to pay off with broken bones any of his lads caught with their fingers in the supply. Clive wanted long-term people who could be useful when he branched out.

Now, Clive telephoned the Sergeant Major. He would have been up since dawn, handling a couple of little things. He picked up the phone at the fourth ring.

'Sergeant Major.'

'Mr Broome?'

'How did things go?'

'Very nicely, sir. I've been to the bank, and I talked to the man you wanted seen to. There won't be any more trouble in Deptford, I don't think.'

Clive imagined the crack of fingerbones.

'That's excellent. I'd appreciate it if you'd drop by later.'

'Very good, sir.'

'Yes, we have another disposal job to do. A lot like the last one. No trouble at all.'

'Fine, sir.'

'Right. See you later. Take care.'

Clive thought for a moment about the other girl, Coral. And about Judi.

In his front room, Clive had a framed print of the Battle of Waterloo, a collection of imported pornographic magazines, a CD player and a VHS recorder and video tapes of all Torvill and Dean's greatest performances. In his kitchen, he had a case of expensive wine, a robot-chef and a microwave oven. In his lavatory, he had copies of *The Official Sloane Ranger Handbook, The Naff Sex Guide* and *How to Be a Wally*. In his work-room, he had a licenced handgun, five thousand pounds in small notes and a fax machine.

In his basement, he had a dead prostitute with her arm cut off.

ten

AS NEAR DEATH as he had ever been, he tried to slither over the beaten earth of the alley. His face hung off his skull in lumpy rags. One of the cuts had been high up and at the back of his head, and a torn curtain of skin and scalp had flapped forwards over his face. It hung over his eyes and nose like a wet scarf. Since his own pain had long since ceased to mean anything to him, he felt almost at peace in the red darkness.

The irony of it was that the men who had done this to him knew nothing about his real nature. They had killed him simply because they were paid to. He would kill them, but without true malice, or even true relish. If people habitually treated each other like this, who could blame the Kind for the way they treated the human race? Of course, it was really his own fault. He knew that he should never have got mixed up in politics.

He had tried to change when they assaulted him, but there had been eight or ten of them and they were very skilled in their profession. Using iron bars and sharp knives instead of crosses and cats' cradles, they had caught him efficiently before he could make himself more dangerous and ripped him apart. They had broken his arms and one leg, and his pelvis was twisted out of shape. Consequently, he could not roll himself over and had to try crawling face up. He grew horny talons, curving them into the hard ground. His hands clawed at the ground like scuttling crabs and pulled the heavy bulk of the rest of his body towards the mouth of the alley, assisted only by the occasional inchworm push of his good leg.

Arriving in Istanbul between the coming of talking pictures and the Wall Street Crash, he had drifted into the restaurant trade, turning a particularly vile brothel into a fashionable nightclub. He hired singers who actually could sing, rather than belly-dancers renowned only for their ability to pleasure simultaneously an inordinate number of patrons, and he replaced the group of criminals, cripples, degenerates and relics who had served as an orchestra with genuine musicians from Paris, London and New Orleans. Finally, he had struck an exclusive deal with Turkey's leading importer of American phonograph records, so that his club would introduce the latest Cole Porter or Irving Berlin song to Istanbul weeks before the Fred Astaire or Paul Whiteman versions became available.

It started to rain, and he began to feel as if vinegar were being pissed into his open wounds. Perhaps he had not outgrown pain after all. The entrails piled on his empty belly must be steaming. Somewhere above, but quite near, he heard music. It was Victor Young and His Orchestra with The Boswell Sisters, performing 'I Found a Million Dollar Baby in a Five and Ten Cent Store'. He stopped crawling, and feeling came back to his misaligned elbows. He tossed his head, and the bloody flap lifted from his face and fell more or less in its proper place. He looked down at himself. He was already covered with flies, and a scraggy monkey, a refugee from some street act, was picking at one of his ankles. It looked hungry enough to forget it was supposed to be a herbivore.

As usual, he had got bored with an easy life, and expanded his operations. He had never entirely taken his establishment out of the business of procuring, and he soon rekindled his taste for the marketing of human flesh. He imported girls, and boys, from Greece, Egypt, various Balkan pretend countries, India, China, even the Socialist Workers' Utopia across the Black Sea. Then, he found his aquaintances became useful in furthering a varied trade in foods, drugs, armaments, icons, rare books, general contraband and murder. Money had always bored him, but his interests also enabled him to build up a fortune in the simplest, least tangible, most negotiable currency in the world – information.

Stiffening his back for the purpose, he sat up suddenly. He dragged his arms from behind him and deposited his hands in his lap. He brushed the dirt and flies off his coiled bowels and pressed the functional mass back into his body. He reached for the cummerbund that had been torn off him during his murder, and wrapped it tightly about his midriff, easing shut the wound that had disembowelled him. His insides realigned themselves, itching and burning by turns. He felt ready to use his arms again and reached for the monkey.

At first, he had dealt only with a mountain of a colonel in the Turkish Secret Police, supplying him with interesting tit-bits about the many foreign nationals who passed through his club. Then, he had delicately approached, in turn, the local representatives of Germany, Russia and Great Britain. There would be yet another war eventually, and Turkey was in such an odd spot on the map. Squeezed between three troubled continents and theoretically neutral, it was naturally at the centre of all manner of legitimate and illegitimate merchant and refugee activities, and the site of diplomacy and espionage on a scale he had not seen since his dealings with the papacy in the 14th century. It had eased the tedium to see the nations of humankind scheme and plot against one another, and to be able to take a hand in the shaping of the War that would change everything again.

The monkey's meagre meat and brief flare of dreamstuff helped, and he was able unsteadily to stand up. He smoothed his forehead and scalp over his skull, and tore away the dead tatters that clung to his cheekbones and neck. They had cut off his genitals and stamped them into the dirt. That was supposed to be a warning to his associates. It did not concern him much. Thorough his assailants might have been, but they had also shown a typically human lack of imagination in their treatment of him. After so many centuries of torture and violence, he would have thought that men would become practised in the artistry of feeding. But no, the race was still saddeningly small-minded.

He had been amused by the opportunity to juggle with
the interests of so many nations and individuals, and had
capriciously exploited the situation. Once he had denounced
an innocent American tobacco trader as a dangerous enemy
spy to the Nazis and the Soviets, and doubled his money by
accepting two commissions to arrange his assassination. But
someone or other had discovered one of his duplicities, or
taken offence at one of his transactions, and had paid a gang
of waterfront knifemen to drag him into this alley and ruin
him.

Soon, he would be whole again. Then, his murderers
would be his meat and drink. And he would find out who
had employed them and feed off him. Then there would be
the War, and wars were what he liked best of all. Europe
would be a killing ground for a while, a banquet for the
Kind. Then, he thought, he might go back to the United
States. He had the feeling, listening to the torch songs of that
nation on his Victrola, that America was about to become the
most interesting country on the globe. The Old World was
using itself up fast. There was life for the taking beyond the
Atlantic, and a vitality which could feed him for decades.

In an upstairs window, a girl appeared. She was not
beautiful, but she was not fat and disgusting either. She
saw him as a stranger loitering in the dark alley below and
routinely exposed her breasts to him.

He stepped into the light, and looked up at her. She did not
scream. In her mind, she said she had seen worse.

'That's what you think,' he said out loud in the wrong
language, one she did not understand. Through exposed and
bloody teeth, he began to serenade her.

'Say it's only a paper moon,' he sang, 'Sailing over a
cardboard sea, but it wouldn't be make believe if you believed
in me . . .'

Fascinated, she remained in the window, waiting for him
to come up to her. She was his instantly. He saw her entire
life, from birth to this moment. Roumanian originally, Macha
Igescu was seventeen years old, working for Demetrios
Malacou. She loved him because he beat her less than her

last protector, never more than once a week. She had had two babies – both sold by Malacou to strangers – and her dreams were befogged by the poppy smoke. She was nearing the end of her professional life. Malacou, she knew, would dump her for that plump-titted Arab bitch, and she would be sold on into some dark dormitory to do her work chained to a cot.

He promised himself that he would find Malacou and kill him for Macha. He would not feed off the pimp; he would just open his throat and let him empty. After all, he was going to owe Macha for his life.

Latching his fingerhooks into the crumbling stonework, he began his climb . . . .

eleven

IN BREWER STREET, all the sex shops had identical notices up in their windows. A Merry Christmas to All Our Customers. The season of goodwill to all men gets everywhere. Anne wondered whether the girls in the Live Erotic Nude Bed Show had to wear Santa Claus hats and reindeer antlers. Weary shop assistants had been busy hanging paper lanterns from the rubberwear, and winding silvery tinsel through displays of sex aids. In a centrally-heated style shop, customers got to choose between purple and turquoise trenchcoats, assisted by young girls with cycle shorts and partially-shaven heads. A record store had a cardboard cut-out of Derek Douane, the teenage ex-choirboy who had inflicted 'Christmas Caroline' on the human race. Anne hurried past his fixed smile, trying not to think of the burbling, thought-destroying tune that could get into your brain and settle for hours. The traffic was snarled, and bike messengers were gleefully whizzing their way through the gridlocked maze of personalised numberplate limousines and delivery vans. In New York, this would occasion a din of honked horns, but the British drivers just sat and fumed in their tincans, waiting for the world to get better. Outside a Chinese take-away, three pigeons pecked determinedly at a splash of frozen sick.

A wino with black toes poking through his mangled trainers aimed himself at her. He skittered through the Christmas-shopping crowds like a pinball, bouncing off walls, lampposts and people, his shaky eyes fixed on her. The grubby hand was already coming out, and the ritual phrase was working its way down from the speech centres of his brain to the spirits-slurred tongue.

'Excuse me,' she said, before he could get it out, 'Could you spare ten pence for a cup of coffee?'

Usually, derelicts retreated in astonishment at this tactic, but the Soho wino was a hardier breed.

'Fuck you, sister,' he coughed at her through black and broken teeth, 'and the horse you rode in on.'

She sidestepped him, and walked on rapidly. She was not happy with her behaviour. She had done pieces on homelessness. She ought to have more sympathy.

'I fought in three world wars for you,' the tramp shouted at her back. She wished Mace was legal in this country.

The capital was turning into a Third World city, she thought. At every central London subway station, there were begging kids, shivering in several layers of clothes, a pleading message printed in biro on a piece of cardboard. Less aggressive than the alky pan-handlers, the kids were even more depressing, fiercely ashamed of their situation, never meeting the eyes of the passersby. The tramp she had dodged was one of the old-style bums, the last of the Summer winos, and was most likely feeling the pinch. With younger, less stereotypically derelict, not obviously cracked people sleeping rough and trying to get into the spare change business, the old and alcoholic would be pushed out of their place in the begging order. The street population was expanding, as more and more people fell through the gaps in the welfare state's safety net. There were ways to get by, but none of them were pleasant, or safe. Soon, London would be just Tijuana, Bangkok or Casablanca with a lousy climate.

The Club Des Esseintes was difficult to find, but she guessed that it was supposed to be. There was a nostalgia shop at the address listed in Judi's diary, with a passport photographer's and a French model agency upstairs. The plaque was screwed to a wall papered many times over with posters for rock gigs and albums. A group called Faster Pussycat, frozen in mid-scream, dominated the pasted-and-torn collage. She had to look at the wall for a full minute before she found the sign. Someone had scraped a hole in Neneh Cherry's midriff so the words were still visible.

Private Club – Walk Down. And in the corner, in little curlicue letters, Des Esseintes.

The shop was full of faded magazines displayed in racks, piles of movie posters and boxes of still photographs. The major display was a selection of one-sheets for films about Santa Claus. In one, the cheery old gentleman was brandishing a bloody hatchet over a naked girl. The ad line boasted 'it's a ho-ho-ho-horror!' You better watch out, Anne thought. Someone had driven a dagger smeared with stage blood through a smiling cut-out of Dudley Moore dressed as an elf. *Phil Spector's Christmas Album* was coming through the shop's speakers, 'Christmas (Baby Please Come Home)' by Darlene Love. At least that was an improvement on Derek Douane. 'Do you have any material on Caroline Munro,' a foreign customer was asking a bored attendant, 'or Rosanna Podesta?' Anne looked around the shop and found the stairwell behind an impressive array of Japanese warrior robots.

The spiral staircase was black, and the walls bright scarlet, but the well was lit only by one bare bulb at the top. Anne went down into the darkness. The stairs fed her into a corridor, dimly lit by imitation candles in electric sconces. The walls were blood red, the floor herringbone-tiled and polished. There were unrecognisable portraits of men in periwigs hanging between the candles. The Marquis de Sade, she supposed, and intimate friends.

A level below the street, she could no longer hear Darlene Love. Instead, there was the tinkle of musak. She recognised the tune and almost laughed. 'You Always Hurt the One You Love'.

The first serious obstacle stood at the end of the corridor, ominous in a black leather hood. His axe did not look like a prop, and there was a coiled bullwhip in his belt. He was wearing polished boots and lumpy tights, with his chest – muscle just running to meat – bare. Anne thought he was unlikely to be impressed by her NUJ card.

She wanted to go home and forget about the whole thing.

Suddenly, she was one of a crowd. Six or seven people had come down behind her, and she walked down the corridor with them, trying to seem at ease. They looked like an ordinary lunchtime group, office workers out for a Christmas drink. The executioner bowed and opened a pair of double doors, admitting them into a cellar bar. Evidently, he recognised some of the club's regular patrons. Anne was swept inside with them. She noticed one young businessman buckling a studded dog collar around his neck.

There had been a sign above the doors. The Inferno Lounge. She had expected a vaulted torture chamber in Hammer Films style, but, at first sight, the room was more impressive. Three walls and the ceiling were covered with a fairly expert mural in imitation of Hieronymous Bosch. Damned souls wriggled, turned in on themselves in the corners, pierced by water pipes near the ceiling.

The furnishings were black, with occasional silver and scarlet highlights. The only light came from a rank of glowing bar heaters and from the many television monitors, which were perched on high shelves above the bar and around the walls, or set into the tables like video games. Under the musak was the muted sound of whipping and slapping and yelping. There was also the rumble of something that sounded like vast underground machinery, grinding away behind the walls.

Anne climbed onto a stool at the bar, and looked around at the customers. There were a few young women in already-dated punk outfits, including one girl with green hair cat-napping upright a few stools down, but most of the people in the Inferno Lounge were conservatively-dressed men. Young to middle-aged white collar types, with briefcases and newspapers. The *Mail* and the *Telegraph*. Mostly, they sat alone, watching the televisions and ignoring their drinks.

Anne wondered which, if any, of these people, was N? She did not know whether Judi was meeting a friend, or a . . . she gulped mentally . . . or a customer. N could have been anyone, including someone on the staff rather than among the clientele.

Up on the monitors, Anne saw an array of sharp video images. An over-aged schoolgirl, complete with braids and ankle socks, taking her knickers down for a cane-brandishing headmaster. A W.P.C. masturbating furiously with a truncheon. Two bored naked women ineptly flogging a tethered third party. An academic explaining the precise uses of a set of antique nipple clamps.

Anne tried to imagine Judi here, to imagine her talking with the other girls, or with the men. She had specialised in receiving pain, Anne knew, not in giving it. She would have had to determine which was any given client's preference. Looking at a thin blond young man in a business suit, while trying not to seem as if she was looking, she wondered whether he liked to hurt or be hurt. He had almost colourless eyes, and was ghost-pale in the videolight. He reminded her of Constable Barry Erskine, the Batterer. She imagined him making fists, and using them on a girl's face. On Judi's face. Again, Anne wanted to leave, but knew she had taken it too far to just go home . . . .

'You can't just sit here, you know,' someone said, 'you'll have to buy a drink.'

The barman looked like a functionary of the Spanish Inquisition, in black robes, picked out with an assorted batch of mystical symbols. Otherwise, he could have been serving in any other unfriendly pub in town.

'Oh,' said Anne, 'perrier.'

The barman exhumed a green bottle. When he unscrewed the cap, there was the faintest ghost of a carbonated fizz. He poured into a tall glass.

'Ice and lemon?'

'Please.'

He picked up the fruit slice and single lump with a wicked-looking pair of hooked tongs, and dropped them in her drink.

'Four pounds fifty,' he said. She hesitated. 'Remember, no one comes here to drink.'

She handed over a five, and received no change. She let the matter drop. She wished she had given the money to the wino out on the street. At least, he would be able to get drunk out of it.

Shit, what a hole.

Some of the young women were approaching the new-
comers, pouting and trying to seem masterful. Even to Anne,
it was obvious that the working girls were unable to take
all this seriously. The thin blond dropped to his knees and
licked a girl's creaking boot, his tongue probing the cracks in
the leather. She had guessed wrong about him: he was into
M, not S. When he looked up, the girl's face was set like a
school pantomime version of the Wicked Stepmother, but
otherwise she just looked ordinary and tired. The would-be
slave kept dropping pound coins into her boot-tops. That
must get uncomfortable.

Casually, Anne began her Nancy Drew act. 'Has Judi been
in recently?'

'What's all this Judi stuff today?' asked the barman. 'Has
she just won the Miss Popularity award?'

Anne pounced, a little too quickly.

'Has anyone else been looking for her?'

'Nina,' the barman said, looking around. It was difficult in
the gloom to make anyone out.

Nina? N?

Anne looked around too. The barman had ignored the
green-haired girl, so she was out. Which of the others could
Nina be?

Anne turned back to the barman, and found that he was,
for the first time, looking carefully at her. She knew he was
realising that he had never seen her before. She glanced at the
doors. The executioner was standing by them.

'You're curious,' the barman told her. 'Open your handbag, love. Let's see your membership card.'

The executioner was coming over now. Nancy Drew had
failed. She would have to start being Clint Eastwood instead,
and she did not think she was really up to it.

'Eric,' the barman called the executioner, 'we have a
trespasser who needs prosecuting.'

These people, she knew, were good at pain. That was how
they made their living.

She dashed her perrier into the barman's eyes, and snatched
his ice tongs. Eric did not move too fast. She hoped he could

not see a thing in his Batman cowl. At school, she had not
been a quarterback, but she had not been a cheerleader either.
She slammed painfully into the executioner, but he did not fall
over.

She grabbed for his mask and pushed it. The eyeholes were
now over his forehead. She backed off, but he still managed to
hit her hand away before falling over his whip and sprawling
on the floor.

She threw the tongs at the barman, and picked up a heavy
metal and leather chair. The barman dodged the tongs, but
did not try to come out and get her. The weight of the chair
felt good.

Some of the businessmen were applauding, and calling for
more. The blond was diverted from his ladylove's boot, and
looking up at Anne, imploring with his watering eyes.

Everyone was staying out of the reach of Anne's chair. She
jabbed it in the air a couple of times, like a lion-tamer. People
cringed.

Anne felt the need to hit Eric with the chair. She brought
it down on him with a log-chopping swing. He grunted and
held his head, still trying to struggle out of the hood.

She threw the chair aside, and pushed through the doors.
She did not know if Eric was after her or not.

She raced down the corridor.

She nearly lost a shoe on the staircase, but made it easily to
the street. For the first time in years, she had a stitch.

Slowing down and trying to get her breath, she walked
briskly through the shop and into the street. The cold wrapped
around her. After the Inferno Lounge, which she now realised
had been overheated, the outside chill was almost welcome.

As she tried to walk away, there was a tug at her smarting
shoulder. Someone was pulling her handbag.

'Excuse me, miss . . .'

twelve

'LOOK,' said Tail Gunner Joe, 'isn't that Bogart?'

It was somebody else, but the observation helped the Monster understand the Junior Senator. Sitting in Romanoff's, an ill-fitting suit and a sweaty grin among so many tailcoats and panstick-smooth faces, the man was stargazing, like any other gawk-eyed Mid-Westerner visiting Sin City – Hollywood, California. It almost made him endearing. Tail Gunner Joe was made for this town. Like the glove salesmen tycoons, the grease-monkey apemen, the waitress demigoddesses and the bogus Russian royalty restauranteurs, the war hero witchfinder was a Great American Fraud. Even politics was not a big enough backdrop for his imagined autobiography. Tail Gunner Joe had to get into Showbiz, and rate more mentions in *Variety* than in *The New York Times*. His was an addictive personality, and the need for fame was as desperate in him as the need for his favoured stimulant, morphine. The Monster knew that the Junior Senator was on his crusade so someone would one day cast Spencer Tracy as him in a film of his heroic life from the dogfights of the war to the pit-bull tussles of the Senate. Like every crooked politician in the United States, he had seen *Mr Smith Goes to Washington* several times, and always identified more fiercely with Jimmy Stewart than Claude Rains. When he had got up in the Senate with his list of 'card-carrying Communists', he had been thinking of Mr Smith.

The Lawyer, a boyish mouse of a man with an intensity that frightened most, was irked by Tail Gunner Joe's lack of concentration. A quiet Jew, he was intent on his papers, and wanted to get the discussion back to the agenda. And the woman, creeping into middle-age with her bobbed hair and staring eyes, was just gaga. Russian originally, she was a prophet of Americanism, and had dignified her sloppy thinking with a neologism, styling herself as the avatar of Objectivism. Even Tail Gunner Joe, who was awed by her intellect, thought of her as a dingbat. The Monster knew there were only two people who counted at this meeting; him, and the Lawyer. They knew that Red-baiting was just a passing thing, and that there was a more important prize to be won through the Committee and its hearings. Between them, the Lawyer and he could own the dreams of America more thoroughly than Louis B. Mayer, Jack Warner or Sam Goldwyn.

'Mr Farnham,' said the Lawyer, 'as I am sure you are aware, we do not want to repeat of the fiasco of Thomas and the Hollywood Ten.'

He nodded. Congressman J. Parnell Thomas had been the chairman of the House Un-American Activities Commission back in '47, the figurehead of the first anti-Communist purge in the film capital. Currently, he was serving an eighteen month sentence, for accepting bribes, in a prison in Danbury, Connecticut, where, by a nasty coincidence even the Monster found amusing, two of his fellow inmates were Ring Lardner Jr and Lester Cole, doing a stretch for Contempt of Congress as a direct result of their appearances as 'unfriendly' witnesses before Thomas and the Committee.

'Thomas was a fool,' he said. 'You can't be St George and have your hand in the till.'

Tail Gunner Joe coughed, obviously not wanting to discuss graft and corruption. The Lawyer ticked off some point on his agenda, and the waiter returned with their drinks. The Junior Senator had obviously been hitting the sauce all afternoon, and was pleasantly squiffed. The Monster had arranged for the party to be taken on a tour of the Paramount lot this afternoon, and the Junior Senator was still excited at having met Cecil B. DeMille and Bing Crosby.

The *entrées* arrived, and Tail Gunner Joe attacked his seafood cocktail hungrily. The Objectivist picked at her salad, and the Lawyer stuck to his soft drink. They were an interesting contrast in repressions, the Objectivist trembling with her neurotic drives, the Lawyer locked tight up inside himself. They both wanted him, the Monster knew.

He sent back the soup to throw a scare into the chef. To him, something as invisible as power was a pleasure only if it were exercised at every opportunity. A new bowl, identically excellent, arrived instantly, along with the apologies of the management and an offer to tear up the bill for the whole meal. He graciously accepted, and lapped up a few spoons of bisque, savouring the taste.

Arriving in California shortly before Pearl Harbour, it had taken him a while to grow into Hugh Farnham. As always, when he remained in one place long enough, he adopted protective colouring. His face set, and he allowed it to change only to simulate the gradual process of ageing. Professional qualifications were easy to come by, and the false details of 'Hugh Farnham''s early life were almost absurdly easy to plant in various records. There were people who would swear to have known him as a young man, even as a child. Now, he was officially 'lawyer to the moguls' – sanctioned by both Hedda Hopper and Louella Parsons – and a big wheel in the motion picture industry, the California state legislature and the coming wave, Americanism. If he had actually been born in a log cabin on the prairies and grown up with the taste of Coca-Cola in his mouth and the prospect of a dignified old age on the White House lawn, he could not have been more American. After so many years of wandering, it did him good to put down roots. This was such a rich and stupid country. He had fed better here than he had for centuries.

The Lawyer still wanted to talk business, and the Objectivist wanted to talk philosophy, but, underlying their conversation, the Monster sensed their desire for him. He was amused that their preferences should be so similar, and relished the stag reels they were playing over and over in their brains. On a basic level they would never be able to articulate, they sensed some of what he was, and longed to submit to his feeding frenzy. The Lawyer, he knew, could never admit to his secret needs, and would even go so far into the closet as to link 'perversion' with the political doctrines he was intent upon helping the Junior Senator stamp out. The Objectivist, however, would sublimate her frenzies into her writing, turning out more and more turbulent, half-literate, half-blathering prose about the failures of altruism, the paramount rights of the individual and the tyranny of the common masses. It was so obvious that the hero of her most famous novel was her imagined version of Hugh Farnham that even one or two of the reviewers had noticed it.

A movie star came into the restaurant, weighed down by furs and diamonds, and trailed by her mother and a discreet entourage. The Monster waved, and the mother, one of the friendliest of the friendlies, beamed a grotesque smile at him. Tail Gunner Joe was impressed that he knew such legendary screen figures, and insisted on being introduced.

'Ginger,' the Monster said, 'this is the Senator from Winsconsin you've been hearing so much about.'

The dancer put on a smiling face as the plump, rumpled politician kissed her hand. The Junior Senator was as sincere as if he were soliciting votes.

'You were wonderful in *The Groom Wore Spurs*,' Tail Gunner Joe, the undiscriminating picture fan, said. The star's smile froze solid, and the Monster tried and failed to remember what her last good film had been.

'I hope you'll be kicking the Reds in the ass,' said the star's mother, claiming the Junior Senator's attention with expansive gestures. She was expensively made up to look like her daughter's bloated twin.

Tail Gunner Joe grinned, even as the Lawyer was wincing, and made a meaty fist. 'Sure will, ma'am,' he said, 'anything to please a lady.'

The star and her entourage swept past. Tail Gunner Joe was warmed with a glow he would retain all evening. He had met real movie stars, and had something to boast about to the folks back home.

'The real problem is in the content,' the Objectivist said, trying to impress him, 'all too often industrialists, bankers and businessmen are presented on the screen as villains, crooks, chiselers or exploiters. The Communists want to put over the message that personal success is somehow achieved at the expense of others, and that every man has hurt somebody by becoming successful. It's pernicious nonsense, of course. The Reds say they want to destroy men like Hitler and Mussolini, but what they really want to destroy are men like Shakespeare, Chopin and Edison.'

It was a neat little speech, and the Junior Senator was pleased with it, nodding as if he understood. The Lawyer had an 'all very well, but . . .' expression, and was holding up his papers again. He was impatient for names, dates and times. The Monster was reminded of a first-time director trying to wrestle a pair of recalcitrant stars into following his script. For him, the Objectivist was just window dressing, of no real interest except for her intellectual credentials. For too long, all the thinkers and artists had been on the left; the crusade had to take the eggheads it could get, no matter how scrambled. The Lawyer was perceptive enough to realise how sham the Objectivist was, and cynical enough to know that, even if he had not been able to finish her last book, there were a million Americans who had and swallowed her bombast as deep thought. If it were not for his cowardice and self-denial, the Monster would have quite admired the Lawyer. Quite.

The dance band was playing 'Mona Lisa', an Oscar-winner the year before for *Captain Carey, USA*. The Monster enjoyed the Academy Awards, and always made sure he got the best seats for the ceremony. The tangle of emotions was so delicious. Winners and losers were meat and drink to him. These days, he just tapped his meals, disdaining to drain them completely, sampling the dreamstuff but sparing the flesh. It was a revelation, how much he could enjoy feeding without killing. In a sense, there was more delight in leaving his broken prey alive.

'Let's talk names,' said Tail Gunner Joe, belching.

The Objectivist's claws came out. 'Yes, let'ssss. You should squeeze Trumbo, Lawson, Dmytryk and Hammett some more.' Her face was tightened as she spoke, her elaborately-applied make-up cracking. 'A spell in prison will have jolted them. They should be ready to turn on their fellow Reds.'

The Junior Senator looked contemptuous. 'Hah. Trumbull, Dimitri and Hackett are nobodies. Who cares about directors . . .'

'Writers,' the Objectivist said, with a little moue. 'They are writers.'

'Writers, then,' The Junior Senator signalled for another drink. The armpits of his lightweight suit were getting alcoholically dark. 'Writers are chickenshit.'

The best-selling novelist knitted her fingers and shut up. The Lawyer enjoyed her discomfiture. And the Monster rolled the little tangle of emotions around in his mouth, like brandy. He had a slight rush.

'What the Senator means to say,' the Lawyer interpreted, 'is that the Committee should make every effort to secure high-profile witnesses. We must not underestimate the importance of the public recognition factor in these hearings.'

'Nobody gives a fuck about who writes pictures,' the Junior Senator growled. 'What we want, dollface, is *stars*. Am I right, Hugh?'

The Monster nodded.

'We gotta get out of this business with Joe Shmoe from Kokomo, author of *Andy Hardy Goes to Leningrad*, or Sammy Kikestein, assistant trainee camera operator on *Pinkos of the South Sea Islands*.'

The Lawyer's face did not move when Tail Gunner Joe mentioned the mythical 'Sammy Kikestein', but he winced inside. Anti-semitism, the man knew, was a two-edged sword.

'If those writers are Commies,' Tail Gunner Joe blustered, 'they should just be taken out and put against a wall. We could all care less about them . . . them . . .'

'Anonymous masses,' the Objectivist suggested.

'Yeah, anomynous. Now, if Clark Gable was a Red . . .'

'. . . not that we have any reason to suspect he is,' the Lawyer put in, addressing his footnote to the Monster.

'No, but if he were, if Katharine Hepburn or William Holden or Kirk Douglas were pinkos. Then that would be *news*. You gotta gimme stars.'

'Gale Sondegaard,' the Objectivist stammered.

'Who?' asked the Senator, spitting pugnaciously.

'An Academy Award winner.'

'Best Supporting Actress. Nothing. Gimme before-the-title stars.'

'John Garfield.'

'A has-been.'

The Monster sat back, and watched them squabble. There was a great nexus of power forming around these people, he knew, and, as Hugh Farnham, he would have to be in the centre of it. But they were such petty tyrants, schoolchildren playing domination games. The Objectivist was squirming, trying to swallow her distaste for the Junior Senator, and to suppress the pictures she was making in her mind of herself spreadeagled naked and bleeding over a rockface as Hugh Farnham savagely drilled her from the rear, the flesh of his body merged with oily quarrying equipment. A founder member of the Motion Picture Alliance for the Preservation of American Ideals, the Objectivist had spun her suppressed kinks into a successful novel and a travesty of a film, and the Monster found it strange to see himself distorted through the broken lens of her mind into the masterful brute played so stiffly in the movie by Gary Cooper. The veins in his cheeks and neck swelled as the Objectivist worked herself up to a crazed interior climax, while trying to pay attention to the Junior Senator. A drop of sweat dribbled from her hairline like a tear. The Monster breathed in her flood of feelings, and was nourished by them.

Here, in Romanoff's, surrounded by fools and knaves, he felt again like the King of the Cats.

'Say,' the Junior Senator asked, 'would you think Ginger would mind if I asked her for a dance?'

The Monster was amused. Tail Gunner Joe was no replace-
ment for Fred Astaire. The Junior Senator was taken with the
idea, and rolled it around his mind for a while, forgetting the
Committee and the purpose of this meeting.

In dreams, Tail Gunner Joe was top-hatted, white-tied and
tailed, swirling gracefully with the movie star; the Lawyer
was in the dark with a wet-mouthed Japanese boy, nervously
certain he was being watched by invisible eyes; the Objectivist
was grovelling in the mud, Hugh Farnham's huge hands
pressing her shoulders down, his pile-driver penis thrusting
brutally into her.

In dreams . . .

In the 20th century, Hollywood was the capital of the
Dreamworld. It was the perfect place for him.

Then, *she* walked in . . . .

thirteen

THE FLAT IN Old Compton Street had a Yale lock and a Chubb, and Nina was not quite up to the relatively simple set of motions necessary to deal with them. She kept her keys in her handbag, and had to root about for a while. Then, she rattled the long Chubb key in its hole, struggling with a rusted mechanism. Her hands started shaking and she could not insert the Yale key properly without putting her bag down and using both hands. She had really not stopped crying yet, and occasionally added yelps of frustration to her strangled whining. She made a hell of a racket.

A door across the hall opened a crack. Anne was acutely uncomfortable in the dingy corridor, fully aware what the invisible neighbour would think. At least Nina lived in Soho, within easy distance of the place where she had accosted Anne. Otherwise, Anne would never have been able to steer her to a safe place and do what had to be done. Come to that, Anne wished she knew precisely what did have to be done.

Finally, Nina got into the flat. Anne noticed a formidable array of extra locks and chains on the inside of the door. If it was hard for the girl to get in, it would be impossible for anyone else. A sensible precaution in her line of business, Anne supposed.

Nina crumpled up and fell into a balding armchair. Anne had to pull the keys out of their holes, pick up Nina's handbag, and lock the door behind them. Anne wondered again how she was going to handle this.

She could not help but find the young girl unnerving. At first, Anne had thought her a shade too chic for the Club Des Esseintes. Her dress looked like the sort of thing Lauren Bacall used to wear to a gangster-owned casino, and her face could have been put together for a *Vogue* fashion shoot. Now, with tear-tracks in the pancake on her cheeks, and her hair turned ratty as she ploughed fingers through it, she looked much more like what Anne realised she was. A junkie and a hooker. Exactly like . . .

. . . exactly like Judi. Nina might be able to pull herself together and make herself presentable when she went out, but Anne suspected that she was finding it increasingly hard to assemble a desirable face. She looked about the slightly messy flat. There had been no card thumbtacked to the door-jamb downstairs and the most expensive appliance in the living room was an Ansafone, so she guessed that Nina was a call girl rather than a streetwalker. By the standards of her profession, she was probably doing quite well. For the moment. Judi must have lived out her last years in rooms like this. Also, she must have been as near the edge as this girl was now.

'Do you know Judi Nielson?' Nina had asked on the street. 'I'm looking for Coral and her.'

Anne had not known any easy way to break the news, and she had not been ready for such a complete crack-up. It was odd, having to comfort a stranger for her own bereavement. And embarrassing, hugging a crying girl in the middle of the pavement, with cursing shoppers flowing around them. Also, Anne was worried that the Club Des Esseintes might send someone after her. The executioner could hardly dash out onto the street in his leather outfit, waving an axe, but he must have street clothes somewhere.

Somehow, she had coaxed the girl's name out of her, and where she lived. Now, she was going to ask her questions. She asked strangers questions every day of her life. Usually, they did not want to give straight replies, but she tried to get them anyway. In this case, she knew she was going to hate hearing the answers as much as Nina was going to hate telling them.

'I'll make some tea, shall I?'

Nina didn't exactly say yes, but Anne went into the tiny kitchen anyway. There was no milk, except for an inch of sludgy cream in a carton, so she used the last sachets of jasmine tea, which she found loose on a table top next to the carton. There was a couple of days' worth of washing-up in the bowl, and she had to fish out, rinse and wipe off a pair of mugs. They both had Royal Wedding pictures on them. There was a disassembled coffee percolator on the draining board. Anne realised that Nina's kitchen looked a lot like her own. They even had the same spice chart blu-takked to a cupboard door.

Looking for clean teaspoons, she opened the drawer by the sink. It was full of sex aids. Grossly outsized rubber penises, a tangle of leather and rubber belts, a dildo with a small model of a leaping dolphin attached to the shaft, vibrating electric eggs, an electrically-operated plastic tongue, various large rings with peculiar attachments and an assortment of unidentifiable objects that might have been instruments of torture. And a plastic case full of little scalpels. Plus several bubble-packs of batteries.

It occurred to Anne that Nina had probably slept with more men in the last month than she had in her entire life. And so had Judi.

She slid the drawer shut, and probed in cold and scummy water, coming up at last with a spoon. She wiped it dry on a kitchen cloth, rubbing the greasy wetness off her hand at the same time. The spoon's underside was discoloured where it had been held over a flame. She wiped it again, very thoroughly. Her knuckles ached, and she rubbed her hand back to life in the dishcloth. She poured the old water out of the bowl, being careful not to dump any of the crockery into the sink, and turned on the hot tap. The pipes coughed and ran. Eventually, steam rose from the washing-up as it was again submerged.

She dumped the teabags in a wastebin shaped like a pair of buttocks, and carried the mugs of tea into the other room. It was not mainly a living room, she realised. It was a bedroom.

Nina still hadn't pulled herself together, but she took the tea easily. She warmed her hands on the mug.

Anne turned on an electric fire. The dust on the elements started to singe and smell. She sat opposite Nina, on the edge of a low chair, leaning forwards, elbows on knees, taking regular sips of the still-too-hot tea. She scalded her tongue.

She had conducted plenty of difficult interviews. Her first session with Mrs Aziz had been especially nervous, as she tried to show some balance, probing for details of any criminal history her dead son might have had. She also remembered the Home Counties councillor who had been placing compulsory purchase orders on private houses he had then sold at a huge profit through his girlfriend's estate agency, the famous writer who had nothing to say about his current book but plenty of comments on attractive young lady interviewers in tight jeans, and the Christian Crusade leader who had been using starvation, regular beatings and harsh punishments to keep his young followers in line.

'My sister,' she began, 'did you know her well?'

Nina swallowed some tea, and shook her head. Anne could not tell if the gesture meant yes or no. Nina put the tea down, clawed her hair again, and tried very hard.

'She was my friend's flatmate. We . . . we worked together sometimes.' Worked together?

'Do you mind me asking questions?'

Nina nodded, 'no, I want to . . . I need to talk. I'm close to the end.'

'What do you mean?'

'It's nearly over, isn't it? Judi's dead. I think Coral is too. We're just girls. Just tarts. No one cares. I wish . . . I wish . . .'

Nina trailed off, hands over her face. Her nails were chewed, old varnish flaked away, and there were prominent blue veins between her knuckles.

'Yes?' encouraged Anne.

'I wish I'd never grown up. I wish I'd stayed at school. I wish I'd stayed with my Mum. I'm only nineteen. I've always been fucked up.'

'Did you know if Judi was . . . was using any kind of drugs?'

'Smack?'

'Heroin, yes?'

'Once, I think so. I don't know.'

'A special kind of heroin?'

'I don't know. Clive would know.'

'Who's Clive?'

Nina halted. Anne knew she did not want to go on. Apart from anything else, the girl was scared.

'Remember, I've nothing to do with the police, Nina. Right now, believe me, they probably like me a lot less than you. Now, who is Clive?'

Nina decided to talk. 'A dealer.'

'Drugs? Does he get heroin for you?'

'Smack, yes.'

'And for Judi?'

'I think he did. He does other things. Judi was with him for a while, but they had a big row and split up. She says he's scary, but . . .'

'Is Clive a pimp?'

Nina was almost indignant. 'We don't have pimps any more. That's stupid. We get beaten up and fucked over enough as it is. We had a girls' co-operative for a while, but now we just freelance on our own. The game isn't like that now. It's mostly just the girls.'

'And you're self-employed?'

'Yes. I'm on Schedule D. I do my own accounts. I've never gone on supplementary benefit.'

'What about Clive then?'

'He fixes us up sometimes.'

'For a commission?'

'No. Well, yes. He has expenses, he says. He puts work my way sometimes. And he did a lot for Judi before they broke up. He's more a friend than a work person. He sent me a Christmas card. It's the only one I've had so far.'

Anne wanted to cry for Nina, to do something for the girl. It was too late for Judi. But maybe she could do something here, something for her sister's memory.

'What did Clive do for Judi?'

'He set her up with some people. Rich people. Weird, if you know what I mean. But we all got paid.'

'You *and* Judi were with these people?'

'Yes. We only went together once. This woman in St John's Wood had a party. She called it an "entertainment". Coral was with us too.'

'Do you remember any names?'

'Well, I shouldn't . . . but . . . this woman was Amelia Something. The last name isn't English. German maybe. Dorf. And there was one really creepy guy. I didn't like him at all. He was called Skinner. Mr Skinner, no Christian name. They called him the Games Master.'

'Games?'

'Do you really want to know? I mean, Judi was your sister and all, but . . .'

'No, I suppose not. You're a nice girl aren't you, Nina?'

'Yeah, so what am I doing like this? I know, I know. It's not easy.'

'It never is.'

Nina looked at her, shrugging. She had a strand of her hair in her mouth, and was chewing nervously. The flat was warming up, but Nina was still shivering.

'Did you know anything about us? Judi's family?'

'Not much. We were watching a film on telly once and she said her Dad had written it or something. It was an old film in black and white. Marlon Brando and Therese Colt were in it. We didn't believe her, and Coral teased her about it. She shut up. I suppose it was true, wasn't it?'

'Mmmm, yes.'

'I knew it really. She pointed out some things you had written sometimes. You're a good writer.'

'Thanks. Judi would have been good too. At something.'

Nina tried to smile, and showed too much of her skull. Her cheeks were too tight over the bones, and there were hollows above her temples. Her eyes were still young, but the rest of her body was ageing fast. Anne remembered Judi's withered look.

'Amelia Dorf is having one of her "entertainments" later this afternoon,' Nina said.

'Are you going?'

'I may have to.'

'Why?'

'Because I'm broke, Anne.'

'I can give you money.'

'Not enough. I need to do some smack. I'm not an addict, but I need it to work sometimes. I'm gradually cutting it out, like Judi, but you can't do it all at once. Clive will be there. He always has good smack. And he's straight with it.'

Anne felt an icy calm. Seizing on what Nina had said, she casually asked the next question, knowing it was the key to the story. 'You say Judi was off heroin?'

'Yes. As far as I know, she had been straight for over a year. She was never a big user. Just a jab once in a while.'

'How did she look?'

'Uh, you mean how did she *look*? Good, I suppose. Pretty. She's a pretty girl. Much prettier than me. As good as Coral sometimes. And Coral is amazing.'

'So, the heroin hadn't affected her in any . . . permanent way?'

'Not really. She lost some weight, but she was looking better lately. When she broke up with Clive, she tried to talk me out of smack. She said I was being stupid.'

'And . . .?'

'Well, she was right, wasn't she. I've always been stupid.'

Nina was looking at Anne and seeing a social worker, a schoolteacher, a Mum. 'Thick, that's me. But I'm not an addict. I'm not. I just need a shot sometimes. Just sometimes.'

'Like now?'

'Yes, 'fraid so.'

'Would you do something for me if I gave you some money?'

'What?'

Nina was alert now.

'The rich people this afternoon? The "entertainment"?'

'Ye-e-es?'

'I'd like you to help me meet them.'

fourteen

S HE WAS WITH a thin, angular young man, who was wearing a slightly too large sports jacket and horn-rimmed glasses. Nobody noticed *him*, but everybody, including the homosexual Lawyer and phallus-worshipping Objectivist, was compelled to stare at *her*. Some fought the urge and carried on talking or eating, intent upon their tableware while their dinner companions' eyes expanded, but most gave in. Even in a crowd sprinkled with authentic movie stars and frequently pinned-up starlets, she drew glances like a magnet draws iron filings. Without needing to look at the dancing star's table, he knew that she must be fuming hatred at the new beauty. All movie stars feared their juniors. He was amused again. Nobody in Romanoff's, himself included, qualified as the woman's junior.

She was, he knew instantly, one of the Kind.

Her hair, so blonde it seemed in this light to be white, was worn unfashionably long, and her evening dress, off the shoulder and floor-length, simple enough to pass in almost any century. Like him, she wore little jewellery. Like him, she excited attention wherever she went. No matter how hard the Kind might try to camouflage themselves among men, they could not suppress the glamour.

Mike Romanoff himself seated her, and her protegé, removing a 'Reserved' sign from a prime table. For an unknown, she was rating unprecedented treatment.

Tail Gunner Joe and the Objectivist were still trading names. She was suggesting Communists and fellow travellers from the Screen Writers' Guild, and he was huffily claiming he had never heard of them. The Junior Senator was greedy for big fish. The Lawyer, he realised, was looking at him and trying to figure something out. It would be impossible for him to even guess at the truth. Compartmentalised and secret-filled the Lawyer's life might be, but he had few dreams, and he could never hope to tap in to the Big Dream he sought to control. The Lawyer's questions about Hugh Farnham were entirely practical, and entirely irrelevant: how much could the man be trusted, how could he be controlled, what could be used to leash him?

She was looking across the room at him, a catlike smile on her lips, her eyes seeming to swell in her face. She had known him at once, as he had known her.

It had been 60 years since the End of the Immortal Empire. Since Giselle's death, he had not encountered another of the Kind. He had heard nothing of the Elders, and wondered occasionally whether he was the last of the family. It would have been so easy, amid the chaotic bloodletting of two world wars and innumerable revolutions, colonial disputes and massacres, for the Kind to die out, and pass from history as unnoticed as ever, its Fall eventually percolating through into the myth-echoes that were all they ever left behind.

Evidently, this was not so.

'King of the Cats,' she said, inside his head, amused at his surprise.

He controlled himself, and nodded minutely, raising his glass to her.

Her protegé was trying to get her attention, and she was brushing him aside. Waiters were flocking to their table, and the young man, left to his own, was awkwardly ordering wine and food for the both of them. The Monster sensed in the young man the seeds of the extraordinary. It could hardly have been otherwise, if this creature were interested in him.

'Outside,' the words formed in his mind, 'on the terrace.'

He was excited by the meeting. He noticed his nails had changed, growing hard and pointed, sharp enough to part the tablecloth. And teeth were swelling in his cheeks, tearing the inside of his mouth. He subdued his body, and excused

himself, reaching for his cigarette case like a Noel Coward
character.

The Objectivist looked at him as he walked towards the
terrace, gliding through the dancing couples. The orchestra
was playing 'A Dream is a Wish Your Heart Makes'. He felt
the tendrils of her desire snapping back at her as they broke,
as he slipped out of the crowded restaurant.

Beyond the curtains he was alone, looking out at the
lights of Hollywood. There were premières out there, and
searchlights stabbed the velvety sky. In the darkness, the
Dreams sparkled.

'Your Majesty,' she said, appearing through the curtains
like a leading lady, 'I am honoured.'

She was mocking him.

'The Kingdom of the Cats is over,' he said. 'I'm Hugh
Farnham, now.'

'Hugh. Very well. You change your names with your skins,
nephew.'

'We all do.'

She made no noise as she came near him, her dress catching
the lights of the city.

'Not all. I'm Ariadne.'

He had heard of her, but not much. Giselle had met her in
Portugal, after the Lisbon earthquake. And, he realised, he had
seen her credits on motion pictures.

'Of "Gowns by Ariadne"?'

She smiled. She was supposed to be one of the Elders, but
she was not above being flattered by recognition.

'I am pleased to meet you,' he said.

'No, you aren't. You were enjoying your uniqueness,
imagining yourself the last of the Kind.'

He said nothing. She was more beautiful even than Giselle,
and stronger even than he.

'We've flourished since your little kingdom fell, you know.
We've changed our ways, while you've stayed the same.'

'Am I to be punished, then?'

She laughed, musically. 'Oh no, Hugh. You may follow
your own road. Perhaps there'll be another Kingdom of the

Cats. You can always rejoin when you get tired of playing with all this . . .'

She extended her arms, including the city in her gesture.

He reached out to her, drawn to her burning ice centre. Feeding was one thing, but this desire was different. The way he felt for Ariadne was not so different from the way the Objectivist or the Lawyer felt for him.

'No,' she said, holding his hand, 'I don't think so. I have other business to . . .'

'Who is he?'

She was taller than she had been, her cheekbones more prominent, her eyes brighter.

'My date?'

He nodded.

'A man of genius, nephew. A lamb among wolves just now, I admit, but a remarkable man. Cameron Nielson.'

He knew of the young man. A playwright, his first works – a two-handed drama about a prisoner and his psychiatrist, and a family saga called *Father, Son and Holy Terror* – had been successful on Broadway, netting two successive Drama Critics Circle Awards, and were optioned by Mark Hellinger at Universal. Along with Arthur Miller and Tennessee Williams, he was expected to shake up the American theatre a little.

The Monster had a taste for geniuses. In his mind, he saw Ariadne opening Nielson's head, and scooping his genius out in grey lumps.

'Not yet,' Ariadne said. 'Later, maybe. But not yet. He has things to do.'

'Why do you care?'

She smiled again. 'I'm a patron of the arts.'

A wind blew by, bringing a chill. Ariadne's dress clung where the wind pressed, and stirred, flapping on her other side. In the starlight, her skin was as dead white as her hair, but her eyes shone, red under green. She was the adult Giselle might have become in a thousand more years.

'And you,' she said, 'will you ride your crusade?'

He nodded. She laughed.

'It'll be interesting. But it'll be the end of you.'

It was like a blow. The Elders were always like that, secure in their survival, contemptuous of the rest of the Kind, treating them like children playing at the edge of the precipice, knowing better but doing nothing.

'I don't think so.'

'Well, maybe not. Maybe you'll last. But your friends in there are a poor lot.'

'They don't matter.'

'That's a dangerous thought. You should be careful about the people you mix with. I prefer the brilliant . . .'

'So do I, they taste better.'

'Not just for that, nephew. They're less prone to envy us. Among humans, the brilliant are freaks and sports. It's mediocrities you should watch. Like your friends back there, arguing about movie stars. When they've finished with the Reds, they'll want to see your head on a pole. Have you read that woman's books?'

He was embarrassed, and shrugged.

'I trust you've not fed off her. She would be such a feeble meal.'

They had nothing more to say to each other, but they stayed on the terrace, politely sampling each other's memories. There were great parts of her experience that she successfully kept him away from. She was much older, much stronger. It was not really new to him, being powerless, but it was hardly relishable.

All she gave him were a few pictures of the world as it had been for her. And yet, she exhausted him in a single draught. All his ghosts were conjured up for her. It was a wrenching, unpleasant experience, but he submitted to it, hoping to impress her. When it was over, she looked at him with an expression he would never be able to wipe from his memory. There was a nannyish kindliness in it, but also disappointment, and – intolerably – pity. She shrugged, her dress rippling from her shoulders, and smiled.

'No,' she said again, 'I don't think so.'

His question was only a thought. Some day?

Her answer was not even that. Maybe, who knows, never . . .

She gave him her hand to be kissed – the Kind always found it hard to dispense with the old manners – and left him, the curtains closing after her. On the balcony, he was alone again.

His fingernails, he realised, were two inches long, and curled into bony barbs. And his mouth was full of blood.

Inside, he was shaking. She had left something of herself in him, perhaps out of tenderness. He hated her for that gesture, and tried to force the images she had spilled into him out of his mind, erasing the centuries with a burning fury.

A girl came out. She had a short black dress, red hair and pale freckles the assistant director who had supervised her screen test thought would not show in Technicolor. She was lighting a cigarette, and shivering. She was here with the assistant director, and was not sure whether she should go to bed with him tonight. He was important, but maybe not that important. Daphne had told her to get an agent, and sleep with him.

'Oh,' she said, 'I'm sorry . . . I thought there was no one out here.'

He laid his hands on her shoulders, and looked into her face. Her eyes moved from side to side, trying to take all of him in. His nails pinched her bare skin, drawing points of blood.

Still trying to wash Ariadne out of his mind, he bent his neck and kissed the girl – Therese Colt – on the mouth, forcing his long tongue into her throat, latching suckerlike to her tonsils.

Therese did not struggle, melting in his embrace as she had done during the screen test with the iron-jawed desert sheik.

He sucked part of her in, finding the Mary Teresa Garrity beneath Therese Colt, and gulped it down. She tasted bitter. After Ariadne, they would all, for a while, taste bitter. He sucked back his tongue, pulling it out of the girl with a rasping slurp, and pushed her away.

He wiped his bleeding mouth with the back of his hand, scraping away skin, then pulled out a silk handkerchief from the top pocket of his dinner jacket, balled it, and used it to mop up the mess. Therese was looking at him with concern, unheeding the part of her that had just been torn loose. Blood was seeping from one of her nostrils, and his nailpoints had opened three twin vents in the side of her dress, exposing more freckles.

'Mister,'she said, 'are you all right?'

He ignored her. She stepped closer, reaching out, but then her knees gave way and she slumped to the floor in a faint.

The Monster grabbed the rail, and took control of himself. Gripping tight, he watched his hands as the nails shrank. He smoothed his hair, and tugged at his clothes, sharpening his appearance.

Therese would recover. She had warmed him, helped him survive Ariadne's indifference. He had taken something from her, but had also left something inside her. Perhaps he had chilled her heart where it needed to be chilled. She would not sleep with the assistant director, but she would become a star.

He left her there, and went back into the restaurant. Ariadne had rejoined Cameron Nielson, and was listening intently as he talked to her. The Monster knew he was talking about his work, for he could feel the young man's burning intensity from across the room. Ariadne had her hand lightly on his arm. The Monster was still shivering. Ariadne gave him the briefest of smiles, and returned her attention to the playwright.

They would never speak again, the Monster and Ariadne, although they would occasionally be in the same city and sense each other's presence. If there were, as she had implied, others of the Kind still surviving, then he never encountered any.

Tail Gunner Joe was drunk and getting abusive, calling the waiters 'kikes' and 'Commies'. He was itching for an injection, the Monster could tell. The Lawyer was making inscrutible little notes. And the Objectivist, deprived of his presence, had gone to the powder room to repair herself.

'And when we've finished hammering the fuckin' Reds,' Tail Gunner Joe told the Lawyer, 'we're gonna go after the fuckin' queers.'

The Monster watched Ariadne lean over to Nielson, and saw the playwright's face rise to meet her kiss.

'Fuckin' asshole bandits oughta be strung up,' the Junior Senator grumbled. The Lawyer was shut up tight, his face not registering everything, but the Monster could sniff his funk.

Ariadne broke the embrace, and nipped playfully at Nielson's ear. He smiled, an odd expression on so serious a young man, crinkling his face like a comedian's. He called the waiter for more drinks.

If he could not have Ariadne, the Monster swore, he would have her protegé. Not now, but when she was through with him.

He would have Cameron Nielson drained and drunk dry, and he would then turn his attention to anything, or anyone, that came from the man. His women would weep blood.

When he was through, it would be as if the playwright had never walked the Earth.

fifteen

I N THE TAXI, on the way to St John's Wood, Nina fell asleep
on Anne's shoulder. The creosoty smell of the girl's hair dye
was pleasant in a roundabout way. Anne almost relaxed.

Nina had lent her an outfit – a short, tight skirt, black
tights, a black jacket not designed to fasten up – and helped
make her up. She had suddenly turned into a teacher, gently
ridiculing Anne's idea of a tarty face, and subtly rearranging
and highlighting her make-up. Anne had to admit she did
not look bad, and hoped she could pass for one of Nina's
workmates. She had tried a pair of Nina's spike heels, but they
had pinched painfully, and she had to hope her comfortable
flats would pass. They were black, highly polished and
matched the rest of her get-up.

It was a dingy afternoon, and slate grey slabs of cloud had
brought the already early sunset forward. The chilly, heavily
padded interior of the cab was comfortably gloomy, lit only
by the orange numbers adding up on the meter as the fare
increased.

Anne found that Nina had, in her sleep, reached out and
taken hold of her hand. Nina's own was cold, but she
squeezed gently. The unconscious intimacy surprised and
comforted Anne. She wished that she could express her
feelings in such a simple, honest manner.

Of course, a cynical footnote inevitably came to mind.
Doubtless, Nina was habitually intimate with strangers in
ways far more involved and far less innocent than hand-
holding.

Anne could not help thinking of Judi.

For the first twelve years of the dead girl's life, Anne had seen her sister, been with her, talked to her, spent time with her, almost every day. And yet, her images of Judi as a baby, as a little girl, as an elementary school pupil, as a young teenager were alternately fuzzy and artificial, like the photographs she had collected in a folder somewhere. Anne was not sure whether her memories were first hand, or had been impressed upon her by the familiarity with those snapshots and the reminiscences of relatives.

Everything else about that period of her life was still vivid – arguing with Cam about trivial things like who should sit in the front seat of the car, being taken for the first time to the theatre for one of Dad's plays and not understanding what was going on in the dark auditorium or the remote stage, being taken by her mother on a holiday for two in the desert where the cowboys had lived and getting bored after a few days with the heat and the sand. But Judi, dead Judi, was quietly fading from her memory like a disgracefully dissolute pharaoh being rubbed out of the history books by unforgiving high priests.

In that folder, there were a number of photographs of babies and little girls, usually caught by the sun among the greens of the garden in New Hampshire, that Anne could not identify. They might be of Judi, but they could as easily be of her younger self. Not until they reached school age, apparently, had the sisters developed any distinctive characteristics of their own.

Much clearer in her mind were the scenes from later life.

Now, it seemed to Anne as if the first time she had really noticed Judi was during the summer after she returned from college. During the three years the sisters had mainly lived apart, Judi had grown into an intelligent, difficult, uncomfortable teenager, chain-smoking at fifteen, reading her way through every book in the house, from *Peyton Place* to *The Romantic Agony*. She had been interested in Anne only in that she would have liked to know the blow-by-blow details of her sister's sex life as a student. She had lost her own virginity, she boasted (confessed?), to one of the local stupids, and was just getting over her initial disappointment

with sex by casting around for less conventional ways of
annoying her family. Now, Anne suspected that at twenty-
one, with two whole neatly-over-and-done-with love affairs
to her credit, she must have been unbearably priggish and
self-obsessed. Love Affair Number Two was going to be her
first novel, but that had worked out less well even than the
real life episode. Judi had read some of her draft chapters, and
gone uncharacteristically quiet, refusing to offer criticisms or
comments. Shortly afterwards, Anne had abandoned fiction
altogether.

Three years later, when Anne had already decided to move
to London and visits to Judi in police stations were no
novelty, she had seen Judi squatting in a New York City
cell with five other prostitutes, dressed in glittery tatters, with
a face like a painted and bruised punk madonna, and dried
blood on her neck and upper breasts. Anne, brought up with
liberal folk myths of the Chicago Democratic Convention,
Paris *soixante-huite* and Attica, had seen the red badge of
courage and threatened the polite lieutenant with a hard-
hitting exposé of police brutality.

'What you don't understand,' she had been told, 'is that
your sister is a specialist.' The policeman, displaying no relish
for it, had tactfully and patiently explained that Judi had come
by her bruises at the hands of clients who had bought her and
paid for the privilege of using her as a punching bag. This
was worse than Anne had been prepared for. Prostitution,
she could just about understand; the rest was beyond her
fantasies, beyond her experience.

She had argued with Judi for hours in an interrogation
room, overseen by a police matron who read *Cosmopolitan*
and looked like a more dangerous Angie Dickinson. Anne
had tried to get Judi to name names and swear out complaints
against the men who had gotten their rocks off beating up
on her. Judi had calmly insisted on protecting her sources of
income. Unlike their father, she did not want a 'rat jacket',
a reputation as an informer. Of course, the NYPD did not
sic Hugh Farnham on her, so she never found out just how
tough she was.

Now, Anne realised how typical Judi was of the family.
Their father had a Nobel prize, Cam was supposed to be
the best in his field and she was herself acknowledged as on
the rise. Judi had chosen to be sado-masochist hooker, but
she was determined to be the best, most professional sado-
masochist hooker in the world. Given a few more years, she
would probably have made more money than any of them.

Anne felt a warm, wet touch at her throat. Still asleep,
Nina was trying to kiss her neck, licking at a patch of skin
with catlike absent-mindedness.

Embarrassed, Anne lifted the girl's head. Nina woke up just
as the taxi driver found the address he had been given.

'I was dreaming . . .'

Evening

one

IT WAS THE kind of quietly well-off residential street where mass murderers live, unnoticed behind the Neighbourhood Watch stickers, until someone turns up a toenail in the rose-beds. The houses were well-maintained, 19th century and 1930s flourishes kept in good nick by careful owners, but there was an overwhelming drabness to the buildings. In the twilight, the only real colour came from the bright estate agents' notice boards posted outside almost every home. The whole street was for sale. This was an expensive part of town – upper upper middle and lower upper – and even the family cars parked in drives were high performance models. But the cracks were beginning to show. There was a stream of rubbish clogging the gutters, as if a parade had passed by with waste-paper substituting for tickertape. A few years ago, that would have been the mark of the scruffy Camden council, but now the rot was creeping into well-heeled Westminster. Even prosperity was not what it had been.

It was not Belgravia, but it was certainly well-off, thank you very much. Quite apart from the usual expenses, mortgages and service charges would be punitive around here. The media and entrepreneur types attracted to the district were unlikely to be rich enough long enough to buy a permanent stake in the prestigious postcode. Anne knew; she had lived in a street like this for a few months, sharing her flat with that psychopath from the BBC, and had had to move on when the *Newsweek* commissions petered out.

Amelia Dorf's house was different. Nina knew it right away, and led Anne across the road to it. It was set apart from its neighbours, like the manorhouse of a village. Built as a home for a large and prosperous mid-Victorian family, the five-storey pile had not, like all of its neighbours, been converted into almost affordable small units. The already formidable garden wall was topped with spear-tipped railings that were probably sharpened every day. The wrought iron gates might have been expressly designed to keep out the most determined and well-equipped lynch mob.

Anne knew that all this meant money, and in an inexhaustible supply. Bank balances like international telephone numbers. Amelia Dorf. She would look through the files when she was in the office. Anyone rich enough to live in this house must have made the news some time in her life.

Nina dealt with the entryphone that had replaced the bell-pull. A snake-neck swivelled above, and a closed circuit camera peered down. A green light winked, and the gates rattled mechanically. Nina pushed them inwards, and they were through before the buzzing stopped. The gates locked behind them.

In front of the house there was a lawn. The centrepiece was an eight-foot tall evergreen topiary dildo.

The front door was open by the time they got to it. Nina and Anne were let into the house by a large and solid man who looked slightly Scandinavian. Anne guessed that he spent most of his days in a gymnasium and knew all the correct Latin names for the muscles he had developed. He wore a quilted floor-length dressing gown that could have passed for a formal ball dress in old St Petersburg. Nina knew him.

'Hello, Anders,' she said, chucking her shiny black coat into his hands, 'this is Anne.'

Anders ignored Anne, but carefully folded Nina's coat with the casual reverence usually found in dry-cleaners or the very best restaurants.

'You're early.'

'It said five on the invitation Amelia sent out. It must be past that now.'

'Typical of you, Nina. No one comes at the time on the card. That's why we always invite for two hours early.'

'I'm sorry, but it's not my fault.'

'It's hardly considerate, you know. We're not really ready.'

Anne took off her own coat, which he took willingly and hung up. She kept her handbag though. Turning from the coat racks, he stared into her eyes in the manner recommended by most 'How to Impress Girls' handbooks. Anne almost laughed.

'Anne,' he said, lowering his glance to her chest, 'you have startled eyes.'

Anne raised an eyebrow.

'You've lived many times, I can tell. We've met before. In the French Revolution.'

Nina chipped in, 'Anders was the Marquis de la Some-where-or-Other.'

Anders took her hand, and kissed her middle knuckles.

'Of course,' Anne said, pulling her fingers free. 'How could I forget? How is that pain in your neck, citizen?'

He looked up, and really looked at her this time. There was a tracery of little scars under his jawline, as if someone had scooped out a pouch of flesh with sharp fingers. He looked too young for plastic surgery, but Anne suspected he was just vain enough to take self-perfection to expensive lengths.

'Now whose eyes are startled?' she asked.

He started ignoring her again. Nina pulled at his heavy sleeve, perhaps harder than she had meant to. His collar shifted, and Anne saw thick muscles with more scars.

'Clive?' said Nina, 'is he here yet?'

'I told you. You're early.'

'But doesn't he stay over sometimes?'

'Sometimes, but not now. I'm staying here now. And a few others. Daeve Pope is here. Clive is with Mr Skinner on business. They'll both be along at tea-time. Do you mind? This is expensive, antique.'

He shook his arm free of her hold, and hugged himself. Anne caught a look of nausea under his patina of health and vigour, as if he could not bear to be touched by another human being.

'Ciao, Nina,' said a short young man, stepping out from a room, 'who's your friend?'

He came into the light, grinning. Anne put his age at about thirty, but he was wearing the striped blazer and straw hat of a public school prefect, and his slightly fuzzy chin suggested he had not started shaving yet.

'Anne,' Nina said, 'this is Daeve Pope. He's a writer . . .'

Nina had been about to say 'he's a writer too,' but Daeve cut her off. 'Perhaps you've seen my work,' he said, 'I do essays for *Kerrang* and *Metal Hammer*. I'm interested in thrash metal.'

Daeve had a cigarette case out. He offered it around too quickly for anyone to accept, and stuck a fag in the corner of his mouth. The cigarettes were a brand Anne did not know, but they must be extra king-size because they were disproportionate, like props from a science fiction film about shrinking people. As he lit up, Daeve looked like a nearly adult-sized child.

'Just thrash, of course. I do not tolerate glam in any way, shape or form. It's the only thing left in rock and roll with the balls to blast and the dick to come through.'

'He's a good writer,' Nina said. 'You can tell.'

Daeve puffed a cloud of smoke, and hung his head on one side, posing. 'Remember,' he said to Anne, suddenly shaking his head up and down so that his boot-black hair flopped over his face and pumping the air with an angry milkmaid's fist, 'just thrash.'

He grinned, tossing his hair back, and took another drag, slipping back into his room like a jack in the box.

Nina looked at the door Daeve had closed behind him, then at Anne. She shrugged. Anders, who had frozen like a stone lion while Daeve was in the passage, came back to life and turned into the sinister butler from an old Boris Karloff movie.

Anders led them down the sparsely furnished hallway, and ushered them into a large room. It was a windowless den, decorated with paper chains and Chinese lanterns. There was a fully dressed Christmas tree, with baubles, lights and presents, and an open fire in an alcove the size of an upright piano.

Behind a glass-topped desk sat an elegant woman in her forties, with purple-streaked hair coiled in a psyche knot and Morticia Addams make-up. She was wearing surgeon's gloves and delicately shaping a Paramount mountain of white powder in front of her. It looked like flour, but a fistful would be worth what Anne had earned in the last year.

There was a naked child squatting by the fire, looking like a tattooed savage in the echt-psychedelic light from the tree and the blaze. He was playing with a pile of expensive toys. He flew a foot-long, perfectly detailed model of Concorde in his hand, and gingerly crash-landed it among the burning logs. He pulled his hand out of the flames quickly and sucked his slightly singed fingers.

The plane's wings melted first, dripping gobbets of molten plastic. Then the beaked body bent downwards and flopped onto the logs. The boy thumped the floor and crooned in ecstasy. He reached for the Starship *Enterprise*.

Anne recognised him. It was Derek Douane, the twelve-year-old ex-choirboy of 'Christmas Caroline' fame. He had his face on the cover of every girls' magazine on the stands. Not since Little Jimmy Osmond had Anne been so personally sickened by a pop singer. Before 'Christmas Caroline', he had had a big hit with a vomitous reggae cover version of 'Puff the Magic Dragon'.

'Ahh, Nina,' said the woman at the desk, Amelia, 'thank you for coming. And, as requested, you brought a friend.'

She got up and shook Anne's hand. Her glove was talcum-powdered with cocaine. Foreign surname or not, she sounded as Anne had once imagined all English women sounded, like Jenny Agutter or Julie Andrews.

'This is Anne.'

'Anne. You'll find us amusing, I hope. And rewarding.' Wrinkles of pertubation appeared on her white forehead. 'Do I know you?'

'I don't think so.'

. . . Anne knew her now. Amelia Dorf. She had seen her before at a press conference. She was on a women's committee formed to oppose the Campaign for Nuclear Disarmament.

The GPA. The Global Peace Something. Alliance? Agency?
Activists? They wanted the West to stockpile as many
atomic weapons as the East, and had, in the Gorbachev era,
been darkly muttering about the increasing threat of Third
World nations with a nuclear capability. Amelia would not
remember her. She was just one of an audience of journalists.
No, Anne knew that Amelia thought she was a familiar face
(and voice?) because she had known Judi . . .

'Ahh, you're American?'

'Canadian,' she lied.

'Canada, right. Where the Mounties come from. Do make
yourself comfortable. We won't really be starting for a while,
so we can get to know each other better before the others
arrive. Nina, you know where the drinks are kept. Get us all
something would you.'

Amelia sat Anne down on a giant cloth marshmallow, and
sunk cross-legged on the carpet next to Derek. She wore a
leotard that showed off her concentration camp figure, and
knee-length alligator-skin boots.

'This is Derek. He's staying for Christmas because he can't
be with his Mummy and Daddy.'

The child star turned and looked at Anne with neanderthal
hostility. His pupils were shrunk to pinpoints, and half his
face was red from being too close to the fire. Amelia plucked
a paper napkin from one of the several cardboard dispensers
scattered around the room and wiped the spittle from his
chin. She threw the napkin into the fire, where it flared like
a meteor next to the softening spaceship.

'You know, bitch,' said Derek in his not-quite broken
voice, 'your tits aren't big enough.'

Amelia slapped him with an open hand.

'Don't be vulgar, Derek. Anne is our guest. We must make
her feel at home.'

Derek didn't mind being slapped at all. He hugged Amelia,
and whispered in her ear. She giggled indulgently, and pushed
him away.

Embarrassed, Anne looked into the fire. The bridge of the
Enterprise was distorting, pulled out of shape by weights

inside the model.

'Can you hear the screams?' asked Derek, baring his teeth like the fly-eating madman in the old *Dracula* movie. 'That's what I like the most. The screams. At my concerts, I make girls scream.'

'I'll bet you do.'

The model in the fire fell apart with a hiss and some plops. Parts of it sizzled, and the logs spat like burning sausages. The stench of burning plastic stung Anne's nostrils.

'That scream there,' said Derek, reaching out to catch the unheard shriek. 'That's Captain Kirk. When the *Enterprise* caught fire, he knew he was going to die and wanted to do all the things they wouldn't let him do on television. He slashed up his captain seat, and whacked Mr Sulu in the belly and shat on Chekhov's face. He was going to fuck Lieutenant Uhura, but his cock caught fire and dropped off. It was plastic like the rest of him. He's melting down into a puddle with the rest of his crew. The blob there is Kirk's cock, and Spock's ears, and Uhura's twat, and Dr McCoy's left leg, and bits of ground-up dilithium crystal. All the crew are just a screaming glob of burning plastic now. Just the same as their starship . . .'

During his rant, Derek had been getting more excited. He reached down and started fingering his stubby penis. Amelia slapped his hand away from his bald genitals and pinched his foreskin. He squeaked and shut up.

'That's enough playing for today, Derek. You've run out of toys. I'll have to ask Santa for some more. Now, go and put some clothes on.'

Derek padded over to a pile of colourful clothes, and obediently started to wrestle with them. Anne wondered what Amelia had the kid high on. His hand-eye coordination was way off, and getting dressed was too much of a struggle for him to accomplish alone. Amelia, treating him like a toddler, helped him with the difficult moves, fussing with buttons, and preventing him from strangling himself with rainbow-striped braces.

Nina came back with a tray of liqueurs. Anne took a glass, but only sipped the thick orange liquid once or twice. The

heat from the fire was already getting to her head, and she
knew that she needed, above all else, to remain in control.
Amelia developed a sudden craving for Christmas cookies,
and told Nina where to find them. The girl left again. If
she had curtseyed, she would have been just like one of the
maidservants on *Upstairs, Downstairs*.

Amelia got back to the cocaine, and went to work on it with
a gold razor-blade. She cut it into white slug-trails that striped
the reflective desktop.

'Would you care to indulge?'

'No thank you,' Anne said, 'Sinus trouble.'

'Ahhh, yes. There's a lot of 'flu going around. It's best
to save it for later, anyway. We don't want people to think
we're piggish, do we?'

Nevertheless, she took a tiny pinch and snuffed it, throwing
her head back. She was like a cook, Anne thought, unable to
resist a lick of the icing.

'There,' said Amelia, seeming not at all dizzy, 'that's better.'
She picked up the blade again, but gripped the wrong edge.
'Ouch, I'm opened . . .'

She held up a gloved hand. It looked like a jewellery store
replica for displaying rings. There was a seeping red line on
the tip of her forefinger. Droplets fell on the desk, rolling
like mercury on the glass, soaking into the cocaine like piss
in snow.

Amelia waved her hand. 'Derek, come here . . .'

The child was at her side instantly. He took Amelia's hand
and professionally peeled back the glove. It came off with a
snap. He stroked her palm, as if playing 'round and round the
garden', and bent his head over. He took the wounded finger
into his mouth and sucked quietly. Amelia ran her free hand
through his bleached blond hair.

'Anne, isn't he lovely?'

'Oh yes, lovely.'

'And he's so talented. He's a singer, you know.'

'I know.'

'And such a nice smile, don't you think. It's no wonder he
has such a following.'

'On the radio, they don't seem to play anyone else.'

'No, that's right. But then again, why should they? He's so much better than all the others. What's his song called? "Christmas Caroline". Such a clever title. Once you've heard it, it goes round and round your mind forever. You keep thinking of it at the most unlikely moments. You never forget it . . .'

'Oh no, never . . .'

> '"Tell me, Christmas Caroline,
> When you say you'll be mine,
> You raise a round of loud applause
> From old Mr Santa Claus.
> We walk down the lane, dear,
> Just us and the reindeer,
> It's such a jaunt,
> And you're the only Christmas present I want."'

In Anne's opinion, Amelia's rendition of the song was superior musically to Derek's recorded version, but unfortunate in that it made audible the lyrics that were incomprehensible in the original. She wondered what Mr Thrash Metal would think of it. Or Cam, who was often said to be interested in the fine dividing line between music and pain. Maybe that was Derek's major achievement, uniting people of such different tastes in their single opinion of him.

'Look at these eyes,' she tilted Derek's head upwards, 'so darling, so knowing. Such a warm little mouth he has.'

At that point, Anne realised that her hostess was certifiably deranged. She was getting fed up with sick people.

'Anne,' Amelia said seriously, almost dangerously, 'don't just agree with me all the time. If you think I'm a fruitcake, please do say so. I hate persons who don't speak speak their minds.'

She smiled sweetly, and suddenly wasn't as out-of-touch and fuzzy-minded as Anne had thought. She had come down off her mental space shuttle and become disturbingly lucid. Anne realised she would have to work harder, conceal more about herself, if she were to get through this.

'Have you ever read *Lolita*?' Amelia asked.

Did Amelia suspect that Anne was not just another disposable tart like Judi and Nina? Was the question a clever trap to find out what kind of person she really was? If so, Amelia had misjudged her tarts. Anne had not read Nabokov, but knew her sister had. She hesitated, and told the truth,

'No, but I saw the film. With James Mason.'

Amelia seemed surprised at even that trace of a cultural background. Anne would have to watch herself, try to seem more like Nina. She tried to pout, and felt silly.

'That's right.' Amelia was too intent on patronising her to notice the face-pulling. 'With James Mason. Humbert Humbert, the James Mason character, is wrong about little girls, I think. They're so boring, so unimaginative. Not sensual at all. Not like little boys.'

Amelia pulled her finger out of Derek's mouth, and rubbed it dry. The bleeding had stopped. She put an arm around the boy. Derek looked at Anne, smiling innocently. With his eyes shut, he looked like a happy imbecile.

Whatever Anne thought of Derek Douane, this was child abuse and an obscenity. Her crusading instincts were aroused.

'No, not at all like Derek,' Amelia continued. 'He's so promising, you know. He'll be quite passionate, I think. A fatal man. They'll all want him. To use him and be used by him.'

Anne was excluded. Amelia's words were directed at her, but she was talking to the boy.

'Wouldn't you just *luh*-love . . .' Amelia caught her voice on the word and had to start again. 'Wouldn't you just love to slit his little throat, and watch the *fuh*-fucking little toad *buh*-bleed to death . . .'

Derek snuggled against Amelia's flat breasts. Anne tried not to look as if she wanted to be sick.

'That, I think would be quite an experience,' said Amelia. 'That, I think, would make me *cuh*-climax like an alley cat.'

She took another pinch of cocaine, and snorted it with a rattle of phlegm. Derek began to hum 'Christmas Caroline', and Amelia joined in on the chorus.

two

O N THE WAY to the pantry to get the Christmas cookies, Nina got lost. The house was big and old, with a lot more corridors and rooms and unexpected turns than seemed necessary, but she had done enough of these 'entertainments' to be familiar with the lower storeys. The route from the den to the pantry was quite simple, she thought. She had to take a walk down a short corridor from the main hallway, go down a few steps to the kitchen. The pantry was just a walk-in alcove off the kitchen. Easy. But somehow, she found herself in a large, empty room. There were wall-sized French windows through which she would in daylight have been able to see the back garden. Now, it was in darkness. There was the vague suggestion of orange light beyond the high wall that marked the rear boundary of Amelia's property; the streetlamps were already on.

Nina sat on the floor and cried. She was in a state. Why was Clive not here yet?

The stomach cramps had been coming back, off and on, all day, but so far she had been able to keep them under control. In her flat with Anne, and in the taxi, she had been able to conceal her pain from the older woman. Now, the spasms were worse than ever.

She was shaking with the cold, but the fire in the den had been irritating and overbearing. Under her heavy clothes, she felt filthy, as if there were a layer of vermin-ridden earth between her naked skin and the fabric.

Things were moving all over her. She scratched and pulled, but could never find the leeches under her blouse or the spiders crawling inside her tights.

She doubled up in pain, and rested her forehead on the carpeted floor. She willed the pains to recede, and gradually they did.

She needed to eat, to shower, to rest, to sleep. Most of all, she needed some smack. She needed Clive. She needed help.

When Amelia had had her serve the drinks, Nina realised just how far gone she was. She had found it difficult to read the labels on the bottles. The delicate glasses had felt thick and awkward in her hands, soft as putty but covered in cutting edges. When pouring, it had been impossible to line up the bottles with the glasses, no matter how close she held the neck of a bottle to the rim of a glass. She had soaked her hand and cuff with *crème de menthe,* and the sticky liquid seemed to have crept up her arm. Her fingers felt as if they were encased in cool wax.

Where was Clive? Good old Clive? Clive the dealer. Clive the healer. Where was Clive?

She scratched her arm, but could not find the stickiness. Her needle tracks were not that bad. Yet. Really, she could wear sleeveless dresses if she wanted to. But not in winter.

Of course, she would have to get off smack in the long run. Or else she *would* look like that girl in the adverts. But she could handle that later. Right now, she neded a fix. Just one more fix, perhaps, then she would stay away forever.

Maybe she would have to do it gradually, taking less each time, taking more time between each time. Perhaps she could get something on the N.H.S.? 'Lady, how about two packs of your old heroin for one of your new improved biological methodone?'

But right now, she needed Clive.

Her stomach clenched like a fist, but there was nothing in there to come up. Her bowels opened like a tulip, but there was nothing there to come out. Her head throbbed like a burst boil, but there was nothing there . . .

Nothing.

She was empty, and only Clive could fill her up. Where was Clive?

Eventually – after how long? – the pains passed, and she was able to stand up. She could feel nothing, as if her entire body were mummified in thick wads of flavourless chewing gum. Moving was difficult, but at least it did not hurt.

Like one of the shambling dead, she left the room and returned to the main hall. Then, without thinking, she found the right corridor. She floated down the steps and opened the door into the kitchen.

Anders was there, supposedly supervising the preparation of an assortment of mixed salads for the buffet. A lumpish Belgian girl called Lise who did menial tasks about the house but hardly ever spoke was grating cheese over a rice dish.

Anders was playing with Daeve.

He had the writer laid out, face down with his baggy trousers around his knees, on a marble-topped kitchen table, and was anally violating him with a large, unwashed carrot.

Anders held Daeve down with a clever grip on the back of his neck. Nina now knew what the expression 'squealing like a stuck pig' really meant.

Anders looked up at Nina and laughed. He was stripped to the waist, and she could see the lunar map of dead skin and fresh scars that was stretched tautly over his Schwarzenegger musculature.

The squealing stopped as Anders plucked out the carrot. Nina knew, as her stomach hit her again, that he was going to take a bite out of it.

'Nyaaah,' he said, chewing, 'what's up, doc?'

three

IT WAS ALL rather pathetic really, not at all the orgy of
degradation she had half-imagined. Amelia had left off
quoting from the wit and wisdom of her favourite mass
murderers, done a few lines of cocaine, and started to whizz
around the room. She was demonstrating aerobic movements
and hostessing for her guests as they arrived.

Anne was sort of expecting blubbery cabinet ministers
and worn clergymen, slavering and ready to practise their
secret vices, but the guests turned out to be unidentifiable
nobodies. For a while, she thought she could have been at
any moderately boring Christmas party.

The women wore Laura Ashley or Ghost dresses, the men
wore expensive jeans. Anne realised that the younger, prettier
members of both sexes had been bought and paid for. She was
supposed to blend in with that group. There were no obvious
freaks, transvestites, monsters or exotic creatures. Well, not
any more than usual.

The guests greedily snuffed cocaine, ate platefuls of designer salad, listened to Amelia's Jean-Michel Jarre CDs,
smoked ordinary cigarettes and weedy joints, and talked
about cars and mortgage rates and money and dry rot
and Eastern Europe and computers and their weight and
Christmas and sex. It was all very '80s, the young, rich and
shallow turning middle-aged, tax-assessed and empty. None
of this had anything to do with Judi.

Derek Douane was being cooed over by a pair of predatory
women in their fifties, not minding their tanned fingers in
his hair, on his face or twanging his braces. Daeve was
lecturing a bank manager on the stylistic differences between

Bolt Thrower, Odin and Meat Market. Anders was playing major-domo outside.

She was trapped, pinned to a bookcase by two smoothly stupid, slightly drunk young men. One, Toby Farrar, was a career army officer out of uniform, the other, Baz Something, was a cricket-playing travel agent. Farrar was short with livery lips and thick black eyebrows, and Something was prematurely bald and thought he was really cool. They were both assholes, and they were both boasting about their early sex lives. Anne stopped listening while they were comparing their masturbatory records, and watched for new arrivals.

'Six times a day,' said Something, 'that was my personal best.'

'Piss on that,' said Farrar, 'that was my mean average.'

Nina seemed to have lost contact with Planet Earth. Earlier, she had taken Anne aside to ask her if she knew when Clive was coming. The girl had not quite forgotten who she was, but had got her mixed up with her sister. Now, she was out in the hallway, stationed eagerly near the front door.'

A veiled woman, with scarlet fingernails, was challenging every man in the room.

'You want to arm wrestle?' she kept saying, 'beat me and you can do whatever you like to my body.'

Anne was surprised that nobody was taking her up on it. The woman had a figure like the young Jane Russell.

Farrar was surprised too. When the challenge got through to him, he disobeyed the first rule of the services and volunteered.

'This is his first time here,' said Something. 'He doesn't know any better, the daft bollock. Watch this.'

Farrar and the woman – whose name, funnily enough, was Jeane Russell – were seated either side of a small desk. Someone put a paper hat on Farrar's head, and he straightened it. She unpinned her veil, and Anne saw she had different-coloured eyes, one blue, one hazel. Everyone crowded around. Something put his hand on Anne's bottom, but did not seem to mind too much when she peeled it off and gave it back to him. Everyone quietened and Amelia turned off Jean-Michel.

In the hallway, Nina was asking someone about Clive.

Jeane Russell held her hand, dainty but thick-wristed, up, and flexed her fingers. She put her elbow down firmly on the desk and leaned forwards.

'Hold on,' said a computer-designing nonentity, 'the final touch . . .' He put two ashtrays full of smouldering butts either side of the field of combat, and sprinkled a few drops of fuel from his lighter on each. Little flames grew. Burning cellophane crackled.

Farrar did not look too happy. Jeane Russell flexed her fingers again.

Farrar drained half a glass of vodka and orange, and grasped Jeane Russell's hand.

Someone said 'go for it' and was promptly ignored.

Farrar and Jeane Russell looked at each other. Jeane Russell smiled, and crushed the man's hand as if it were an eggshell.

Farrar yelped at the sound of grinding bones, and looked around in dazed fury. Jeane Russell brought his arm down as easily as a barmaid pulling a pint and dropped his hand into a burning ashtray.

Someone who knew what she was doing produced a pitcher of iced water for Farrar's hand. She also used it to put the fires out.

'Shit,' said Farrar, 'you bitch!' He tried to slap Jeane Russell with his left hand, but she backed out of the way and just laughed at him.

'Anyone else?' she asked. No one came forwards.

'How does she do that?' Anne asked Something.

'I don't know,' he said, holding up his own once-ruined hand, 'she just does.'

Farrar came after his friend. 'You bastard, you could have warned me. Look at this . . .'

The officer held up his wedding ring between thumb and forefinger. It was a squeezed oval, and cracked top and bottom.

'Cathy will do her fucking nut . . . .'

four

CLIVE DID NOT like the idea of spending the early evening with Amelia Dorf's crowd of goat rapists and rich sickies, but as an entrepreneur he knew the importance of maintaining a personal relationship with his best customers. Besides, there was a good chance of turning up tonight's cunt at Amelia's 'entertainment'. Then he could leave early, and get on with the Business.

He was listening to electro-funk on the car stereo. He liked music with a rhythm.

The Sergeant Major had handled Coral pretty well. Since it was two-in-a-row time, he had taken a lot more precautions with this one. By the time she showed up in that rubbish dump on the Isle of Dogs, there would be little left that was recognisable. With luck, she might be buried forever under the wet newspapers, stinking food remnants and empty cornflake packets. Mr Skinner would be very pleased. This job was one of his 'specials'. He had certainly got his money's worth.

Later, Clive had to go to a club and watch the Sergeant Major and some of his army mates. They were very well organised. They would pretend to get pissed and start a fight. There would be a lot of damage and a few people would get hurt, but the lads would be away by the time the police could get round to the place.

The manager had been trying to set himself up in the Business when he knew full well that Clive had the franchise. He needed to be reminded of the way the world was arranged.

Also, it would be a thrill for the cunt. 'Want to go to a club and see some damage done?' That would be a good pick-up line. Very good.

Clive wanted to see the manager with a broken nose, blood on his dicky bow and frilly shirt front. Maybe the Sergeant Major would go in for some Greek dancing, and smash all the house DJ's records instead of plates.

He was buzzed through the gates, and parked neatly in front of the house. There were quite a few cars ranked in the drive. Someone with safe sex on the brain had draped a pillow-case over the glans of Amelia's silly dick-shaped bush. He set the car alarm, and went up to the door.

Before he was even inside Amelia's hallway, some harridan was leaping him, kissing his face with dry lips, pulling at his lapels. Her breath was foul.

'Clive. Oh God, Clive, it's been so long . . . it's so good to see you. Clive, you've got to . . . I need . . . I can pay . . . Clive, I . . .'

It was Coral's old flatmate, Nina Kenyon. Luckily for him, Amelia's bodybuilding freak had been handling the entryphone and was there to pull her off him. He put her down.

'It's all right, Anders,' Nina said, 'I'm sorry. I just need to . . . could we be alone, please?'

'Clive?' he asked, obviously awaiting orders to hurt someone.

'It's okay, Anders. I can deal with this.'

'Fine.' The muscle mutant waddled off. Nina was all over him again, but more ingratiating this time, controlling her desperation, soothing the wrinkles she had put in his coat, unwrapping his scarf.

'Clive, I'm sorry. I didn't mean to come on so . . . I need you . . . I need a hit . . . please, Clive . . .'

He had dealt to her fairly steadily. When she was flush, she had been stupid enough to pay over the odds. When she was broke, she had been stupid enough to plead for credit. She used to be a good cunt, now she was a dressful of dead fishmeat.

'Let me get my coat off, for fuck's sake. It's expensive. Used to walk around on a camel's hump.'

She pulled his topcoat off, and took the scarf. She fumbled, dropping them on the floor and picking them up, sorrying wildly, before shoving them onto the rack with the others. Clive reckoned she was well past skin-popping. She was up to two or three needles a week, and had gone without for maybe 48 hours. She would cut off her right arm and give it to him if he came over with as much as a single bag.

'I can't do business here,' he said. 'It's a party.'

'Clive, come on. Clive, please. I need some smack. Not much, just enough. It's the last time. Please . . . *please* . . .'

'Nina, fuck off. You still owe me from the last time. Remember. You don't have a tab any more, it's all used. You have to clear that before I can even think about transacting with you again. Now, leave me alone . . . .'

She had dragged him into a room that turned out to be empty. At least she had the sense not to do her grovelling and pleading in front of other people. She would not let him go. She opened her purse.

'I've got money. Look. Anne gave it to me. Here . . .'

'I don't know any Annes.'

'Here, look . . .'

She held out two freshly crumpled ten pound notes, one in either fist. He prised them free, smoothed them, and pocketed them.

'Fine, Nina. Now we're even. I'm glad to see you're learning a little responsibility. It's important . . .'

'No, Clive,' she screeched at him, 'it's not for last time. You don't understand. It's for this time. Now. Clive, please . . .'

'No, Nina, that was for last time. *The* last time. I should never have extended credit to you then, and I won't do it again.'

'I don't have any more.'

'Then I don't make a sale.'

'You don't understand, Clive . . .'

'I think I do, Nina.'

'Clive, what about if I were to . . .'

'No, that won't do. It'll have to be cash. You've depreciated recently, gone down against sterling.'

'Clive, I . . .'

He left her babbling and crossed the hall to the party. He kissed Amelia and gave her a Christmas card. It was a privately printed cartoon of Santa Claus having sex with Rudolf the Red-Nosed Reindeer. Amelia tore the envelope open and laughed.

In the den, Clive calmed down and practised his charm again. He exchanged a few pleasantries with Jeane the Amazon, and collected on a small cocaine deal with a Senior Lecturer in Romance Languages. There were some people you could trust, after all.

Cocaine. There was another staple seller. Like Moet et Chandon or Chanel No. 5. The preferred drug of old money, and, by extension, of the *nouveau* mob. His most loyal cocaine customers were in the City, Whitehall and the Palace of Westminster.

Nina came in soon after, flapping her arms like pterodactyl wings, and pounced on a girl he had never seen before. Anne? She looked like a good cunt. Nina had her hand in the other girl's handbag, and was begging her for money in exactly the same terms she had used on him while begging for heroin.

Even if she came up with the money, Clive was not about to hand over a bag in the open. She was so far gone she had got seriously stupid. But it was all his own fault really.

Now, he had the Sergeant Major and his sales force to deal in person with small customers like Nina. She was a hangover from the old days, when he had had to hustle the stuff himself. He had several like her and they were very nearly impossible to ditch. Of course they died from time to time, so there was a light at the end of the tunnel.

'We got totally wrecked yesterday,' said one of his old-fashioned die-hard dope customers, 'and rented out *Santa Claus – the Movie* on video. It was the most moving experience I ever had. They ought to hand out gear instead of ice cream to the kids'

'Yeah,' said his Tonto-hairstyled girlfriend, 'we had a megalaugh.'

A deep-voiced character with five o'clock shadow all over his face and fists like Popeye the Sailor grabbed the girl by her Indian beads and slammed her up against the mantelpiece.

'I just hate it,' he growled, drooling between yellow teeth, 'when people misuse the suffix mega.'

He banged her head backwards, knocking down a domino row of Christmas cards.

'It denotes quantity, not size,' he growled, dropping the girl. He stumped off, in search of split infinitives and incorrect usages of the adverb 'hopefully', and the Last of the Hippies picked up his Moonchild or Starbeam or whatever, and calmed her down.

Nina was back, with a fiver and some change.

'Clive, I'm really sorry about earlier . . .'

He would not take the money. She put it in his lap. He picked it up and dropped it in a bowl of fruit punch. The coins sank between the bananas, apples and mushrooms.

'Nina, just fuck off will you.'

'Clive, I need you. I'll do anything. Please . . .'

He stood up and slapped her. Hard. Everyone shut up and looked at them.

'Now look what you've done, you stupid cunt. You've spoiled the party.'

'Yeah,' said somebody drunk who just wanted to be nasty, 'you tell her. Break the cow's arm.'

This, thought Clive, might be fun.

He took a double handful of Nina's jacket, above her breasts, and tore. Tiny buttons flew, and she clutched herself. She shook her head wildly. Her hair was a frightful mess. Her make-up was streaked.

The man who had agreed with Clive grabbed Nina's jacket collar and tried to rip down her back. Someone else pulled her necklace, and imitation pearls spread underfoot. There was a lot of screaming and laughing.

Nina was passed from person to person. Everybody tried to take something – a scrap of clothing, a lock of hair, a false eyelash, a brooch. They pinched and kissed and cuddled and laughed and swore.

Nina was beyond hysterics. Her mouth opened and closed, but Clive could not tell whether she was making any noises. Everyone else sounded pained and crazy enough.

He stood back and watched. Someone started singing 'Oranges and Lemons', and everybody joined in. Clive was surprised that he remembered the words. All those years of *Listen With Mother* must have sunk in.

> 'Oranges and lemons,
> Say the bells of St Clements,
> I owe you five farthings,
> Say the bells of St Martins . . .'

Amelia was in there, jostling and tugging with the worst of them. And Anders, showing off his strength by tearing only at the thick material of Nina's suit. Only Nina's friend, Anne, stayed out of the game, and she was not doing anything to stop it. Clive looked at her, and she looked at him.

He poured a drink. Chateauneuf du Pape. It was supposed to be very good, but all wine tasted alike to him.

Nina was on the floor now, sobbing, and the others had a rugby scrum over her. Already, there was blood. The girl had had her hands over her face and was rolling from side to side. She could do little to protect herself.

Soon it would get out of hand. But it had got out of hand before, and Clive had coped with it.

Judi and Coral. Now, *that* was out of hand. And Clive had coped with that.

He would ask for even more money this time.

One of the men had his fly open and his dick out. He was going to take a leak on the girl, but Amelia pulled him out of the circle with a cry of 'not on my carpet'.

Everybody backed off now. It was the last verse of the song. Jeane the Amazon picked Nina up. The girl was a mess.

> 'Here comes a candle
> To light you to bed,
> And here comes a chopper . . .'

Then Mr Skinner came down.

five

'To . . .'

This was sick, sick. Anne knew she ought to do something, ought to intervene. But . . .

'. . . chop . . .'

She looked at the young man, Clive. He was anonymously handsome, studiously calm and trying to be detached. He wanted to be apart from the humiliation he had engineered. Men like this, a man like this, had taken Judi apart . . . .

'. . . off . . .'

Was this man to blame? Judi's ex-. Ex-what? Boyfriend? Pimp? Drug pusher? Here he was, enjoying the party, watching the games. And Judi was dead. She could see him sweating. She guessed he was almost bursting with pleasure . . .

'. . . your . . .'

Then, he came into the room. The Monster. But he could not be the Monster. He could not . . .

'. . . HEAD!'

The Monster parted the circle of people, and took Nina from Jeane Russell. No, not the Monster. Just a man. He held Nina. Everyone shut up, except the girl. The man stroked her face and hair, soothed her whimpering, kissed her bruises, shushed in her ear. No one interfered.

'Mr Skinner . . .' Amelia's sentence trailed off into empty air. The man had looked at her, and shut her up.

Skinner. Anne had heard of him, and not just from Nina. One of the guests had been talking about him. He was supposed to be someone you were afraid of. She could understand that.

Of course, he was not the Monster. He was not Hugh
Farnham.

Actually, the resemblance was minimal. He was a big man
too, and his face had that same patched-together lizardy
look. But that didn't make him Hugh Farnham. He was
conservatively dressed, in a dark, three-piece business suit.
He wore a tarnished gold watch chain across his waistcoat.
He had a dark, fur-collared coat draped like a cloak over his
shoulders.

He included Nina in his coat, an angel wrapping a child
in its wings. He looked at Anne, smiling slightly, then at
everyone else. He spoke, in accentless English.

'A specimen, I suppose. Of what, though? Vice un-
rewarded?'

'Mr Skinner,' said Clive, 'we . . .'

'Yes. I know. You were playing. Just playing. You know I
don't like you to play games without me, but you went ahead
regardless. You know you need your Games Master. Without
me, you do crude, unimaginative things like this . . .'

He showed them Nina's face, lowering his fur collar away
from it. She was empty, used up.

'You don't understand pain. You can't appreciate it. You
let nasty little personal grudges creep in, and you taint the
experience. You have to go beyond that, transcend revenge
and pique and cruelty and cowardice. Pain is of and for itself
alone. I've told you this before, but you are a small-minded
lot, really. I despair of you.'

Anne looked around her. The guests were completely
cowed, like golden calf worshippers contemplating shards of
Moses' broken tablets. This was astonishing. Skinner released
Nina from his protection and set her down in an armchair.
She allowed herself to be posed like a mannequin, but drew
in on herself when he let her go.

Anne had met presidents without a tenth of what Skinner
was using. And she knew that he was barely stretching
himself. These were just make-believe decadents.

'She was bothering us,' said Clive, almost whining, 'she
wanted . . .'

'Yes,' Skinner paused, 'what did she want? What did she want that you have but wouldn't give her?'

Clive did not want to answer.

'The drug?'

Clive swallowed. 'Yes, she never paid . . .'

'Never. I think not, Clive, but let that pass. Heroin is interesting stuff. You supply only the finest, don't you . . .'

Someone made a joke Anne did not get, '. . . only the best, because graded grains make finer flour . . .'

And Daeve said, 'Heroin, it's what your right arm's for.'

There was only one sceptic in the crowd. Toby Farrar. It was his first 'entertainment', Anne remembered. He had not learned the applicable procedures yet. He stepped forwards.

'Who the fuck are you, fruitbat?'

He pulled at Skinner's empty coat sleeve. The expensive item slithered off his back like a shed snakeskin. It fell to the floor. Skinner's shoulders expanded. He grew taller.

The circle reformed, around Skinner and Farrar. Anne was part of it now, with Derek Douane on one side, and Jeane Russell on the other. Should they join hands?

Farrar knew what he had got into now, and stood to attention. He was still holding the coat sleeve. Skinner prowled around the man, his head in close like a drill sergeant chewing out a quivering private.

'Who the fuck am I, friend? I'm just another fruitbat, Major Farrar.' His head bobbed independent of his body. 'No one at all really.'

Skinner raised his hand to Farrar's face, and put his thumb in the officer's left eye. He pressed, just hard enough, and drew back from the falling man.

Farrar swore, and got up, holding his hand over his face like an eyepatch. Red tears stained his cheek. The hand came away bloody. He had not lost the eye, but the upper lid was neatly sliced. Toby Farrar's wife would think he had been in the wars.

'Clive, what is your complaint against this girl?'

'Credit . . . she wanted credit . . .'

'And?'

'. . . and that's not the way . . . not the way I do business.'

'Of course not. You all know Clive Broome, don't you?
He's an honest businessman. His terms are hard, but equit-
able. Cash for drugs.' Clive winced. 'Or cash for sex. Cash
for pain. Cash for anything, really. Anything you want. He
provides quite a service.'

Someone muttered, '. . . the swindling bastard!' It was the
man who had first joined in when Clive started on Nina.
Obviously, he wanted to see blood, and didn't much care
whose it was.

Now Clive was in the circle with Skinner. Farrar was back
with the rest, holding a handkerchief to his eye. He had been
converted.

Anne did not like Clive, did not care what happened to
him. If he had had anything to do with the way Judi died,
then she wanted him to suffer as much as possible. Did that
make her the same as Amelia as the others?

'What's wrong?'

'I told you, Clive. I'm disappointed. You are promising.
But you don't have a philosophy. You don't have purity.'

Skinner put a hand on Clive's shoulder. Anne knew he
was not disappointed or annoyed or anything. He was just
playing. He was just hurting people for his own amusement.

Or maybe there was more to it?

'What do you want from me?' Skinner asked everyone.
'What do you want from your Games Master?'

There was quiet.

'Do you want to be entertained? Do you want to be hurt?
Or do you want to learn? Do you even know what you want?
You must want something, or else you are nothing. Nothing
at all.'

He stood by Nina. She was curled up in her chair, head
down, coughing a little.

'This girl, Nina. You want to see this girl suffer? You want
to see this girl hurt? To see this girl hurt herself? You want to
see . . . to feel . . . what?'

It was Amelia who came forwards. She was the repre-
sentative.

'Yes, Mr Skinner,' she said, 'take her. Then show us something. Show us something we will never forget. Help us know ourselves.'

'Very well. Clive?'

'Yes.'

'Give me some heroin please'

'What?'

'Heroin.'

'But . . .'

'I think you can trust everyone here. They all know what you do for a living.'

Clive searched his pockets, as if looking for a train ticket. Someone laughed. It was obvious he did not have pockets full of drugs.

'You have some, of course?'

'My car . . .'

'Yes. The compartment under the passenger seat in the front, right? Very clever. The keys please.'

Clive fished them out of a pocket, and handed them over. Skinner looked around, and picked his man.

'Major Farrar?'

Farrar came forwards. He was not in pain now, but he still had a red tear of blood on one cheek. He looked like a lopsided clown.

'It's the BMW. You'll have to peel back the carpet. It should be easy. Clive?'

'It's in a malteser box.'

'Good. You understand, Major? Bring the heroin here.'

Farrar knew how to obey an order. Skinner crouched in front of Nina.

'Now you'll get what you want. I'll look after you.'

She shrank in her seat. Again, Anne felt she ought to do something but could not think of anything.

They all stood around in silence. The computer salesman suggested they play 'Twenty Questions' or 'I Spy', but a glance from Skinner shut him up.

Farrar came back with a small boxful of heroin. Skinner picked out three sachets.

'That's too much,' said Clive, 'she might . . .'

'So?'

The dealer almost smiled, and visibly relaxed. He was out of the circle. Nina was in it again.

Skinner gave Nina's handbag to Amelia. She emptied it on the floor, and picked out the junkie kit. Bent sugar spoon, a length of rubber tubing, and hypodermic needle. She dumped them on the arm of Nina's chair. The syringe was a proper hospital model, not a disposable pipette.

Skinner laid out the sachets in a row next to the kit. Nina was too far gone, too traumatised, to pay any attention. Even heroin could not reach her.

'Clive,' said Skinner, 'do the honours.'

'I'm not very good at this. I just sell it, I don't use it.'

'Very wise, I'm sure. But you must be familiar with the business end.'

'Yes. I'll need a bigger spoon.'

Amelia handed him something from a silver service. He examined it. It was unusual, a dinner-size replica of a teaspoon, with a carved apostle at the end of the handle.

Clive spilled some of the powder as he heaped it in the spoon, and could not hold it steady over his lighter flame, but finally he got it liquefied. The spoon would be ruined.

'It's a good idea to mix it with citric acid,' he said. Nobody offered him a lemon slice from their perrier.

Amelia rolled up Nina's torn sleeve and tied the tourniquet tight around her upper arm. Veins stood out bluish against pale skin. Anne saw the beginnings of tracks.

Nina was still pliable, uninterested in her situation.

Clive drew the heroin into the syringe, filling it to capacity.

'She'll overdose,' he warned.

'Not if she's strong enough,' said Skinner. 'Give it to her. She doesn't have to use it. The decision is hers.'

Nina bent and unbent her bare arm. She looked around. She was coming back.

'Clive . . .'

'I'm here, Nina. Here's your smack. It's all right now, all right.'

'Uh?'

'You don't have to pay. It's all been taken care of. Now, be a good girl and take your medicine.'

He put the syringe in her hand. It rolled in her fingers, but she quickly got a hold on it. She smiled.

'Nina, it's up to you,' said Skinner.

'Nina,' said Anne, 'don't . . .'

Skinner swivelled to look at her. His eyes were nothing special, but he was fearsome. Perhaps he was the Monster?

'Don't what?' he said, smiling.

'. . . don't . . .' Anne tried to say.

'Don't *die*?'

'. . . no . . . yes . . .'

'It's up to her, isn't it?'

Anne could not say anything. Skinner was looking at her, and she felt a caress of terror. Was she to be next in the circle? The Games Master was taking an elaborately casual interest in her. After a long moment, he turned away, and paid attention to the current victim.

Nina held the syringe properly now. A drop appeared at the tip of the needle. No air bubbles. She looked at the others, she looked at the syringe, she looked at Anne.

'Don't . . . please.'

Nina broke. She erupted out of her chair, yelling, and charged for the door. She shouldered her way between Anne and Derek. The child, laughing, fell over. Anne was jolted, but Jeane Russell held her up with a painful grip.

Nina was out of the door, and the syringe gone with her. The cry receded, and her clattering footsteps became distant. She had gone upstairs. Nobody moved.

It was a big house. Anne knew Nina could easily find a place to kill herself in private. Poor thing.

'Clive,' said Skinner, 'you, and this girl – Anne, isn't it? – you go and bring Nina back. Stop her from wasting herself if you can. It's important. We'll keep the party going while you're gone.'

Clive knew enough to do what he was told. He took Anne's arm and dragged her out into the hallway, towards the stairs.

She did not fight.

Inside, she was cold.

The Games Master knew her name. Skinner knew who she was.

six

H E DID NOT know why but, upstairs, Amelia's house reminded him of a jungle. It was remarkably clean and well-maintained, and all the lights worked but Clive felt as if he ought to be wearing a pith helmet, and carrying a hunting rifle that could bring down a charging rhino at fifty paces. With the American girl as a bearer, and that dopey cunt Nina as rogue quarry, this was a skew-whiff safari.

Every time he had been led through the house previously, it had been different. The mix of the original architect's unusual commitment to the concept of asymmetry, the previous inhabitants' rabid fetish for amassing ridiculous quantities of Victorian bric-à-brac and '30s kitsch, and Amelia's own declared desire to keep her environment in a state of constant flux had turned the place into a confused and confusing labyrinth.

'We'll never find her,' he told the girl, Anne, 'let's just hang about out of earshot for a few minutes and go back.'

She looked at him in a queer, incisive way he did not like at all. He wondered who the fuck she was.

'I don't think that guy Skinner would like that.'

'So?'

'So you're scared of him. All of you are.'

'That's not true.'

It was not true. Was it? Mr Skinner was weird, unpredictably dangerous, even, but he was just . . .

Just what?

If anything, Mr Skinner should be scared of him. After what Clive had done for him, he would be forever in his debt. In his power.

'I can handle Mr Skinner.'

'Yeah,' she said, unconvinced, 'right.'

'Let's try and find the second floor. The lights are on up there.'

'This is the second floor.'

'Not in England.'

'Oh yes, you people have to have a nothingth floor.'

There was something about the girl. She was not a loser, like Nina, or a sickie, like Amelia. She was sharp. Clive had got so used to being able to fool everyone in this circle that he was unnerved by her obvious clear-sightedness. The rest were wrapped up in a fog, from drugs or cracked minds, but Anne knew exactly what was going on.

Of course, there were some things she could not know about.

She had got him on Mr Skinner, though. Really, he had to admit that the man scared him. Clive liked to hurt people as much as the next person, felt the need to confirm his power over others, but Mr Skinner was a specialist, an expert. He could hurt capriciously, pointlessly, even against his own interests . . .

Like now. Mr Skinner needed Clive, and yet he was punishing him, making a great show of his obsolescence. This search party was crazy.

'Why you?' Anne asked him as they climbed the stairs. 'You're his type.'

Christ, did she know *everything* he was thinking? He suppressed the urge to respond, to tease an answer to the question out of himself. He did not want to think about it.

For what was he being punished?

The second floor landing was spacious, a gallery almost, but much less cluttered than the lower parts of the house. Passages fed off left and right. As far as they could see, the walls were plain white, with evenly spaced-out black doors. It all looked like an enlarged version of those laboratory mazes they let rats loose in.

He decided that Anne was probably a very good cunt. Americans were all easy. Except Judi. She had been difficult.

Perhaps this expedition did not have to be a total waste. He had screwed girls who hated him before, and had always got something out of it.

He stepped near the girl, and put an exploratory hand on her hip. He tried his nicest smile, and prepared to whisper his suavest come-on line.

'You have a lovely smile,' he said, 'may I taste it?'

She took his wrist between thumb and forefinger, and held his hand up between them as if gripping a putrid fish by the tail. She turned her thumb- and fingernails in and pinched, probing for painful pulses between the bones. She let go.

'Look, Clive, I don't like what you do for a living, I don't like the way you treat girls at parties, I don't like your taste in shirts and I don't like the way you look. Therefore, I suggest we concentrate on finding Nina.'

He could not help asking himself: what was wrong with his shirt?

'What's the point?' He said, rubbing his cuff over the place she had gored him.

'Maybe we can stop her hurting herself.'

'It's too late for that. I know a lot of smackheads. She's got to have stuck it in her arm by now. She's dead, only she'll be able to move around for a bit longer. Not much longer.'

'You kill many this way?'

'Fuck off,' he said, suddenly angry. 'Who do you think you are, Joan of Arc? I'm just like anyone else. I sell people what they want.'

'But you have to make them want it first. You have to make them want to die.'

What was this girl doing at one of Amelia's dos? She certainly did not blend it with the crowd. Clive thought she might be a rare type of pervert who gets off on vociferously condemning all the vices she actually practises. He had heard of that brand of peculiarity before. But she did not strike him as a girl who would get much pleasure out of flagellating herself with self-loathing and trembling hypocrisy. She was more the grit in the cream type, born to be a pain in the backside, always getting at you.

'Okay,' he said. 'Let's stop arguing and find the girl. I still think she's on this floor. She'd want the lights on.'

'Fine. But the corridor is lit up both ways. Which did she take?'

'It doesn't matter. She'll be in one of the rooms. We can go through them easily. I reckon they only have one door apiece, so she'll be trapped. Not that she'll be able to do much about running away. She'll be on a bed somewhere, out of her skull.'

They took a passage to the left, opening each door in turn and flicking on the interior light-switches for each room. This floor apparently was a private gallery of some sort. The first room was hung with explicit 18th century paintings, depicting the classical rapes of chubbily nubile girls by an assortment of animal and half-animal deities. The second was a showroom for garish '50s juke boxes.

'Have you noticed,' said Anne. 'There are no windows.'

'Amelia is nutty. She's always having the builders in to fiddle around with something or other. She must have had this whole floor bricked up from the outside.'

'Why?'

'I told you, she's nutty.'

The next room was full of mounted animals. They were stuffed and posed in all manner of positions, demonstrating sexual unions between incompatible species. It was supposed to be funny, but Clive thought Amelia's kinkiness could get monotonous after a while. Anne did not pass comment, and he shut the door.

'What is it with this Skinner?' asked Anne. 'What does he do?'

'He's just . . . just rich, I suppose. Rich and twisted.'

'There's a lot of that about.'

'I know.' Clive wanted to go on. He had never had anyone to whom he could talk about Mr Skinner. Not even the Sergeant Major. Not even Judi. There was no one he could really trust. 'But he's different . . .'

'What do you mean?'

'Amelia and the others. They're just playing. Mr Skinner

is serious. With him, all this . . . all this stuff is important, almost as important as being alive . . . .'

'And you? Do you like these games?'

She was good at asking questions, he realised, good at getting answers. Just like Judi. He did not like that.

Judi had always tried to rub his nose in parts of his life he just wanted to let lie there and be profitable. He was glad he had got rid of her. Admittedly, she had been the one who left, but, in the end, he had been the one to do the getting-rid-of. Poor Judi. Poor old, dead Judi.

He opened a door.

'Jesus Christ!'

The room was a walk-in freezer. Hanging from ceiling hooks were butchered human carcasses. The opened door jarred one, and they swung to and fro, bumping into each other like the elements of an executive toy. Lifeless knuckles scraped the floor.

Anne reached in and turned on the lights. The fridge was not as cold as it ought to have been.

'Bacon, I suppose,' she said.

She touched a corpse. He could see now that it was a distorted papier maché sculpture, luridly coloured in red. The ribs were wooden struts, thinly papered over. The cooling coils on the walls and the spreading stains on the floor were painted.

'Francis Bacon, I mean.'

'It's fucking sick!'

Clive had thought it would be Judi and Coral again, on a much larger scale. Even the Sergeant Major would have problems with this much cuntmeat.

Actually, after the first shock, the sculpture did not look real at all. The limbs were out of proportion, and you could read the newspaper headlines under the thin red paint. But, somehow, it was worse than real.

Who the hell had Amelia got to make this anyway?

'Nina,' Anne shouted. 'It's Anne. I want to help you. It's all right.'

Her voice did not even echo in the passages.

Around the next bend was darkness. The lights were not burning.

'She must have stopped here,' Anne said, 'or doubled back.'

'No, we'd have run into her.'

'Maybe.'

Anne called out again. There was no answer of any kind. Clive wondered why they had not heard anything from downstairs. It was odd that the party should get so quiet. There was no music, even.

Then, he felt the world shift on its axis, and knew that a new reality had slotted into its place. New physical laws, new moral dictates, new topographical patterns. It would be a major adjustment, and he did not know how to cope with it yet.

'There's something wrong here,' he said.

'She could be on another floor.'

'I don't think so . . . Let's give up and go back downstairs.'

He turned his back on the darkness to argue with Anne. That was when, with a glass-cracking shriek, the harpy brought him down from behind. A talon punctured the flesh under his chin, and tore . . . .

seven

CLIVE SPUN around and collapsed at the same time, heaving from his shoulders in a spasm which threw Nina off his back. Anne tried to catch the girl, hoping to embrace her from behind and pin her arms, but missed getting a sure hold on her. She was slammed into a wall by Nina's weight and momentum, and felt the shock of the impact in her teeth. Knots of pain throbbed in her spine.

Nina was still screeching. It was an inhuman, continuous sound, containing hatred, rage and triumph beyond expression in words. It was a horrible sound. Anne remembered her brother's première. Cam's concert should have started by now.

She reached for the back of Nina's ripped jacket, but only managed to get a handful of hair. Nina stood up, and the hair was pulled through Anne's fist. It was as if a steel rope had been scraped across her palm.

She looked up at Nina and could see that the girl did not recognise her. She was completely feral, a tie-dye splash of blood across her front, her fingers bent into claws. She turned away, and ducked into the darkness. Out of the light, she shut up. Anne heard rapid, birdlike footsteps. Then nothing.

She looked across the passage at Clive. He was half-sitting, half-slumped against the wall, vainly trying to move.

Nina had stabbed him with the syringe. It hung unpleasantly from his ruined throat, broken. The glass was cracked, the handle loose, and the needle bent. It had been emptied, but was more than half full now. With blood. Clive's jacket and shirt were stained, and little squirts rose and fell from his wound with each heartbeat.

Anne guessed that he had a severed artery. She got up, steadying herself against the wall, and took a few experimental steps. Her back did not ache that much. She had not been damaged.

Clive rolled his eyes, and tried to speak. Blood leaked out of his mouth, but nothing else.

It had happened too quickly to be absorbed. Anne knew that Nina had stabbed Clive, but she was not sure whether she had doped him as well.

He was an ugly mess, and he was still alive, but Anne could find no emotion to feel for him. She had seen her sister ancient and dead on a stretcher this morning, probably because of Clive or someone like him. She did not even have any squeamishness left over.

He moved feebly, trying to lift a hand to probe his wound.

She felt uncomfortable, watching him die and unable to care about him. She did not know what, if anything, to do for him. So she left, and went after Nina.

She did not want to think about him any more.

eight

I T DID NOT hurt, so he knew it must be serious.
   He saw Anne look away from him and leave his field of
vision. He could not turn his head. A light came on, banishing
the darkness around the corner. She was following Nina, the
stupid . . .

Everything was clear. He was trapped in his body, as surely
as a crashed motorist could be held in a wrecked car by a
locked seat belt. Unless he got himself free soon, he would
die . . . .

He concentrated on trying to stand up. There was some
feeling, not much, in his knees and upper thighs. He pulled,
and managed to bend forwards at the waist like an oarsman.
He could touch his toes. He got hold of the polished tip of one
of his shoes, and tried to pull himself away from the wall. His
head was between his knees and he could smell the blood. The
wetness was pooling in his lap.

Then, for a moment, his back and shoulders were working
properly. He achieved some sort of upright position, although
his treacherous legs deserted him immediately. He staggered
through the open doorway, into the painted freezer, feeling
his knees giving out with each inept step. To steady himself,
he hugged a sculptured torso. An arm came loose and fell off,
revealing scrunched up newsprint where there should have
been ligament, bone and muscle. He knew he was bleeding
all over the work of art.

Someone else came into the room and sat down on a plain
wooden chair to watch him struggle. It was Mr Skinner,
calm and hungry. The man's face gave nothing away. He
was neutral. He was not going to help Clive out of his

crumpled BMW, but he was not going to kick the bent door shut on him either.

He knew Nina had poisoned him as well. He had never had heroin before, but he knew enough junkies to recognise the effects. Although the pins and needles in his legs could perhaps have been from loss of blood. Purple lines floated on the surfaces of his eyes, coming briefly into focus, then retreating into vague smudges.

Purple haze, he thought.

Finally, the pain came,

First it hit him where Nina had, just below his jaw. From this nucleus, it swiftly spread throughout his head and trunk, leaving only his limbs in an unfeeling limbo. He almost passed out, but his eyes would not close. He kept on fighting . . .

Fighting for what?

. . . kept on fighting to stay upright. The lumpy statue in his arms was crumbling. Large chunks fell around his feet. Something gave way like the bottom of a carrier bag, and the bulk of the papier maché was squeezed out. He realised that in the centre of the soft fake torso was a hard real butcher's hook. The remains of the sculpture slipped through his arms, and he sank onto the sharp iron prong.

It went into his upper belly, and caught under his ribcage. He felt himself pulled out of shape, his innards adopting new alignments.

The hook was a curved icicle. It was uncomfortable rather than agonising. The ice spread through his chest, forming around his beating heart.

His hand and arms were free, but his knees and ankles had long since given out. He could feel nothing at all below the hook's point of entry. He jerked downwards, his entire weight on the hook and chain. It held. He did not fall.

He swung his left arm up in a reverse backstroke, and grasped the chain. He felt the links pressing into his palm. He hauled, taking some of the weight off the hook, but not enough.

Then he felt for the pain in his neck. His hand seemed like a flesh mitten, fingerless and clumsy. He wrapped it around the syringe, ignoring the jagged glass which tore his skin.

Mr Skinner had come closer. Now, his face was only inches away from Clive's own. He was as near as a lover or a parent could ever come. Clive felt delicate feelers worming through his mind, draining his pain, his fear. It was a great relief. He felt arms around him, lifting his body up, easing him off the hook.

He pulled the syringe out, and weakly flung it away. The bottom half of Mr Skinner's face was suddenly reddened. Clive heard the fountain, and knew that he had torn something important. He saw an arc of blood, and knew that it came from his own neck. It was oddly like going cross-eyed and seeing the bridge of your nose. Then, the blood got in his eyes.

Clive shook his head, and cleared his vision. Mr Skinner was smiling an impossibly wide smile. Fifty or sixty perfect, pointed teeth gleamed between his parted lips. Then his face faded until, at last, only his smile was left behind.

nine

'NINA!'

The girl had darted into a dark stretch of the corridor, and could not be found easily. Anne trailed her fingers along the wall at shoulder height, but there were no switches or dangling cords. She could still see, dimly, which meant that there must be a light source somewhere near. Somewhere.

'Nina!'

She went forwards, step by step. The floor proved untrustworthy. She had already found a few unexpected steps, up or down, and slammed a toe against a new level. It was all fairly pointless, like the needless ha-has of a carnival funhouse.

She stopped and listened. The house was silent. It was as if the whole place were deserted and derelict.

What were Amelia and her guests doing? She hoped that they had not dispersed from their downstairs room. Could they be playing some sadeian variation on hide and seek? Could they be in the dark, waiting for her?

'Nina, it's me. Anne.'

The girl must have calmed down. She must be within earshot, but she was keeping quiet. She had been hysterical, now she was probably close to catatonia. Anne thought Nina had found a hiding place and was lying low. She could imagine the girl curled up in a cupboard, trying to breathe noiselessly, willing her heartbeat to be less loud.

God, the house was quiet! Admittedly, this was a placid residential district, but there should be some exterior noise: occasional traffic, water dripping from the eaves, distant carol singers, murmuring electrical appliances. There was nothing. The walls must be ten feet thick.

She found the light. It came from a tributary passage that lead off from the main corridor at a curious angle. The rooms must be not quite square. A funnel of light fell from a circular ceiling hole, drawing attention to the skeleton of an ornate spiral staircase. It was a rickety old piece of work; presumably intended for servants banished from the regular stairs. It could not have been easy to hump awkward loads up and down the wobbly death trap. There were grinning gnomes worked into the iron filigree, running downwards helter-skelter.

Nina would have been drawn to the light, just as Anne had been. She must have gone upstairs. Anne started upwards on the shaking staircase, but had to stop abruptly. The hole extended a foot or so above the level of the ceiling, and then ended. There was a dim fluorescent tube in the recess. She could not go up, only down. The floors below were dark. Carefully, she descended into an unknown, unlit room.

She stepped off the bottom stair onto a carpeted floor. The light above her was remote and useless, blocked off by the triangular edges of the staircase. In the dark, she took little steps, her hands out before her. She found a wall, and hugged it. She edged sideways, clockwise. After getting into and out of three corners between stretches of flat wall, she found a door. And by it there was a switch. She turned on the light.

The room was bare, except for the staircase, and a pair of indifferent watercolours of dead flowers that hung on the wall opposite the door. The paintings were at eye level. Why had she not jostled them while feeling her way around?

It did not make sense, so she gave up thinking about it.

The door was not locked. The passage outside was unlike the ones on the floor above. It was as wide as a small room, but there were bulky pieces of old furniture against the walls between the doors, and Anne was forced to squeeze through a narrow and irregular middle path. Hard wooden angles pressed into her.

'Nina.'

On the floor, she found a scattering of porcelain shards. Several ornaments from a displayed collection of unpleasant little figurines had been swept off a small table. The girl had

come this way, she was sure. Again, Anne started looking
into every room for Nina. All the doors were unlocked. The
rooms beyond were filled with more forgotten furniture.
This must be where Amelia shifted everything when she
was having building done. A few of the pieces were properly
stored, with dustsheets and numbered tags, but most of the
stuff was just crammed in every which way.

Progress was slower than it had been upstairs. Welsh
dressers and tallboys kept getting in her way. And she was
alone.

Would Clive die? Could she have helped him?

This was not much of a party. Anne knew she had to expose
Amelia and her friends. The magazine would not go for it;
they could not afford the lawsuits. But she had friends on the
tabloids, the *News of the World*, the *Daily Mirror*. Pop stars
and society hostesses in S and M games that led to death.
Deaths? She could keep Judi out of it, but ruin a good few
careers, businesses and marriages. There would probably be
multiple prosecutions. The Global Peace Whatever would
lose a lot of credibility, she reflected. Maybe not: those
far right moralists had plenty of ways of surviving nasty
revelations and expelling offenders from their ranks. She
now believed that her sister had died, if not through the
direct actions of the people downstairs, then at least through
her unhealthy associations with them. What she had seen done
to Nina would have wrecked anybody.

Scum. Scum. Scum.

The rooms were like the passage, packed with antiques.
Most of them were in states of disrepair. Crippled chairs
with missing feet and tufts of stuffing coming through the
cracks; dead, useless grandfather clocks with faces but no
hands; embroidered hangings eaten with mould patches that
made hunt scenes resemble maps of unknown worlds. But
there was no dust, no dirt, no cobwebs. All this was looked
after, preserved in its current state of decay.

She opened a door, and found herself in the Bacon room.

. . . but surely that was upstairs. No, she must have
invisibly ascended through those upwards-sloping corridors

and irritating little steps, and come down again on the spiral staircase. For the last few minutes, she had been travelling in parallel to her previous route. The junk rooms alternated with the gallery chambers like the opposing teeth of a zip-fastener. Only the Bacon room interconnected both strata of the house. It had two doors. Clive would be beyond the other. Dead?

Despite everything, she had to see him. She could not immediately do anything for Nina. Perhaps she would be able to stop the bleeding. Maybe even save his life. Save him for the Old Bailey and whichever penal dustbin they locked dope peddlers in.

Anne had once written a piece about prison conditions. After a tour and a few interviews with convicts, she was in favour of sweeping reforms. But she wanted Clive to get dumped into a *grand guignol* Devil's Island with whip-wielding guards, running filth in the cells and neanderthal yard bosses. She hoped he would be gang-raped in the showers every night. A liberal, she remembered someone saying, is just a reactionary who has not been mugged yet. Tomorrow, she realised, she would be socially conscious again. Tonight, she would have elected Dirty Harry as chief of police. Shit, she wanted out of this mess.

She opened the other door . . .

'Clive?'

. . . and found herself in a part of the house she had never seen before. It was either a passage or a long, thin room, a stone-walled storage space lined with gunpowder plot-style wooden barrels. It was more like some sort of cellar than an upstairs room.

Obviously, there was more than one Bacon room.

She looked around, carefully this time. One of the dummies was fully dressed. She should have noticed it earlier. It was not at all like the others in the room, like all the ones in the other room. They were all dismembered portions, with exposed ribs and piglike pink hides.

It was the figure of an old, dead man. She was reminded of Dorian Gray at the end of the book, unrecognisably decrepit,

identifiable only by the rings sunk into the fleshy fingers. This
statue was shrivelled inside its suit, hanging from a hook in its
chest.

She did not want to touch it, but she had to.

She had expected it to be weighted, to feel cold and heavy.
But it was an obvious fake, papier-maché light. The wrinkled
skin, while rubberised to lend some semblance of naturalism,
was dry and fragile.

It was a repulsive piece of work, but paradoxical. The
concept was violently unpleasant, extravagantly horrible. But
there was a bland expression worked into the prune-like face.
It was like a sentimental 19th century vision of peaceful repose
after protracted suffering, the miserable on Earth rewarded in
Heaven.

Of course, the statue was in modern dress. A suspiciously
stained smart dark suit, just like Clive's. In fact, the costume
was exactly like Clive's, down to the horrible shirt and
expensive shoes. It was another of Amelia's bad taste jokes.
And now the effort would be wasted, since its subject was in
no condition to be either offended or amused.

Anne was tired, and fed up. It could only be about eight
o'clock – her old-fashioned watch, unwound this morning,
had stopped – but she felt as if she had been up all night,
working to meet an insane deadline. All she wanted was to get
this whole thing over with, so she could go home to Kentish
Town and sleep in her own bed.

It would be cold though. There was no one in the apartment
to turn on the electric blanket.

Downstairs. She would go downstairs and tell Amelia
what had happened to Clive. She knew what would happen.
Skinner would take over. The guests would disperse. Ambu-
lances and doctors would be called, the right people would all
be bribed, and the sordid mess would be efficiently covered
up. She would never be able to prove a thing. Whatever. She
did not care.

Leaving the Bacon room, she made her way through the
junkyard corridor. She thought the spiral staircase would lead
her down to the party.

. . . but she could not find the room. It had been distinct from the others. It was comparatively empty. She turned corners she was sure she had never encountered before. Had she taken the wrong route? Every room she looked into was the same. She came full circle around the house, and opened a door to find herself looking up again at the dangling corpse statue.

Now, she could see that it even *looked* like Clive. Or rather, as Clive would look if he were to live to the age of one hundred and fifty and then die. It really was a wretched thing.

She tried to picture the door of the room with the stairs. Had it been disguised to blend into the wall? Could she have missed it by mistaking it for one of the panelled wardrobes? Did it have an exterior handle? She could remember nothing.

Anne felt an urge to throw the kind of temper tantrum she had been able to get away with when she was six years old. She wanted to whimper in frustration and break something. But there was no one around to be made uncomfortable, or be coerced into helping her out. She was on her own. Anyway, her father and Cam had invariably known when she was faking. The Nielsons had always been a family of know-it-alls.

She walked through the Bacon room again, avoiding the central figure, deciding to try the place with the barrels.

. . . but now here was a main passage beyond the door, spacious and well-lit. A few yards down, the passage broadened out and became a mezzanine. There was the main staircase she had climbed with Clive a while – how long? – ago.

Could there be Bacon rooms, more or less the same, dotted throughout the house in order to creatre confusion? If so, then Amelia Dorf was an incredibly subtle and sadistic bitch. But, of course, she had known about the sadistic part. As for the subtlety, that seemed quite alien to the woman who coochy-cooed over children she wanted to mutilate. It was now obvious that Amelia had never been in charge.

Anne knew exactly whose fault this, all of this, was. She remembered his unremarkable eyes. And she remembered that he had known immediately who she was. Whatever game was being played now, it was between them, between her and Skinner.

Now, the walkabout was over. The rest of the party was just a flight of stairs away, in the room off the main hall. She heard a tinny phonograph. The record was 'Mr Sandman' by The Chordettes. It always gave Anne goosebumps, especially when the unidentified male voice answered the girls' plea for Mr Sandman to bring them a dream with a drawn-out, ever-so-slightly creepy 'ye-e-es?'

. . . but the main hall was not one flight of stairs down. Peering over the balustrade of the mezzanine, Anne saw a huge conservatory, thronged with man-sized plants. The far wall was a large expanse of ornamented glass, with pitch blackness beyond. Heat rose from the depths, and every smooth cold surface was damp with condensation.

Shit, this house was crazy! Anne realised now how jumbled up and contrived the interior was. The architect must have been an opium fiend.

The Chordettes finished. Something rustled in the undergrowth. Anne cautiously went down the stairs.

'Nina?'

Tropical blossoms turned towards her, stamens quivering. It was some species of voice-activated flytrap she had never heard of. There was a crackle of static, like a public address system at a church social, then another record started. Mama Cass crooning 'Dream a Little Dream of Me'.

Anne was annoyed.

'Stop playing stupid games, assholes!' There was no answer, just the song. 'Clive is hurt. He might be dead.'

She knew it was not a game any more. She wished she had a gun, the more powerful the better. She would have been happiest with a flamethrower.

Something clattered on the tile floor, behind a frothing bed of shrubs. The flesh of the plants was waxy, with green highlights from the directional lamps. The whole place was artistically lit. Anne glimpsed a different shade of green, moving among the vegetation.

She looked around for a blunt instrument. Something heavy and barefoot was padding around the conservatory. Something not human.

Then, the foliage parted. A giant cat's head poked out. Its eyes gleamed as if the irises were neon rings. It was a tiger, dyed green. Its fur was arranged in punkish spikes.

She made it to the staircase, and dashed at random back into the bulk of the house.

This could not be happening. Could not, could not, could *not!*

ten

AFTER CLIVE, he was full but unsatisfied. And he knew in his bones what that meant. This had all happened before. It was time to make a new start. He would need to feed beyond the point of gluttony, and then retreat to await the change. He would have to build himself up, because the change would take it all out of him.

There had not been much to Clive. But he had been young and in good condition. His physical substance had been a tonic, but already the hunger was coming back.

His clothes were too small now, pinching him at the neck, the waist and the crotch, stretched tight over the shoulders, the chest and his muscled limbs. It would not last. The feeding he had had from Clive was only a momentary boost. Already, he felt himself dwindling in his suit. Soon, he would be completely spent.

As for the rest of it, Clive had been a disappointment. At the moment of extinction, he had held the young man's mind up like a pierced coconut and let all the thin milk trickle out. Compared with Judi, there had been almost no yield. Down deep, Clive was unimaginative, inactive, petty, unquestioning. Judi was still with him, still struggling against the dark. Clive was already less than a ghost, less than a memory.

Still, the surges of animal strength pleased him. He scooped a handful of marble out of a bannister as if it were plasticene, and briefly enjoyed the traces of the many fingers that had brushed over this patch of cold stone down the years. He dropped it, and it bounced down the stairs. Someone was coming up.

'Mr Skinner?'

It was Amelia, looking eager. She was forever busily seeking out new gratifications, forever unaware of the weasel he always discerned nestling in her skull.

'Amelia. I asked you to stay downstairs with the guests. There are rules, you know. It would be much simpler if you obeyed them.'

'But . . .'

'I know I don't always explain myself, but you must always do what I say. I have reasons. These things are vitally important.'

She stepped over the marble chunk, and walked up to him. Even standing on the same broad step as him, she seemed pitifully small.

'Clive and the girl. It's been at least an hour. And Nina . . .'

'I found Clive. He's gone. Anne is lost, but I know where she is.'

'Nina?'

'She'll turn up.'

'Shouldn't we . . .?'

'No. There is no point now.'

'You look flushed. Have you been overexerting yourself?'

She reached up and touched his cheek. He felt a slight tickling as his old skin blistered. There was no pain, but he flinched from the contact. Amelia's unsubtle lust for him darted out of her like static electricity. He was repulsed by the scramble of images in her mind. She reminded him of the Objectivist.

They were standing on the main staircase, two flights up from the party room. He could hear the nervous chatter of the guests. He could make out all the separate conversations. Other sounds caught in between the meaningless words. Drinks being poured, a plastic cup crumpling, someone beating a fingertip tattoo on a table.

He had them all fixed in his mind. There were sixteen people in that room, standing, sitting, lying. Anne was getting out of the conservatory. Nina was curled up under a bed upstairs. Amelia was with him. Clive was used. There was no one else. The nearest house was empty. No cars or people moved in the street outside. Beyond the garden was a fairly busy road, but all the passing drivers were wrapped up in their tincans, insulated by Christmas drinks and trivial pursuits.

It was perfect.

He held up his right hand, stretching his fingers, and took Amelia's face in his grip. Her puzzled expression was covered. The thumb hooked under her chin, and the fingers pressed the top of her head an inch above the hairline. His nails grew, curving into her.

She could not speak, but he saw her panicked eyes staring from the spaces between his long fingers. Her cold nose pressed into his palm. Muffled sounds came from her throat.

'Shhh, Amelia. It's over. You'll always be with me now. Isn't that what you've wanted?'

He squeezed and pulled, taking off the front half of her head. He ignored the raw, splintered mess, and leaned forwards as if to kiss where her lips had been. He caught the weasel escaping as an insubstantial wisp, and inhaled it in through his nostrils.

He was not interested in the meat, just the flavour.

She was sour, but strong. Not as nourishing as Judi, but an excellent appetiser for what was to come. She had always been ruled by her desires. He savoured the weasel on his palate for seconds, and then breathed her into his lungs. She was still startled, but almost comfortable. She had been easy to incorporate.

He threw the face away, and went downstairs to join the party. He was ready now. Ready to give in to his feeding frenzy.

eleven

<u>H</u>ERE BE TYGERS. In St John's Wood? She had seen it, but she did not believe it. On the mezzanine again, she turned and looked back, down into the conservatory. There was no animal that she could see. The shrubs were not even disturbed. The song finished, and the loudspeakers just hissed. The place was completely undisturbed, if not completely undisturbing.

Anne wondered. Had she somehow been drugged? She had drunk only perrier at the party, and eaten nothing. But she could have been slipped something somewhere, through a pinprick. Had Clive done anything? And what kind of dope produced that kind of idiotic but vivid halluciantion? She did not want to think about it; that would only make her more disorientated.

The time is out of joint, she thought. 'Oh curséd spite,' she said aloud, 'that ever I was born to set it right.'

There was nothing awry in her mind now. She could remember *Hamlet* and the dates of important battles in the Revolutionary War and the names of Disney's Seven Dwarfs and the telephone numbers of old boyfriends and the faces of people she had known in college but not seen in years and the deadlines for the three pieces she had been working on . . .

Millions and millions of bits of information were still in her head, correctly labelled and neatly stored, but she could not work out the geography of this house, she was seeing green tigers and she was afraid in a way she had not been since childhood.

She was afraid that the Monster was going to get her.

In another part of the house, the screaming started. She could not work out how far away it was, but the shrill was enough to hammer into her skull like nails. There were many voices, screaming differently, loudly raised in a badly orchestrated cantata. Somewhere, violence was being done. If there was a tiger, it was loose now among the party guests. Loose and hungry.

It was time to get out. She could call the police – call Inspector Hollis – make a fool of herself, level hysterical accusations, have a breakdown, go to bed for weeks, miss Christmas. But first, she had to get out. She had to get out of this house.

The main staircase must be near, somewhere in the centre of the house. If she could get to the main hall, she could automatically open the gates from the instrument panel by the front door.

That would mean getting past the party, getting past whatever was happening to the guests.

The screaming was dying now. A few stragglers kept it up for a few seconds, then there was nothing. Just quiet.

She had not been able to work out where the noise had been coming from. It might even have been just another sound effect. Presumably . . .

She stopped thinking, and turned away from the mezzanine, plunging back into the corridor maze.

twelve

UNDER THE four-poster bed, Nina was safe, curtained
from the nightmare by the bedspread. The monsters
could not get her here.

But, cling as she might to the bolster she had taken with
her to stop her screams, she could not stop shaking.

She did not know whether she had used the smack. She
remembered the needle going into flesh, but she was not
sure that it had been her own. Her right arm had gone to
sleep below the tourniquet.

In the dark, she imagined red-eyed rats scurrying around
her, lashing her with their tails.

She heard her own heartbeat, alarmingly rapid, and she
heard the sea in her ears.

She was crying like a baby, sobbing for her Mum. The
monsters were prowling in the bedroom, searching for her.
She heard their hissing breaths, and the hard, sharp noise of
their hooves on the polished floorboards. She prayed they
would not think of looking under the bed.

Mr Skinner was inside her mind, whispering, alternately
cajoling and scolding her. He held his coat open, and called
her to him. He had everything she needed. If she got to him,
she would never have to worry again, never have to want
again.

She tried not to listen to Mr Skinner. She tried.

But he was persuasive, kindly, paternal . . .

The rats nipped at her flesh, biting through her ripped
clothes, sinking sharp little teeth into her skin. The monsters
argued among themselves in monster language, tails lashing.

Mr Skinner was calling for her.

Her heartbeat was still quickening in a crescendo. Soon, it must peak, and stop . . . .

Mr Skinner's coat was warm, welcoming. Wrapped in it, she would be able to sleep again, to dream sweet dreams, to wake up refreshed between clean sheets.

The rats got to her face, and she screamed inside herself, pressing her face to the bolster. The vermin were inside the pillow, biting outwards, clawing at her tight-shut eyes, scratching her tear-tracked cheeks, forcing their furry heads into her mouth.

One monster wanted to lift the bedspread, but his friends were contemptuous. They locked grinding horns, and scuffled.

Mr Skinner was singing, old songs from the '30s and '40s. He was like the bandleaders her Gran remembered, in a crisp collar, soothing through a megaphone.

Nina wanted to go to him.

'Yes,' she said aloud, 'yes, yes, yes!'

Mr Skinner finished his song, and bowed. Flashbulbs went off from the audience.

She was his. As soon as she got to him, she would be his.

She tried to get up on all fours, and bumped her head on the underside of the bed.

Her heartbeats were like a constant patter now, and she felt pains inside her chest and head.

The curtains parted, and light gushed into the dark space. Under the bed, Nina realised, was where the monsters lived. They were not afraid to come in after her.

Her heart stopped. For an eternal moment, she waited for its next beat . . .

thirteen

ANNE HAD GIVEN up the rational approach, and picked a passage at random. When she came to an intersection, she had ignored it or taken a new direction without bothering to think about it. She had passed through a few rooms. Now that she was looking closely, she realised that most of the rooms in the house had two doors. Each was a fat little passage in itself. She had not found any more Bacon rooms. Most of the decor in this part of the house was modelled after Hollywood's idea of elaborate period furnishings. Nobody real seemed to live here.

In a Versailles bed-chamber, attended by dressmaker's dummies in brocade jackets and periwigs, she found Nina. She had unconsciously put into practice the Winnie the Pooh principle, which rules that the most effective method of searching for a lost person or object is to get lost oneself on the assumption that some force of nature brings all forgotten things together in ignored niches and unfrequented locales. Of course, now they were both lost.

Nina was half-hidden under a four-poster bed, trailing silk sheets behind her like a bridal train. She was sprawled, hugging a sausage-shaped pillow like Linus' comforter. Anne could see that she was biting deeply into the pillow. Earlier, Nina had been stretched a good many notches too tight; now, she had snapped, and was flapping limply.

Her cuff was still undone, and the tourniquet had made her hand and lower arm into white marble, but Anne could see no new puncture. She guessed Nina had been too overwrought to shoot up. Maybe, she had successfully fought the need.

'Nina . . .'

The girl cringed at Anne's voice, and chewed the pillow. She had been crying, and was still shaking badly. It was difficult to tell whether she was retching or sobbing. She rocked back and forth.

Anne crouched, and gently tried to pull the pillow away. Nina was reluctant to give it up. Anne coaxed, and stroked her hard jaw. Finally, the girl let her teeth unclench, and relinquished a wet mouthful of cotton.

She put the pillow down, and hugged Nina. The girl responded, gripping Anne in a desperate embrace. It was like a wrestling hold. She tried to soothe the girl, and Nina relaxed. Anne unknotted the rubber tubing from her arm, and pulled the tourniquet loose. Nina's upper arm was ringed with red, but she bent her elbow and wriggled her fingers, getting the circulation going again. They stood up, and Nina half-sat on the edge of the bed. She stretched and lay back. She was nearly asleep.

'No,' Anne said. 'We have to get out of the house. We can't stay.'

'I'm tired.'

'I know. So am I. But we can't stay. This is a bad place.' Anne knew she was treating Nina like a four-year-old, but could see no other way to cope with her. 'I think something's happened downstairs. Did you hear the noise? I don't think we're safe here.'

'Then . . . let's . . . go home . . .'

'Yes, let's. Home. Come on, get up. I'll help. Here . . .'

She lifted Nina, getting the girl upright. Anne made sure the girl was not hurt. Nina had given up completely. She did not protest when she was led towards the door.

'This house,' said Anne, 'it doesn't seem to make sense. Where is the main staircase? Do you know?'

Nina smiled wanly. 'Through that door, turn left . . .'

'Are you sure?'

Nina was waking up. For a moment, she was supremely confident. 'Of course. Come on, don't be a slowcoach.'

Anne found herself being led. Nina was right. The main staircase was there, and two flights down, so was the main hall. The place was empty, quiet and normal.

'That's crazy,' Anne said, 'I'm sure I came this way . . .'

'Crazy? How?'

'It's nothing. Nothing really. I just got lost.'

They went downstairs, carefully and without incident.

'Anne?'

'Yes?'

'Hold my hand.'

'Sure.'

They touched fingers, and got them entwined. Anne kissed Nina on the cheek.

'Eugh,' the girl croaked, 'don't get soppy.'

'I won't.'

They were downstairs now, in the hall. It was not a fake. Anne saw her own coat hanging up on the rack with the others. There was no noise of any kind from the party room. The door was closed.

She knew she would have to take a look.

'Stay here,' she told Nina, letting her hand go, 'this will be over in a moment.'

She held the doorhandle, took a deep breath, and opened the door.

. . . the room was a mess, but there were no people there. Drinks stood abandoned. The Christmas tree was broken, having shed a layer of needles and broken baubles onto the presents. Food and cigarette butts had been trodden into the precious carpet. The open fire had practically died. The lights were still on, and a cassette was clicking in a tape deck.

Nina took her hand again, and tugged her away from the open door. 'Has everyone gone?' she asked.

'I think so.'

'Should we find someone to say goodbye to?'

Anne turned away from the party room. 'Let's not bother. Let's go.'

'Amelia usually pays. A hundred pounds. Sometimes more, if you've been . . .'

'We'll bill her later, okay?'

'Okay.'

They got their coats. Nina wanted to keep holding hands, and hurried the sleeves over her arms so they would not be out of contact for long. It was a bit embarrassing but Anne was glad of it.

The instrument panel looked complicated, but all the switches were neatly marked. The monitor showed the street outside in snowy black and white. There was no one about. Anne flipped the switch that opened the front gate, and the ironwork brushed the bottom of the video image.

'There,' she said. 'Easy.'

Nina opened the front door by hand and stepped outside, pulling Anne after her . . .

It was very dark, and Anne felt something slap into her face and stay there. She lifted it aside – it felt like a heavy curtain – and still could not see anything. Nina's grip tightened. The door had shut behind them.

'Anne, where are we?'

She did not know.

In her coat pocket, she had a pen with a little light in it, for taking notes in theatres and other dark places. She felt for it, and brought it out.

The glowworm lit up both their faces. Nina was frightened again. There were mobile shadows above her nose and eyebrows. They were in a large wardrobe. The curtain had been a crinoline, hanging from one of two rails that ran just above their heads.

'This . . .'

'. . . doesn't make sense. I know.'

There was no handle on this side of the door. Anne tried to get her fingers into the jamb, but could not. It appeared to have locked itself.

'We'll suffocate,' said Nina.

'I don't think so.' Anne pushed aside an armload of dresses, finding only another rank of old clothes. 'I don't think this is a regular closet. It's deep. More like a passage . . .'

'There's a way out?'

'At the other end. Right.'

On Anne's side, there were women's clothes – elaborate ball gowns with mock jewels sewn into the bodices and rustling, puffy sleeves and skirts. Nina faced a succession of sombre gentleman's wear – black evening suits, heavy overcoats. A few brass and silver buttons gleamed in the minimal light.

There was not much space. They could not go side by side. Anne took the lead, and dragged Nina. The girl's hand was cold now, although it was quite stuffy in the passage. It was not an easy progress. The clothes had not been disturbed for a long time and were as thick and tangled as jungle foliage. There would be untold vermin nesting in the folds of material.

Anne would have had good use for a machete.

A few of the wooden hangers had rusted wire hooks which bent and broke as they passed. Bundles fell down, stirring up dust. Nina had a coughing fit. The fallen clothes were as difficult to wade through as thick mud.

They must have penetrated twenty feet into the passage, and there was still no hint of an end within reach.

Anne felt the wind knocked out of her. She had blundered into a suit that was much more solid than most. She staggered back, and had to be steadied by Nina. A dark, hanging shape blocked the way. Holding up her light, Anne saw a cavernous opera cape with a Mephistophelean magician's tailcoat hanging inside it. And inside both was a large corpse.

Nina had a minor convulsion. Anne's hand felt crushed.

'Anders!'

It was, but, for all his weight, he looked hollow. Anne touched his dead white face, and felt nothing that had been alive.

'No,' she said, 'it's a sculpture. I've seen them before. Look, it's supposed to be Anders grown old . . .'

The hair was white, the neck muscles flabby. The face was minutely wrinkled, the flesh beneath semi-liquid.

'Let's go on.'

Nina was hesitant.

'You don't have to touch it.'

They ducked, and squeezed past. There were others. Some were unrecognisably altered or mutilated, but most were obvious caricatures of people Anne had seen at the party. Not only were they made to look lifeless and tormented, but they were crammed into mouldering fancy dress costumes. Toby Farrar wore the braided tunic of a Hussar, and even had a jaunty helmet perched on his head. Jeane Russell was an unsuitably voluptuous fairy queen with gossamer wings and golden spangles on her bare, withered arms. Derek Douane was got up as a Dickensian urchin, with a broken neck and a dirty face. Daeve was a knobbly-kneed schoolgirl in a navy blue pinafore, with red spot freckles on his cheeks and straw-coloured ropes attached to his beret.

It was hot in the thin corridor, and the hanging husks made going forwards practically impossible. The two girls paused, grimy and breathless, in the middle of the sick display. Nina tugged Anne back, towards the way they had come from.

'We can't give up now,' Anne said. 'Try to ignore these things. They're not real.'

'There's a thing in here with us.'

'What?'

'A thing.'

Anne listened, but there was no noise at all.

'It's an animal,' said Nina.

A tiger?

'I don't think so,' said Anne. 'Let's go on. It can't be much longer. We must be nearly there.'

They struggled a little further. Baz Something dangled absurdly, in the ballooning pants, curly-toed slippers, tiny waistcoat and bulbous turban of an Arabian Nights eunuch. His paunch bulged over a sash. At the end of the line was the computer salesman, dressed up as the Queen of Hearts. His death was supposed to have been messy, and there was a lot of realistic blood all over his costume. In the centre of his chest, where there was a heart motif on his tunic, there was a ragged hole disclosing his real heart, which looked to have been squeezed by an iron fist.

Nina screamed, horribly loud in the confined space.

'One of them touched me,' she said. 'Touched my hair.'

She tried to put her arms around Anne, but could not. A body got in the way. Anne banged her elbow on a solid wood wall.

'They're just statues.'

Anne pulled Nina along. They left the bodies behind them. The passage was wider now, with room for four racks. There were enough costumes here to keep the Paris Opera going for five successive seasons. But it was easier to move forwards.

'They're after us. They're not dead.'

Nina was whining. Anne wanted to slap her. She was at the end of her patience. None of this was helping.

Her light was carried forwards. It picked out a face, and they stopped. Nina's hand-grip was painful again. The face smiled.

'Good evening, Anne.'

It was Skinner. He looked more like Hugh Farnham now. There was some scarring on his cheek. Anne thought it was growing as she stared at it. She had nothing to say.

'I knew your sister, you know.' The bastard did not even look evil. 'Intimately.'

She could not look away from him. He smiled blandly again, without much enthusiasm. He was as tired as she felt.

'Skinner, what the fuck are you playing at?'

'Playing?'

She remembered it was not a game any more.

'Playing? That's for imbeciles like Amelia Dorf. You and me, Anne, we don't play games.'

'Yeah, right.'

Nina yanked her arm hard, pulling Anne's shoulder painfully. She turned away from Skinner. The other girl had plunged behind a curtain of fur coats. Anne was pulled into the clothes and lost her balance. Then she was down, and Nina was on top of her. The pen-light rolled away. Nina let go of her hand. Anne felt fingers in her throat, squeezing hard. She reached for Nina's hands, and grabbed what she hoped were her little fingers. She bent the fingers back. There was a squeal, and she was released.

Anne tried to get up, pulling on a coat, but Nina was still pinning her to the floor. There was still some light. Looking up at Nina, Anne saw a dead face. Just like the other effigies.

The scuffle at the Club Des Esseintes aside, she had not been in a fight since elementary school. The trick with the little fingers was the only thing she remembered from a piece she had once written on self-defence courses for women. She was no good at this. She rolled from side to side, trying to get the Nina Thing off her chest.

She got hold of a fallen ulster and stuffed it into Nina's face. It wrapped around her head. The Nina Thing tore at it, but Anne was released. She pushed the girl hard, and heard her fall over.

The struggle had been silent. Neither girl had grunted or sworn. There had only been a few sharp yelps of pain. Skinner might not even have been there.

Skinner?

Free of Nina, Anne got her head down and charged. She did not connect with Skinner as she had expected, and fell down. She scrambled along on leftover momentum, using her hands and knees more than her feet.

It was dark, and the passage was narrower now. She brushed the walls with both shoulders, and even banged her head when she tried to stand up.

There was something behind her, coming after her, coming to get her. The Nina Thing. And it was not alone. The others, the guests, were there too, in a pack. They were not alive, but they were not dead enough either.

She considered lying down on the floor, covered with fallen dresses, and waited for their touch on her neck. But she could not make herself give up. She kept on.

She kept on until she ran into a wall of loose boards. They fell apart, wood splintering, nails wrenching, and she burst out of the side of a building.

She stumbled and fell, her palms striking wet, dirty concrete. She felt cold night air on her face.

Entr'acte

<u>one</u>

I N HIS DREAM, Cameron Nielson Jr saw life as a motion picture, unspooling steadily in the white-hot gaze of the bulb, the past piling up like celluloid string on the projection booth floor. CAMERON NIELSON in *The Cameron Nielson Story*. A Cameron Nielson Film. From the Cradle to the Grave with CAMERON NIELSON. 'It'll run and run,' Cameron Nielson.

His early years had been mainly montage. The young composer practises his scales while waiting for a big break. The young composer at odds with his family, who want him to follow a less daring course. The young composer working late into the night, notes flowing from his stylo. Women, leaving. Landlords knocking on doors, demanding money. Dishes piling up in a sink. Fingers in close-up, struggling with a recalcitrant piano. Electrical equipment accumulating around the traditional musical instrument. The reflection of a soldering iron in protective goggles as the musical weapons are forged.

Variety headlines spin out of the papier maché mist and chart the rise of a career. Fatherly, distinguished men scoffing at the hero's genius in smoke-filled clubs, plotting his come-uppance, but ultimately being swept away by the rollercoaster force of his obsessive talent. Early successes are built upon, as different audiences are superimposed, each clapping a little louder than the last, a crescendo rising. The young composer called out of his electronic cocoon after a performance and taking his bows with the other musicians, a rare grin on his sweating face. A devoted woman, her face a blur, clapping from the wings.

And throughout it all the music, first heard as an eerie sketch inside the hero's head, skeletally indistinct and bone china fragile. Then, as the young composer experiments at his consoles and keyboards, taking on some meat, becoming stronger, deeper. Finally, in a triumphant climax, bursting forth strong and unforgettable, exploding from his mind into reality, in THX sound, blasting at the acoustics of every concert hall in the world.

Then, amid the frenzy of music and applause, a clinch with the devoted woman and a fade to a painless old age. The composer, with talcum powder-white hair and a young face, dying content in his bed, surrounded by adoring and grieving children, his music living on. Under the end title, a pan across a series of busts in some Elysian hall of music. Palestrina. Bach. Beethoven. Mozart. Brahms. Wagner. Mahler. Stravinsky. Schoenberg. Stockhausen. CAMERON NIELSON. *The End*, in curlicue letters. A CAMERON NIELSON PRODUCTION.

'Cam?'

'Uh?' He jumped a little as Alexia slipped the *boutonnière* into the lapel of his tailcoat.

'You were dreaming,' she said.

He concentrated. He was calm. Before a concert, some people went to pieces, chain-smoking, hands trembling, shaking whisky out of the bottle. Cameron Nielson Jr became the still centre of a hurricane, as collected and single-minded as a great neurosurgeon before an operation.

'I'm sorry. I have to carry the whole piece in my head.'

Alexia smiled. His *boutonnière* matched her corsage. She had been his personal assistant throughout the preparation for the performance of the *Telemachus Symphony*, and they had slept together, three times. He was beginning to find the sex interesting, and had already started to wonder whether he should try to make her position permanent. The English girl was efficient and brought him just the right touch of warmth. He knew that he could be an ice-cube at times – God knows, Beethoven, Mozart and Wagner had not been easy to live with either – and Alexia took the chill off him.

She patted his lapel, straightening the flower, and kissed him like a little girl.

She was very English. His father had married an English girl, after divorcing Cameron's mother. The Nielsons were all drawn to this country. Perhaps it was a genetic thing. In all likelihood, Anne would settle for an Englishman. And Judi . . .

He drove his family out of his head, and let the music flood back. As a boy, he had been certain that he was adopted, or that his mother had taken a lover. Once, well after her marriage to his father was over, he had even asked her, but she just laughed at him. He remembered the red-cheeked embarrassment, and his subsequent determination never to let it show again. For a while, he had even resisted his name, scratching out the Jr on any documents with his full name on them, and signing himself C. Eugene Nielson. Now, that seemed cowardly. He simply had to stake his claim and fight for it, making sure by his works that everybody knew who Cameron Nielson *really* was. The brilliant young composer, not the burned-out playwright.

'Not long now.'

'No.'

'Nervous?'

Alexia did not know him well, he realised. 'Of course not. It's too late for that.'

Performing this piece was as complicated as launching a space shuttle, involving synchronised computer systems, traditional orchestral instruments, African drums and as many technicians as trained musicians. Cameron was not merely the composer and conductor, but a theremin soloist and the director of operations. There were human elements involved, and that would give the piece an immediacy, but so much of it was pre-programmed, with tapes played and sounds conjured by infallible computers, that most of the work was already done. The performance itself was important, but it was almost of academic interest. *Telemachus* was already a thoroughly achieved work. Presenting it to the public was like unveiling a finished sculpture.

'Then why are you whistling?'

He realised he had been, and clamped his lips. It was a habit he had had as a child. A bad habit. His nanny had scolded him over and over, but he had never been able to stop. She conjured up a bogeyman, Mr Whistle, who pulled out the voices of little boys who whistled, leaving them only with their whistles. That had been before Dr Spock. He had been terrified, but still unable to stop. He had dreamed about Mr Whistle, picturing him as a child-sized man in a Little Lord Fauntleroy outfit, with floppy velvet bows and knickerbockers, his head a white eggshape, featureless but for a shark's gash of a mouth. He knew that he still whistled sometimes, but the bogeyman could not scare him any more.

'It's an old thing with me, Alexia, I'm sorry.'

'Don't be,' she said, smiling. 'I think it's cute.'

'Cute? That's not an English expression.'

The girl stepped back, away from him. 'Obviously I'm being polluted by an American.'

There were good luck cards on the dressing room table, from tutors, colleagues, a few friends. There was nothing from Dad, of course, nor Anne. He could not expect their interest. But there was a note, heart-stoppingly cheerful in its brevity, from Judi. It must have been mailed a few days ago, with a second class stamp. It had stopped him dead, for a moment.

'Here's another one,' Alexia said, producing a square envelope, 'delivered by hand. Sorry it's a bit bent.'

He slit it open with his finger, and glanced at it.

'Best wishes for your career,' it read, 'from . . .' Mr Scribble?

'Mr . . . I can't make this out, Lex. What do you think?'

'Begins with a W,' she laughed. 'Looks like Whistle.'

Before he could stop himself, a piercing howl was forced through his teeth.

'Sounds like Whistle too.'

He suffered a flashback, an out-of-place reel from an old dark house horror movie, or maybe a nightmare being offered for psychoanalysis to Ingrid Bergman. The young composer wanders through a haunted mansion, trying to exorcise the spirits of his tyrannical father and castrating sisters. Molten watches tumble out of wardrobes, cellos sprout spider-legs and scuttle musically in the shadows, faceless conductors lash out with scorpion-tailed batons. All very symbolic, with theremins on the soundtrack. And also in the house is the Monster, Mr Whistle, obscene drool leaking onto his embroidered vest.

He dispelled the images, and hugged the girl, almost desperately.

'That was a surprise,' she said. 'I knew you weren't the composing machine they say you are.'

They? Who were they? Who had been talking?

'I'm sorry,' he said, embarrassed.

'It's all right. This is a big night. You have a right to be nervous. What with your father, and your sister. No one could blame you.'

Was she already making excuses? Did she know something about the performance he did not?

He let her go, and walked to the mirror. As always he wore the traditional evening clothes. He liked the reference to the classical tradition. His white tie was perfectly tied, his shirt-front stiff with starch and studded properly.

Alexia whistled this time, off-key. A wolf whistle. Cameron forced a smile.

The digital clock was counting down towards the performance. On the closed-circuit monitors, he saw the technicians taking their places at the instrument banks. The stage was dominated by a cracked mask with blank, blind eyes. Telemachus, himself. Cameron thought the face looked like his father. The instrument monitors were reading normal as the equipment started up. Alexia brought him his headset, which he slipped on like a minimalist space helmet. He was becoming part of the machinery of the piece. He checked his watch against the clock, and mentally ticked off the functions as they were performed.

7:31.

'It's nearly time,' Alexia said, needlessly.

The orchestral musicians were filing out, also formally dressed. Minerva Beaton, the cellist, had resisted *Telemachus* at first, refusing to become part of the machinery of the piece, but those arguments, hateful to Cameron's memory, were over now. She had had to be converted, but now she was a true believer. She would serve the symphony.

'Who's that?'

Alexia pointed to a shape moving on one of the monitors, just behind Minerva. It was shadowed, and small.

'There shouldn't be any children backstage.'

There was a gleam in the dark, as if reflected off a large eggshell. Then the shape was gone.

'There's no one there,' Cameron said quietly. 'No one at all.'

'No,' she said. 'There was . . .'

'It was just a glitch,' he said, too forcefully. Alexia held his glance for a few moments, a furrow between her eyebrows, and dropped the subject.

7:33.

Light was flooding the monitors as the curtains rose. There was polite applause as the mask came into view, and the performers settled.

'Ready?'

He nodded, and left the room, Alexia a few steps behind. The door was held open for him, and he threaded his way through all the backstage equipment. Alexia took her canvas chair in the wings, her bug in her ear so she could relay if necessary his almost subaudial commands to the technical people.

7:34.

Cameron Nielson Jr stepped out on the stage just as the initial applause was dying, and climbed the dais with leisurely ease, settling down behind the theremin stand. He nodded to each of the performers. There was a flicker of applause for his appearance, but it faded away on schedule, leaving him three seconds of silence by the clock on the theremin before the first tonalities sounded out.

Then at precisely 7:35, the nightmare began.

two

IN HIS NIGHTMARE, the device with the beeping alarms misfired because, by 7:59, the audience was laughing too loud for their watches to be heard. The tittering started during the first five minutes of the piece, and grew.

The music was his, and emerged as written from the apparatus he had designed for it, but it was changed. The effects he had carefully measured were misjudged, comical, obscene, absurd. Minerva Beaton could hardly keep her long face straight as she sawed her cello. The eerie, longing notes of his Telemachus theme sounded like whoopee cushions.

Beyond the lights, Cameron got the impression of audience members thronging the exits, trying to get out of the concert hall. He tried to keep going, his hands wringing sounds from the theremin. Painful feedback boomed from the amplifiers, and he realised he was whistling again, the sound dreadfully enlarged by his headset and hurled out into the auditorium.

Telemachus looked down blindly on his humiliation. And the childsized intruder shifted in the shadows around the stage, mocking him from the darkness.

He started coughing, and blood spatted across the note-dotted creaminess of his score.

Somehow, he made it through to the end.

There was no crescendo of applause, just a lone volley of claps. Alexia was trying to make him feel better.

He wrenched off his headset and fled the spotlit stage, pushing past the girl, hiding his red face in the dark.

When the last resonances of the symphony had died, all that was left was an electronic whine. It sounded like an idiot child whistling. Somebody turned it off.

The film sped up as Cameron ran out of the building, still in his tailcoat, and tried to lose himself in the streets around the Barbican. His shiny shoes pounded the sidewalks, and neon signs flashed the names of increasingly seedy nightclubs at him. It started raining in sparkling sheets, the technicians pouring water down from above his eyeline onto him. Rich, orchestral music, a kitschy concerto in the style of Erich Wolfgang Korngold, thundered on the soundtrack, vibrating his teeth.

Mr Whistle was still dogging him, not pursuing but just keeping up. The bogeyman did not need to do anything more to him. His fate was complete. In the space of a few cuts, he had a thick growth of stubble, his shirtfront was soiled with liquor, his hair was wild and his tails were tattered. He had a bottle of cheap booze in his hand, and was swigging from it.

He was in a flophouse, his coatsleeve wrinkled up above his left elbow and his shirtsleeve ripped away. The vein pulsed in his arm as the makeshift tourniquet drew tighter. Judi, her face white with Gothic make-up, handed him the glowing syringe. As the needle slid into him, he whistled sharply, hurting his ears. Rain washed Judi's face away.

Then, the sun came up and the nightmare shifted gears. He was in a gutter, cold clean water running around him, washing the grime and sleep from his face. A figure loomed over him, haloed by the sunlight, and picked him up, her arms slipping tight around his chest. Her blonde hair shone gold.

'Lex?'

She did not try to soothe him, but she took him away from Skid Row, pulling him into a kingsize bed with freshly-laundered sheets. He was naked and clean again, his pains salved. The music came back. Things were not as bad as they seemed . . .

In the long run, they were much worse.

The night before the wedding, Cameron Nielson Jr burned his manuscripts, one by one. Alexia stood by and watched him do it. Acting as his agent, she had got him a commission to score a 15-minute TV documentary about autumn leaves.

He thought he could do it. A sub-Elgar theme was whistling in his mind. In the burning pages, he imagined his electro-acoustic instruments sparking and self-destructing like a spaceship set at the end of a low-budget science fiction film. He reached for a more conventional musical palette, strings and woodwinds.

They were married in church, in the West Country village where Alexia had grown up. Her parents were delighted. Anne was there, representing his family, and his Dad, his spirits lifted by his recent turn for the better, sent a cable of congratulations to the groom and a mash note to the bride. Turning from the altar, Cameron could not see Mr Whistle among the congregation, but did think he glimpsed Judi, loitering embarrassed near the back.

After the ceremony, Alexia kissed him and loved him. He was enfolded by warm feelings. There was gentle applause, and flashbulbs popped. The orchestra played only harmonic music. Everything was easy.

After the honeymoon, Alexia was pregnant and he was progressing well on the film score. His work proved acceptable, and further commissions resulted. No one knew his name, but people hummed his tunes. He wrote the theme music for a British television serial adapted from a Barbara Cartland novel. He wrote a 30-second piece for a shampoo commercial that enabled him to buy a house in the country. With his wife and Cameron Nielson III, he had a comfortable life, cocooned by money and anonymity. He never thought of performing again, or of serious music. If there was something lacking in his life, he did not know what it was.

Meanwhile, thanks to a series of startling medical break-throughs, his father was recovering from his debilitating strokes. He almost literally returned from the dead, and his personal memoir, *Facing Death*, was the strongest thing he had written since the '50s. A 75-page essay, it climbed the *New York Times* bestseller list and was *the* talking-point book of the year. Following that, there was a revival of interest in Cameron Nielson Sr, and most of his theatrical works were staged in New York and London. *The Rat Jacket* broke box office records on Broadway with Dustin Hoffman and Al Pacino, *The Crunch* was directed by Peter Hall on Shaftesbury Avenue, and *On the Graveyard Shift at Sam's Bar-B-Q and Grill* was remade by Steven Spielberg with Marlon Brando as Sam, Robert DeNiro in Brando's old role and Meryl Streep as Angela. Cameron's father began writing plays again, and managements competed for the rights to stage each new mature masterpiece. He was pleased for his Dad, and things were better between them. When Martin Scorsese filmed *The Rat Jacket*, Cameron Nielson Sr tried to get his son the job of writing the score, but the deal fell through. Cameron did not mind about that, even when Harvey Broadribb, who had been at Juillard with him, won the Academy Award for his work on the movie.

Anne sent him a signed copy of her first book, *Remembering Judi*. A non-fiction account of their sister's last years, *Remembering Judi* won the Pulitzer Prize and was a hardback bestseller. It was turned into the highest-rated Made-for-TV movie ever produced, catapulting Nina Kenyon, the young unknown cast in the lead, to multiple awards and international stardom. After that, Anne became a novelist, won the Booker and the Whitbread in the same year with different books, and was given her own television show. He wrote the opening and closing signature tunes for the program, but they were dumped after the first season and replaced with 'something a little more distinctive'. He wrote more shampoo, hairspray, deodorant and sliced bread commercials.

On a visit to England, Cameron's Dad met Minerva Beaton at a dinner party arranged by Alexia and wound up marrying the cellist. She reminded him of someone he had known as a young man. At the age of forty, Cameron was presented with a baby brother, Todd Nielson, upon whom everybody doted. When his own son was old enough to go to school, Alexia took up painting, working her way away from representational landscapes into suggestive abstracts based on the British countryside. Her work was too unconventional for immediate popular acceptance, but Cameron could tell how good she was, and was supportive even when she was discouraged. Anne and Dad both bought her paintings and displayed them prominently, and Cameron used his fee from a sanitary napkin commercial to finance an exhibition in London. Alexia was critically acclaimed, and several major galleries purchased her, but she did not become immediately collectible. She joked that she would only make money fifty years after she was dead, and he told her that money did not matter.

Cameron went to a lot of receptions, private views, book launches, first night parties, movie premières and testimonials. His father, sister, wife and stepmother – Minerva became a much-in-demand soloist and had a big-selling jazz-classical crossover album – were always being honoured, and he always tried to turn out to support them. He got used to people asking him 'and what do *you* do?' He needed less and less to work, his commercial and film scores earning him a steady residual income. He did not miss his music, and could barely remember his performing days. Alexia and Cameron III gently chided him for his whistling habit, and he developed an aversion to his own work. Even when Alexia, who remained a young woman even as her hair silvered, tried to point out the strengths of his pieces he mentally tuned out. He had spent his life designing inoffensive wallpaper, he realised, and he was not really ashamed of that.

Cameron III asked for a guitar for his 13th birthday. Cameron wanted to give him a computer, but Alexia prevailed and soon the house was full of twangs and scales again. His son was obsessive about music, mastering classical, folk and rock modes with alarming rapidity. At sixteen, he put together his first group and, with a cash present from his grandfather, put out a record of his own songs. It got a lot of airplay from John Peel, and was written up extensively by the music press. A major company signed him up, and he had a series of top ten hits while building a serious reputation. Elvis Costello called him a genius, and Jonathan Demme made an in-concert film of his appearance at the Hollywood Bowl. Cameron III was embarrassed by the *Smash Hits* following and tried not to be a teen idol, whereupon he was celebrated all the more. Cameron knew how good his son really was, and encouraged him to break free of the pop straitjacket. Cameron III recorded duets with Stevie Wonder, David Byrne, Frank Sinatra and Kiri Te Kanawa. Then, he wrote a West End musical based on his aunt's *Remembering Judi* and it transferred to Broadway, with Nina Kenyon making an impressive singing debut in her original role, finally outgrossing everything written by Andrew Lloyd Webber. On *The Tonight Show*, Johnny Carson did a whole monologue on the theme of, 'yes, but who is Cameron Nielson *the Second*?'

Todd Nielson became a medical researcher, and finally did something about the ageing process. Their father was one of the first beneficiaries, and the whole family was able to gather at his 100th birthday party. Cameron talked with Minerva, who was being magnanimously tolerant of her husband's much-publicised affair with Nina Kenyon, and with Anne, who was well into the tertiary stage of her fourth marriage (to Didier Bishopric, a society restauranteur) and just back from the Betty Ford clinic after a spell of amphetamine dependency. The family had asked him to compose a tune for the party, but he had declined. He did not do that any more. Finally, his son stepped in and wrote a song, 'Not Out', that would become an anthem for the new generation of active centenarians. However, thanks to a nervous disorder, Cameron Nielson III was unable to play at the party and, at the last minute, Cameron agreed to step in. After his son's band, joined for the occasion by Minerva, played 'Not Out', with Nina handling the vocal, Cameron sat at the piano. Everybody sang 'Happy Birthday to You', drowning him out. It was a great occasion.

Cameron III's condition got worse, and his uncle Todd recommended specialists. Alexia was tormented, and poured her feelings out on canvas, producing some of her best work. Cameron spent a lot of time sitting at his piano with the lid down, his fingers resting on the wood, whistling unconsciously. The specialists tried increasingly radical treatments, but his son did not recover. In the nursing home,

Cameron III wrote an album's worth of his very best material, railing against the darkness that was crowding in on him. At the funeral, Cameron's stepmother played the cello while he stood with his arm around Alexia, feeling drained and empty.

Anne overdosed alone in her penthouse, describing herself in her last note as 'just another dead junkie.' Their father wrote a tragic play about his daughters, and Nina, grown old enough, played 'Amy', the character based on Anne. There were characters equivalent to Victoria Page, Judi and Todd, but no one in *An American Family* resembled Cameron. There were new arts by now, shared dreams that could be shaped by the skilled. Susan, Anne's daughter by Didier, became one of the first geniuses of the form, moulding her night fantasies into unforgettably affecting tapestries of emotion and narrative.

The Museum of Modern Art in New York held a major retrospective of Alexia Nielson's paintings, but his wife did not live to see it. She succumbed to an unexpected cerebral haemorrhage at the easel two weeks before the opening. Her last, unfinished work was uncharacteristic: a portrait of her husband, prepared as a birthday surprise. He insisted it be exhibited, although it lacked a face. Several journalists who covered the event assumed that Alexia was Cameron Nielson's daughter and that he, despite his name, had married into the family.

Hugh Farnham was discovered in a retirement home in Florida, living under an assumed identity, obsessively chewing on his rusks. He agreed to a televised debate, hosted by Dan Rather, with Cameron Nielson Sr. Farnham was still feisty on the show, but Cameron Nielson, looking younger now than his son, was as skilled as a great matador, and finally evened the score with his former tormentor, driving him to tearful contrition. Waving a fist at the camera, Cameron Nielson recited the names of those blacklist casualties he had avenged at last. At the reception after the show, Todd, learning for the first time of the ancient history of his family, spat in Hugh Farnham's face. The old inquisitor slunk into the night, spittle still dripping from his cheek.

Cameron, needing nothing, sat around the house, surrounded by other peoples' books and music and art. A journalist interviewed him for a book about his family, and when *The Nielsons* appeared, it made no mention at all of his professional life. He did not mind.

He whistled, tunelessly. Alone, with no worries, he whistled. The whistling became louder, more piercing, more painful.

Sitting at his piano, he howled. He looked down and saw he had battered his fingers bloody against the wooden lid.

He was coughing.

The whistling sounded like feedback, and his hammering on the piano became a dying round of applause. He was in the light, but there was darkness all around.

One of the perils of dreaming too much was that you got flashbacks afterwards. He tried to clear the phantoms from his head and grasp reality.

He looked up and saw Minerva at her cello, and Alexia, young and alive again, in the wings.

He was not sitting at a piano. It was a theremin.

The whistling stopped, and the music began.

three

H IS HANDS hovered above the instrument, refusing to
move, but the opening notes of the symphony came from
the theremin.

Nobody noticed that he was not contributing. Tapes cut
in and overlaid the unearthly siren-call of the electro-acoustic
instrument, and Minerva's cello answered the melodic ton-
ality with a delicately offhand echo.

Cameron was sweating. His hands were stuck in space, a
foot away from the theremin. He felt as if he were pressing
against a strong, polarised magnetic force.

But the theremin played its part by itself, as if it were
programmed to.

The *Telemachus Symphony* swelled. The audience were
hypnotised by the piece, each member, even those cynical
about 'so-called "modern" music', knew they were present
at a historic event. This was a première that would be
remembered forever.

It was for Judi, Cameron decided. He must make that clear
to the press. And for Dad.

Now, perhaps, they would understand.

His wrists began to ache, and his nails were empurpled with
blood.

Anne. He must tell Anne.

He was not a total ice-cube. This music proved that.

The symphony continued, greater than anything he had
ever done. It was greater than him. He was not needed any
more.

His hands were released, and he dropped them to his lap.
The theremin was playing itself with passion, with feeling.

For the first time, he understood his own work. His face was wet with tears.

Minerva's solo came and went. The trick with the watches was more than a technical stunt, it actually worked in the context of the piece, sucking the audience even further into the spell.

Quietly, humbly, Cameron took off his headset and set it down on the floor. He slipped off his stool and backed away from the theremin stand. No one noticed. The music had them all.

He turned. A single globular tear crept from the white blank of Telemachus' eye and ran down the giant mask.

Alexia was sobbing gently in the wings, stifling herself into silence. The music went on, and on.

Cameron left the stage, unremarked, and stepped into a carpeted, brightly-lit corridor. He could still hear his music, as if it were very far away.

He needed a cigarette.

He felt light-headed, as if he had been awake for days on end.

Looking for a concession stand, he turned a corner. The bogeyman was waiting for him.

It was a long time since he had seen Mr Whistle. They had both grown up. Mr Whistle's clothes had grown in size with him. He was a tall, broad man now, but he still wore knickerbockers and velvet. His face was different, almost human, but he still had a shark's mouth.

'Hello, Cam,' he whistled. 'Long time, no see . . .'

Cameron felt small again. The music was fading. Mr Whistle seemed to be growing to giant size, his huge head scraping the ceiling. He was forced to bend at the waist, looming over him.

'You have such an interesting family,' he said. 'So varied, so talented . . .'

Cameron remembered his dream, remembered the thickly-populated nightmare life he had led, trailing off into a bland and dusty future.

Mr Whistle smiled, teeth cutting his lips. He wiped his

mouth with the back of his hand and tore away a ragged stretch of skin.

'Just think of me as the Ghost of Cameron Yet to Come . . .'

Could he hear laughter from the auditorium? He was clutched by dread.

Was it all coming true?

'We stand at a crossroads, Cam,' Mr Whistle said. 'You, and your entire family. You know how I served your father, and let him live. You know how I loved your sister, and made her die. They each had a choice. As do you . . .'

He was held fast again, his whole body wrapped in an invisible field.

'And Anne?' he asked.

'Her too. I'm dealing with her even as we speak. As a ghost, I'm not really here. I could tear you in two, but I'm not really here. It's one of my many talents.'

Cameron did not doubt his old bogeyman. He remembered Mr Whistle's ways.

'You're whistling, little boy,' the Monster told him.

He was. He could not stop himself.

His half-heard symphony was a background for his tuneless whistle.

'You know what I do to little boys who whistle?'

Cameron was a child again, the hell of life before him. Growing up, exams, acne, practice, arguments, girls, alienation, scales. He could not go through it all again.

'I take their voices!'

The whistle died in Cameron's throat.

'That's better. You won't need to speak. This is a yes or no question. You can nod or shake your head.'

Cameron realised that Mr Whistle looked a little like Hugh Farnham. He was a bogeyman for all the family.

'Consider yourself lucky. I've given you all a choice, but you're the only one who is getting it straight, all cards on the table. There are no subtle, metaphorical struggles here. This is a simple deal.'

Cameron tried to hear his symphony, strained his ears for it. The music was there, but very faint.

'You've seen a possible future, stretching out from this evening. I can't guarantee it will be exactly like that, but you must have got the picture. You can expect a long and happy life if you give up serious music. Simple, isn't it? Which would you rather died, you or your music? You know how your father chose. He has had the benefit of a fine son and beautiful daughters, but there have been no more great plays.'

The music was growing louder. It was inside his head, but throughout the building too. He tried to get a fix on it. It was strong and clean. It expressed the feelings he had never allowed himself. He could not let it go.

'So, let's get this clear. Nod your head if you want to live, without music . . .'

Cameron held still.

'Live? Die? Music? Happiness? It doesn't mean much to me. I get mine either way.'

Mr Whistle rested a large hand on Cameron's shirtfront. He flexed his fingers. Cameron felt an electrical tingle.

He had decided. Not until now had he really known how much it all meant to him. He was older now than Mozart had been when he died. He still had a lot more to write but, considering that he was bowing out with *Telemachus*, he thought that he would not leave a negligible *oeuvre* behind him.

'Well, Mr Ice-cube . . .? What can I do?'

Cameron's throat started working. It was agony, but he got the words out.

'You . . .'

Mr Whistle knew what his decision had been. Static crackled between his fingers, and Cameron felt the bolts charging into his heart.

'. . . can . . .'

The killing force came. It exploded inside him just as the last notes of his symphony died away. As he fell, a smoking black handprint on his chest, he heard the standing ovation building. They were calling for him, whistling shrilly, stamping their feet.

He smiled as the life went out in him, looking up at the already transparent Monster.

'. . . you can *whistle!*'

Night

one

'BA-BA-BOMP-BA-BA,'
Anne tried to stand up. It was not easy. She nearly lost a shoe pulling her foot out of the hole behind her.

'BA-ba-bomp-ba-ba,'

It was dark in front, but there were indistinct swirls of painfully bright colours to the left and right. Stained glass and neon, Technicolor and Dayglo, fireworks and foil-embossed paperback covers.

'BA-ba-bomp-ba-ba,'

The scat-singing was loud, but it was fighting several other pieces of music in an arrangement that was less contrapuntal than cacophonous. It was merely the nearest and loudest of five or six clashing noises. The scum skimmed off the top of an ocean of din.

'Ba-ding-a-dang-ding,'

This was not St John's Wood.

'Ba-ding-a-dong-ding,'

This was somewhere in the centre of town. The West End. Soho. It did not make sense.

'Blue *MOOOOONNN!*'

Her eyes hurt. She covered them, blinking purposefully.

'Dib-da-dib-da-dib-dib,'

It was dark inside her head.

'. . . moon, moon, moon . . . blue moon . . .'

Each 'moon' from the backing vocalists was a needle pushed through the bridge of her nose, probing for the forepart of her brain. It did not hurt as much as it should have.

She took her hands away from her eyes, and looked again.

The world got clearer, as if someone were twiddling the focus of her retinae. Her eyes tuned in, but her mind could not match them.

She leaned against a rough, damp wall, feeling an icy draft on her ankles. It was very cold, and she was very tired. She felt hung over, and a million miles from the bed she wanted to be asleep in.

How the hell had she got here?

And where was here?

She was in a narrow passage that crookedly connected two busy streets. It was irregularly paved, and lit only by an open window a few storeys above. There were no doors in the walls, but she could tell from the noise that the building she thought she had come out of was a pub. The boards she had broken through were an entrance to the cellar. She tried to superimpose this place on Amelia Dorf's house, but could not make the images jibe.

There was nothing coming after her any more. She thought that the cellar was empty. It was dark down below, but she could make out the shapes of beer kegs. No monsters, no people. They had given up.

But it had all been real. She could still feel the points in her throat where the Nina Thing's fingers had fastened. She must have plenty of other scrapes and bruises.

She got out of the passage, and found herself somewhere she recognised. She was back in Brewer Street. There were crowds of people about. Ordinary, real, non-monstrous people. The pubs had not let out yet, so it must be not be later than eleven. She had thought it must be well into the small hours. The streets were not exactly reassuring, but they were safer than the old dark house, or the wardrobe of death.

Next to the pub was a loud strip club. Bare coloured bulbs flashed on and off around a come-on sign. 'Beautiful Girls XXXXXXX Totally Naked.' There were black and white posters under glass, just a shade more indecent than allowed by the law. So much for the Clean-Up Soho Campaign. The silver paper stars pasted over nipples had peeled and slipped to the bottom of the case, leaving the pouting, overdeveloped girls with gluey smudges on their breasts.

'Come in and slobber over our fat ugly bimbos,' bawled a fat ugly young man in jeans and a windbreaker, standing in the middle of a yellow-lit foyer. His breath was steaming in clouds, and he stamped his feet in a crooked little tap-dance step to keep his doubtless numb toes warm. 'Get your rocks off as they get their clothes off. Sex, sex, sex. Get your lovely, steaming, thirst-quenching, piping hot, country-fresh sex here! You can't get things like this in Russia, you know. It's a free country here. Sex, sex, sex. God save the Queen, and all who sail in her . . .'

The bored black woman in the club's ticket booth looked up from her knitting magazine and laughed. Nobody was being lured in. The spieler noticed Anne.

'Fuck off back to your own turf, lovey,' he shouted, 'you're putting the shits up the punters. You've got a look on you like Dracula's bleeding daughter!'

He raised his hands, crossing his fingers to make a crucifix.

'Back! Back, I thay!' he adopted a Karloffian lisp. 'Begone hellthpawn!'

Anne retreated, and was jostled along the pavement by a group of colourfully-dressed Chinese kids with '70s punk haircuts. They chattered and laughed, being rude about Western passersby who could not understand their language. Anne knew she was being discussed, anatomised as a freak.

She wondered just how awful she did look. She did not feel all right inside. She realised that she had not eaten properly in twenty-four hours. Just half a breakfast and a sandwich in the Nellie Dean ages ago.

The Chinese kids piled into a pub, pushing and kicking each other. A gust of beery hot air hit her. She wanted to be sick. A young man in a smartly hideous jacket tried to come out while the kids were trying to go in. He was buffeted from side to side, and swore in what Anne thought was an Australian accent. He pushed her, and headed off on a determined course for somewhere.

She tripped, and tottered at the edge of the kerb. She

stepped into the gutter and got her balance. A McDonald's carton crumpled lousily under her shoe, and her heel squelched into a half-eaten Egg McMuffin.

The music mix was more offensive out in the open. Anne could pick out random snatches of disco, Derek Douane, reggae, acid house, rhythm and blues, funk, Kylie Minogue and '60s oldies. The result was a sweaty medley, harsh and brittle on the surface, but cheesy and rotten underneath.

Every shop in sight was open, selling sex. She walked towards Wardour Street. That would be quieter, calmer. She could get her bearings. There were a few clubs at the lower end of the street, but it was mostly owned by monolithic movie companies. She went past displays of posters and stills for upcoming films, gradually calming herself. Heroes posed with guns: Sylvester Stallone, Kurt Russell, Rutger Hauer, Clint Eastwood. If she could get to Tottenham Court Road tube station, she could get home almost on automatic pilot.

First, she needed to make herself human again. She crossed the road, dodging a limousine with a personalised number-plate, and squeezed into a long, thin pub called The Ship. It was full of leather and PVC-clothed young people, banging their heads in time to the music. This was one of the overspill places for The Marquee, just down the road. Daeve Pope would have been in heavy metal heaven.

A battered man in a woollen hat, one eye almost closed by a bruise, was appealing to the drinkers.

'Are there any East End boys here?'

He was ignored. Anne tried to get past.

'Come on now. East End boys. I need some help. One of our own's been done over. Gimme some help. Come on.'

Some of the patrons were getting annoyed. The would-be lynch mob leader grabbed an arm and was shaken off.

'Where's the old East End? I need some fucking help.'

'Listen,' said a cockatoo-plumed girl, 'we wouldn't fight for our country. I don't see why we should go to war for our fucking post code.'

'Bitch. One of our own is bleeding . . . .'

Anne got out of the mini-drama and went upstairs to the Ladies. It was empty and relatively clean. She locked herself into a cubicle and took a leak. It was good just to sit down, and she was tempted to rest her head against the partition and get some sleep. It would be so easy just to give up for a while.

She pulled herself back together again, and hauled herself out of the cubicle to make full use of the facilities. A girl with a superheroine costume was holding her face up to the mirror, tracing a cobweb pattern on her pale cheeks. Anne looked at her own face. It was pretty ghastly. She washed. The dirt and the make-up came off easily, and there were no obvious bruises underneath. Even her neck, which still hurt, was unmarked. She had lost her handbag somewhere, but her wallet was still in her inside jacket pocket, and she had some make-up things in her coat. The coat, mercifully, was large enough to cover the clothes she had borrowed from Nina. She lipsticked in her usual modest mouth and combed her hair. Her reflection looked like her again. She even practised smiling.

Walking to the station, past the brightly-lit boutiques, cinemas, remainder bookshops and tatty souvenir stalls, all decorated for Christmas and building up to the January sales, she found herself having to think about what had happened to her.

Drugs. It was something to do with drugs. Maybe they had doped her perrier at Amelia's, with LSD or some other hallucinogen. Then, after she had taken her tour of Nightmare City, they had brought her into the middle of town and dumped her.

But it did not feel like drugs. She had done acid once, at college, and it had not been anything like this evening's entertainment. What she had just been through was insane and illogical, but also unambiguous and actual. It felt real.

Not LSD, then. Maybe something a good deal weirder. Something expensive and experimental, like Inspector Hollis' designer dope.

Hollis. She must call him in the morning, give him all the names she had found, and let the police handle any investigation. This evening had proved her incompetence as Philip Marlowe.

A taxicab cruised by with its light on, and she decided to signal it. It would be faster than the underground. But, as she pulled her hand out of her pocket, she remembered. She had given Nina all her cash, and the girl had thrown it at Clive. If she wanted to get home in comfort, she would have to find a cashpoint. The taxi was gone. There was no point in bothering. She turned her back on the street and descended into the underground station.

Underground. The tube. That was how she thought of it. Not as the subway. She was turning British. Writing a piece a few weeks ago, she had had to think very hard before remembering the American expression for council housing.

It was still quite busy. She found her travel pass in her top pocket, and slipped it into the automatic gate, muttering 'open fucking sesame' to the machine. It refused to accept the bent card, and she had to find a barrier run by a human being. The robots were doing a lot of turning people back, and the guard-manned point was thronged with a wedge-shaped queue of complaining travellers. Anne hung back, but got past in a minute or so.

She would take the Northern line to Kentish Town. It was only six stops. Her flat was only a few minutes' walk away from the station. Then, she would sleep.

She was underground. Going down. Please mind the gap.

As she descended the escalator towards the platforms, she noticed the digital clock in the ceiling. In the station, the time was 10:37.

She did not have to wait long for a train.

two

THE MAN opposite her was nodding, muttering to himself, just this side of being asleep. There were dusty stains on the lapels of his suit jacket, and his too-small cloth cap was creeping backwards on his scalp with each roll of his head. He had a bald spot, under a straggle of brown hair, and a ratty Fu Manchu moustache. His arms were wrapped around a full carrier bag on his lap. Anne could see bottle-necks and wrapped sandwiches. A stick of French bread stuck up, resting against his head like the neck of a cello. He did not look well at all.

There was no one else in the carriage; unusual on this part of this line and at this time in the evening. In Central London, this was a peak travel hour. The restaurants and movies and theatres would be starting to turn people out. A lot of service workers would be clocking off. The train should be at least half full. She should still have been able to get a seat, but she should not have a carriage practically to herself. It was unusual, strange; but unusual and strange were not words she was prepared to apply to anything short of a surreal Hell on Earth after her day.

Tomorrow, it would all seem crazy. Next week, she would have talked it through with three or four different people. Hollis, Mark, Nigel and Clare at the office, maybe even Cam. She would prod them, and they would rationalise things, give explanations, make jokes, suggest she calm down. It would all start to seem more like a bad trip, a bad dream. Now, she knew that it had not been a hallucination, it had been real. Soon, she knew she would be thinking in terms of shock, stress, guilt reaction, grief, anxiety, a clouded mind. Eventually, she would convince herself.

But . . .

At the next stop, Goodge Street, a young couple and an old man got on. The girl wore tiny earphones, and had a Sony walkman slung in a holster from her belt. Anne heard the tinny thrash of muted music. A demon drum solo was turned into the nagging p'tum-chk p'tum-chk of a dripping tap. The two kids stayed by the doors, necking. The boy stroked the girl's side, twisting the walkman lead around his fingers in a one-handed cat's cradle.

The old man, shabby and bearded, sat one seat away from her. He stank of paint-stripper. She knew she was about to be hassled.

'Excuse me . . .'

She was too tired. She ignored him.

''scuse *me!*'

She really did not need this. She looked up at the advertisements above the windows. A faded bra ad was dotted with circular orange 'this poster degrades women' stickers. Right on. This city degrades women. The old man touched her sleeve. He had spider-shaped scabs on his knuckles, and several beercan tab-pulls bunched on his ring finger.

'Miss?'

She gave up, and turned to him. He smiled. His beard was grey-white, but discoloured yellow around his mouth as if he had been drooling thin custard. He had ill-fitting false teeth like the Civil War issue dentures Walter Brennan used to wear in Westerns where he was the feisty old-timer.

Walter Brennan never pissed in his pants, though. Walter Brennan never gargled with methylated spirits, or wore the same ragged T-shirts for months on end, or slept in a cardboard cocoon in a condemned house, or bothered young women on the subway.

'Miss?'

'Yes,' she said, non-commitally.

'Miss, do you have . . .'

His voice did not quite work properly. His beard and teeth got in the way. He hawked phlegm, and started again.

'Do you have a sister at home . . . *just like you?*'

She did not understand. 'I'm sorry?'

'A sister.'

She tried to make out an expression on his creased face. There were lines of dirt embedded in his skin. His nose was red. He was a clown, a bum. But there was something almost intelligent in him somewhere, something deliberate and malicious.

She had to get rid of him.

'Fuck off, creep!'

'Sssssssister!'

The train stopped again, Warren Street. There was a pause, the automatic doors unclenched. More people got on. The wino looked away from her. There was quite a crowd.

Please, she thought, let someone sit between me and him, let someone sit next to me.

Someone did, but it was no relief.

The new man was young and huge. He smelled of stale faeces and tomato sauce. He wore an army greatcoat, not big enough to cover his blubbery belly although it was buttoned across his chest. He was a skinhead, and had a line of swastikas tattooed around his neck. His hand was deep in a damp newspaper parcel.

'Want one, darling?' He said, shoving a bundle of vinegary chips up to her face. The stodgy strands were long and thick and twisted, spotted with mobile gobbets of ketchup. Looking at the food was like staring into an abdominal incision.

'No thanks.'

'Go on. You could do with some building up.'

'It's okay, thanks.'

'You'll need all your strength.'

She had heard that the British ate fish and chips out of old newspapers, had seen it in films about the blitz. But that was a long time ago. Now, fish and chips came in plain white paper. But the skinhead's food was wrapped up old-style.

The wino leaned and leered at her from behind the cover of the chip man's mighty stomach. The rails were bumpier than usual this evening. She was being shaken thoroughly. The strap-hangers were swaying unsteadily, as if the metal floor were running in wavelets. The wino chuckled silently. She realised that the strange thing about him was that he was not drunk.

Anne looked away. The carriage was pretty much full now. Almost every seat was taken, and there were plenty of standees. The necking kids had gone. Most of the passengers looked down-and-out, or rowdy, or indefinably depraved.

By the doors, where the couple had been, three teenage boys were scuffling and messing around. One swung from a chromed pole like an ape. They had rosettes and long tartan scarves. One wore an oversize silk jockey's cap with a little teddy bear pinned to it. She thought they were Scots.

Football fans, she supposed. Football hooligans, they called them over here. Dear old staid, conservative, non-violent Britain. Soccer fans were its contribution to the global tradition of random violence. Back home in the States, sports followers were fanatics, exercising an insane competitiveness on the stands, pouring out aggression through their team's performance. But outside the stadium, the hostility evaporated. Over here, 'what team do you support?' was tantamount to a declaration of war. This sceptre'd isle, this happy breed, this bunch of foul-mouthed assholes . . .

One of the kids started winding his scarf around his head, mummifying himself. His mates laughed, and helped him tie the topknot. The teenage monster lurched and bounced a beercan off his head. One of his mates took the dented tube away from him and opened it, splashing froth over a window. The mummy staggered stiff-kneed down the aisle, arms outstretched in a drunken monster impression. He was laughing.

The man opposite woke up suddenly. His cap fell off. The mummy tripped over his legs, and only saved himself from falling by grabbing one of the row of dangling blackjacks above the seats.

'Mind my bloody chips,' shouted the NF paratrooper, hugging his food. The man opposite was holding on tight to his groceries. His bag was ripped, and tins fell out.

The mummy clawed blindly with his free hand, groping for the chip man's voice. He clutched air in front of Anne's face. She tried to recede into her seat, to keep out of it.

'You a fucking bloody Nazi boy, Jummie?' burped the mummy in an unmistakable Glaswegian accent. 'You a pansy for Hitler, Jummie?'

'He bends over for the SS,' said the mummy's cap-wearing friend, making an obscene fist, 'you can tell. He's a glove puppet. It's official.'

The mummy tottered over her. His scarf was loose at the chin. He took the flapping, tasselled end and slowly unwound. Anne looked up to see his face. The scarf came away and fell on the floor, twisted in a multiple S.

His face was dead. He was a noseless, lipless, leather-cheeked horror-comic-from-the-'50s dead person. Eyes like red poached eggs rolled in their hollows. A pink, healthy tongue stuck out between the exposed teeth.

'Hey, you, Jummie,' he said to her. 'Gissa kiss, love.'

Anne knew she was back on the Nightmare Express.

She tried to stand up, but the chip man held her arm, pinning it to the seat rest. He had the face of a potato now, coarsely vegetable with pitted depressions instead of features. Something pressed her right shoulder down. She was completely stuck.

She looked, and found that the shoulder-holder was Jeane Russell from Amelia's party. She had a belted trench coat over her fairy queen outfit. Her face was full and red now, almost bursting. She was evenly speckled with silver glitter.

The zombie hooligan leaned over her.

'Gisssssa kissss!'

The tongue was impossibly extended, pointed and wet and more alive than the rest of the thing. It poked out and wriggled like a slug. He bent to kiss her. She squirmed.

The trained stopped again. Mornington Crescent. The doors opened and closed impersonally.

The hooligan froze, and withdrew. The holds on her arm and shoulder eased.

'Gissa kiss?' It was whining now, pathetic.

'Uh-huh,' she said, 'not on a first date.'

From now on, she had decided, she would fight back. She did not like being a victim. She was going to take back the night. At least, she was going to try.

The station was not Mornington Crescent. As the train pulled out, she saw gleaming white, bare walls slide past the windows. No movie posters, no multi-lingual Telecom ads, no London Transport signs.

More passengers had got on. Her travelling companions had quietened, as if someone in authority had arrived. Anne knew that she was the only live person in the carriage. She recognised a few faces from Amelia's party, but most of the dead people were strangers. One startling apparition a few seats away was masked, and got up like a Chinese mandarin, with clacking claws for hands emerging from generous silk sleeves.

There were plenty of vile smells, and the train was colder than it ought to be.

The wino pulled his clothes apart, exposing old wounds.

'See,' he said, 'stigmata!'

The chip man kept lifting handfuls of soggy potato to his head, but instead of shoving them into a mouth he was plastering them onto the featureless mass, sculpting himself a parrot nose, acromegalic brows and a Kirk Douglas chin.

But it was still a tube train, grubby and battered. Those advertisements were still there, plugging temp agencies, breath fresheners, computer dating, a lurid paperback about anthropophagous slugs, holiday firms . . .

'Okay,' she said, looking about at the others, 'what comes next?'

At the other end of the carriage someone started moving, coming towards her, weaving past the standing dead, eyes fixed on her. It was a girl, in a better state than the others. She could almost pass for human. Almost.

Anne stood up.

'Judi?'

three

ANNE STARTED forwards, to hug her sister. She thought better of it, and held back. She felt awkward. Judi smiled.

'I know what you mean, Annie.'

Judi looked better than she had in the morgue. Actually, she looked better than the last time Anne had seen her alive. She had been on drugs then. Now, she did not need them.

'The only thing I shoot into my veins these days is formaldehyde, Annie,' she said.

Anne stepped backwards, the train rocking under her feet, making her unsteady. Judi had always tended to know what she was thinking, but now she knew her sister really could read her mind.

'You don't know the half of it, Annie,' Judi said. Her ironic smile and quizzically raised eyebrows excluded the rest of the dead people. The sisters had instantly re-established their old understanding and intimacy. 'It's weirder than you think.'

Anne could have laughed, but did not.

'I don't fucking believe it, Ju.'

'You'd fucking better try, because there's a lot more coming your way. I'd hate to spoil it for you.'

'Skinner?'

'Yeah, Skinner. It all comes down to him really, but I guess you knew that already.'

'I suppose so. How . . .'

'. . . did I get into this? Don't ask, Annie, don't ask. It's a shitty story.'

Judi had her young face back again, and it looked good. Her punk/kabuki make-up was professionally applied and striking; her black short hairstyle was stylish and street chic.

She was ready for a dusk-to-dawn party, self-possessed and poised enough to appear in a hairspray commercial.

'I had your bag,' Anne said, but I left it somewhere. At that club, or at Nina's flat. I don't remember.'

'That's okay. I don't need those things any more.'

She was perfectly turned out: patterned black tights, black pointed ballet shoes, snug black mini dress, and an expensive Marlon Brando black leather jacket with the arms hacked off to turn it into a waistcoat. Her arms looked pink and strong. She wasn't feeling the cold.

'It's a shame about Nina,' Judi said. 'She was a good kid. Dumb as hell, but a good kid.'

The waistcoat was slashed with unnecessary zips that glistened like moist scars. The shoulders were padded like a flak jacket, with fringed epaulettes. Useless straps hung undone. Peace signs and Anarchy symbols were picked out in steel studs. Judi's hands were in Kangaroo pouch pockets over her stomach. Her fists pushed the leather out. Anne could make out the ridges of her sister's knuckles.

'Annie, did we have a good childhood?'

Anne looked away exasperated. Only Judi could get to her so quickly, and only this discussion could push her over the edge. It always came up at the very worst of times. They had last gone through the pointless business in the visitors' room of a police station. Now they were practically in the afterlife, and here it all was again . . . .

'On a scale of one to ten, how would you rate our parents? Individually and as a combination? With regards to each other, to us as a combination, to us as individuals, and to society as a whole? Could they have been any worse, do you think?'

'Ju,' Anne realised they were back to their little kid names now, 'Ju, I don't really think it matters any more.'

'Maybe not, but it's interesting. Do you think we would have been better off if Dad had been a small-time failure. As opposed to that special big-time type of failure who looks like a success until the last reel and then turns yellow and runs?'

It was embarrassing, having this talk again, and in public. The dead were listening intently, enjoying the psychodrama. Any moment now, Judi would be turning them into a jury, appealing for their verdict on the Nielsen family. What a ridiculous way to behave.

'Ju, I'm sorry.'

'What for?'

'All of it. Dad, Cam, me, Vicky. I'm sorry. We should've . . .'

'It's too late for should've, Annie. Should've, could've, would've. It was all so complicated, you know. Even before Skinner. We came into it all too late to make any difference. Dad could never write it out, you could never think it out . . . .'

Anne was crying now; not just politely staining her cheeks, but leaking profusely from her eyes and nose. She got a handkerchief from somewhere, and wiped herself, but it did little good.

'You know who we should have had as a father, Annie. I thought it out once. Ibsen. Old Henryk wouldn't have fallen apart in front of Farnham's Witchfinders, Annie. Or screwed up his kids like we were screwed up. Or written that fucking awful *Graveyard Shift* thing.'

Judi was crying too. Little, disciplined tears that ran beautifully over her make-up mask without ruining it. The death-faced hooligan had his arm around her now, comforting her, consoling her. He looked reproachfully at Anne, huge eyes moving in their orbits.

'We should stick with our own kind, Annie. Stick to your own kind.' Judi accepted the hooligan's chaste cheek-touch of a kiss. 'And you can see what my own kind is these days . . . .'

Jeane Russell also cuddled up to Judi, patting a shoulder with a diaphanously gloved hand. The whole carriage was behind Judi. Anne was alone.

'Ju . . .'

Judi gently shrugged free of her attendants, and came towards her. Anne realised that she had backed against the end of the carriage, against the door to the driver's cabin. Judi came to her, smiling with closed lips.

'Annie,' she breathed, 'let's give up and go with it. Get it over with.'

Judi took her hands out of her pockets, and brushed her fingers up and down the front of her waistcoat. She tugged at her zips, opening little pouches in the leather. Some of the zips crept open by themselves, tooth by tooth. Silver-edged lips twisted slightly, and opened. Things were moving inside the waistcoat, pushing outwards, distending the leather, reaching for the air.

The first one came out of a mouth just under the right epaulette. It was a tongue, then it was a crooked finger, then a snake-headed tentacle. The lump at the end was shaped, but featureless. The tentacles were blind and probing. They were not part of Judi, but they came from her. Judi diminished, as her substance flowed into the protuberances. Anne could see the blobs of unformed flesh moving down the tentacles through peristalsis.

'You have to go with it, Annie.'

Judi's face was shrinking again. She was starting to look she had done in death. Old and unidentifiable. The bulbs were swollen now, turning a fleshy red. Trails of yellowish fluid dribbled from the pockets, and ran down the waistcoat. Judi was leaking badly.

'Come on, Annie. Let's make up.'

Judi was feeble now, unsteady. She was not up to coping with the motion of the train. Tentacles from the region of her waist wrapped around poles, and she stayed upright. The new growth looked strong. They had the power of constriction, and Anne guessed they would be sticky to the touch.

A tentacle waved towards her. It was like a bloated anemone frond. The train was slowing down, coming to a station.

Anne grabbed the tentacle, and yanked hard. It was warm and unpleasant in her grip, but it did not slide free. She felt a mild nettle sting. Judi gasped, and bent double. The tentacle came out of her body as easily and unendingly as a roll tape measure. Anne swallowed the gulp of hot bile that came up in the back of her mouth.

Judi was coming apart inside her waistcoat. Anne pushed the thing that had been her sister away. It went into the crowd, deflated and insubstantial, and was caught as they surged forwards.

'Annie!'

The shout died as Judi's emptying clothes fell on the floor. Rivulets of yellow filled the grooves in the floor.

The dead were coming for her. She kicked out in imitation of martial arts movies, putting her hip behind the blow and landing her foot sideways into the hooligan's stomach. It did not give, but bones broke like sticks somewhere inside him. He was in the way of the rest of them.

The train was in a station. The single door beside her slid open, and she pushed herself out of the carriage. She stumbled on the steady stone of the platform, and put a hand out to stop herself slamming into the curved wall. She took the impact on her wrist.

'Mind the gap,' said an automated voice, 'mind the gap.'

The train moved out, its doors still open. She saw hateful faces pressed to the windows. Judi looked lost among so many dead people. Sparks flashed under the wheels. The noise of the train receded and went away.

She had stopped crying.

four

IN THE DARKNESS of the Dream, he floated. His feeding frenzy exhausted, he was torpid, unable to pay attention to the rat in her maze. For the moment, he was the shaper of her world, the worker of her destinies; but he was too tired, too caught up in his own changes, to follow her progress as conscientiously as he should have done.

A swarm of ghosts gyred around him in a multiple helix, allowed some measure of self-determination by his preoccupation, furtively snatching their existence from his body and his mind. The strongest of Amelia Dorf's guests had already been processed and were settling into their new shapes, raw recruits in his army of phantoms. The lesser personalities – Clive, Anders, Amelia – were completely absorbed, gone forever unless he should choose to make the effort to reassemble them. They would do his bidding, more or less, and for the present they would have to cope with Anne.

Of course, she had her own ghosts, as she must almost be ready to realise. She would hardly have been able to get as far as she had already without a very strong image of the outlines of the world, of her own personal dream. She had even been able to effect an imperfect superimposition of her reality upon his own. He had come across very few others not of the Kind, with that strength of vision. He wondered whether it was a hereditary factor, passed down from her father, gained by him through osmosis. After all, he had been one of Ariadne's protegés.

Anne Nielson was an extraordinary woman, as he had known for years. Her father, when he came up before the

Farnham Commission, had proved extraordinarily resilient, but he had still caved in, and then he had proved richly satisfying. More recently, the lesson had been reinforced by delicious, dangerous Judi. Even the son had had a tang to him, although he had proved surprisingly hard to digest at the end. It was a varied and satisfying meal, but the last dish would be the most exquisite, the most sustaining. He would need to fast, to recuperate, to change, before he would be ready to take her.

He had sifted through Judi's memory, had scooped into Anne's mind, but could find no traces of Ariadne. The girls had never met their father's one-time patron, had never even heard of her. Cam had a vague memory of a glamorous 'aunt', who had once taken a remote interest in his father, but it was no more than a shadow. He was disappointed somehow. Perhaps he should seek out Ariadne. By the standards of the Kind, their sole meeting had been almost yesterday. It was probably too soon to see if she had changed in her opinions of him. No, the best he could do was to fortify himself with the Nielson family, and wait a century or two. Everything would change in time. Things changed faster as time progressed, he had noticed in this dizzying century. He would meet Ariadne again. Things would be different between them.

Like an Elizabethan tickling the back of his throat with a peacock feather to induce vomiting so he would be able to face the next enormous course, he brought up another cloud of ghosts. Insignificant, meagre, thin and tasteless presences who could safely be ignored, who could safely be set free. Most of them came apart like butterflies in a whirlwind and were dispersed; some struggled for infinite moments, trying to summon up enough reserves of strength to achieve reality, before they were spent. A few tried vainly to coalesce into a hardier entity. Amelia fluttered against his lips, entreating to be let back in. He blew her away.

He had only sampled Cameron Nielson Sr during the hearings, then let the man live out a diminished, unproductive life. There were no more prizes for Cameron, no more

Pulitzers, Critics Circles, Nobels. And he had never taken home a statuette on Oscar night. He had had the playwright in his power, and been tempted to astonish the court and the television audiences by sucking him dry on the stand. But, rather than feed, he had just taken away Nielson's reputation, his genius, his worldly stature. He had even been rather touched by *The Rat Jacket*, that last flare of Cameron's talent, and had been amused by the author's recreation of his Hugh Farnham persona as the intellectual, bullying cop. Had he known that the man should be allowed to father his children? Or had he been too cautious, too frightened of his increasing visibility?

This was a strange century. He could no longer run his course in one place, and simply leave a continent to start again. The faces, manners and origins of notable men were too highly publicised. He could change his appearance, but not enough to become immediately unrecognisable. From now on, he would have to devote himself to private achievements. That would limit his amusements, but nevertheless he was confident in his ability to find purposes to suit him, enthusiasms to pursue, people to relish . . . It would be a long while before he turned into one of the Elders, hiding away in a living death, nurturing their effete Dreams, too fastidious to get involved with the tumult of humanity.

A wraith approached him, and latched on like a bat, suckling greedily from his surplus, desperate for a shape, for an identity. It was Judi; she had been seriously ruptured. He let her have her fill. She was important to him, a link with Anne, a shared ghost. He touched Judi's conscious memory, curious about the meeting on the train. She put up a token resistance, but, knowing that she only existed on his sufferance, opened her mind to him and let him prowl.

The train scene was fresh and painful inside Judi. His admiration was excited by Anne. She was picking up the knack. It was such a simple thing, to go against the consensus reality, but so few human beings could work up the willpower. Given time, she could learn to shape the Dream to her will. But, of course, he would not give her time. Hers would be an untried talent, an unfulfilled potential. Even in its protean state, however, it would make the business of feeding off her protracted and tiring. But incomparable.

He twisted, and descended in his dream.

He delved deeper in Judi's memories. He considered Anne as a child, as a schoolgirl, as a college student, as a would-be parent substitute, as a journalist. Judi had read practically everything her sister had ever written, including an uncharacteristic series of pieces on tin toy collecting, sofa beds and other arcane subjects published under a pseudonym (Angela Buonfiglia) taken from one of their father's plays. Further back, Judi had envied Anne her college boyfriend, had always tried to impress and amuse the older girl, had briefly tried to copy her clothes and food preferences, had longed to be asked to share her toys so that she could express her devotion through generosity. He tried to dilute Judi's images of her sister with objectivity, with his own observations, with Cam's tightly-guarded feelings, with the pathetic and stupid judgements of Clive, Amelia and a few of Amelia's guests, and with the slight tastes of her he had sampled at the entrance to the maze. He had less than a tenth of the jigsaw puzzle pieces, but even the fragments of a picture he was able to put together made him ache for Anne. He was motivated, he would have to exert himself . . . .

His feet settled on the concrete of the tube platform. He reined in his multitudes, incorporating them. Even Judi. He was alone. He had seldom been more powerful this close to a change.

Anne had gone. There were no egresses in the featureless white tile walls. The tunnel was the only way out. She had chanced the darkness. She was a clever girl, to realise that there would never be another train in this station.

Already, the rails were softening, the circular tube was becoming ovoid. His presence froze the decay, but it would start again when he followed Anne into the tunnel. In time, the station would resolve itself, healing as invisibly as a wound in the deep of his brain. The overhead lights started going out, but that did not matter to him.

He stepped off the edge of the platform, onto the track. He knew which way his rat had bolted. Balancing on the dead third rail, he tightrope-walked after her, into the tunnel.

five

SHE KNEW SHE was not in a tube tunnel any more. The wall she had been feeling her way along in the dark had given out. There were no longer regularly spaced Christmas emergency lights to give an outline of her surroundings. The narrow path she was walking was not bordered by a shiny track. If she stopped to sit and rest, she could feel cold earth and a few scrubby patches of grass either side of the rough strip of asphalt.

Above her, around her, was total darkness. There was no ceiling, there were no walls. The darkness was infinite. She was out in the open somewhere, but there was no trace of light. No stars, no fireflies, no streetlamps, no fires.

There was no wind, but the still air was freezing. She wished she was wearing thick trousers rather than a skirt and tights. Preferably arctic survival gear. Walking through the chilly night was like wading through pampas grass. The cold was as sharp as a straight razor. She could not feel her toes. Her hands were deep in her coat pockets, fingering the last patches of warmth near her body. There was probably ice on her cheeks where she had been crying.

She kept on walking, picking up her feet and putting them down. Going somewhere.

It had not been Judi on the train. At least, it had not been all of Judi. Just as it had not been all of Nina in the wardrobe. Just ghosts.

But no one believes in ghosts really. Not M.R. James/Jacob Marley/white sheet-type ghosts. Ibsen-type ghosts, maybe. Not that she had ever actually read old Henryk, or seen *Ghosts*. Judi had one-upped her in the literacy game again.

Then there was a light ahead. Three indistinct lines, shaped like a soccer goal, silhouetting an oblong. It was some kind of a building, with the light source squarely behind it. She could make out the hard black edges, and see how the light diffused around them.

It was obvious that she would not like what she found there. That much she had picked up from the way things were going. But she was glad to have proof that she had not gone blind in the dark.

The building was further away, and bigger than she had guessed. She could not measure time that well any more, but it took a considerable while to get there.

This side of the building, there was a single, small light. It was above a door, above a weathered sign she could not read.

Knowing she would regret it, but knowing she had no choice, she took the door handle and turned. . .

Something sizzled above her, and hissed. She really was blinded, by the light this time. She turned away, into the darkness, electric blue and orange lines imprinted on her eyes. They faded quickly.

She looked upwards. There was a neon sign, flashing on and off, crackling slightly. It was familiar.

SAM'S, it said in big letters, BAR-B-Q AND GRILL.

She pushed the door open, and went in.

six

WORLDS AWAY, across an ocean, it was late afternoon, time to take hot chocolate to an invalid. Outside, it was just dark, and there was thick, Christmassy snow on the ground. She had put up decorations all over the house, although the invalid could only get to two or three rooms. The tree was in his bedroom, and she had made paper angels for the bathroom. She had put fake snow and a silver star on the mirrored door of the medicine cupboard. She had finally arranged with the agency for a substitute nurse, a single girl who needed the triple overtime, to take her place over the holiday. But she would be back before the New Year, doing her best to make the old man's last months mess-free and painless. Tonight, she would sit up with her patient in his study and watch *It's a Wonderful Life* on television. It was on every Christmas, and was one of her favourite films. She remembered seeing it many times as a child, and was looking forward, after several years, to rediscovering its pleasures. She found it hard to believe that her patient had ever worked in Hollywood, had known people like Jimmy Stewart and Gloria Grahame. There were signed and dedicated photographs of them in his collection, unframed and unsorted after some long-ago house-moving. Also, photographs and letters from names she knew: Lauren Bacall, Tennessee Williams, Alistair Cooke, Arthur Kennedy, Paul Robeson, Jean-Paul Sartre, Cole Porter (another invalid), Lee Strasberg, Adlai Stevenson, Elia Kazan. She wondered whether they all had letters and pictures signed by him. As soon as she entered the study, she knew that he had given up. He was slumped into his chair, his blanket on the floor, a paperback book by his foot, spine-broken, pages down. She tried to find a pulse. Nothing. He was gone.

seven

IT WAS THE original Broadway production, with most of
the cast that had gone on to be in the film. She had walked
on somewhere in the third act, after Sam's stroke. Lee J. Cobb
would be sitting the rest of the play out in his dressing room
while the other characters revolved around the void left in their
lives, in the centre of the play, behind the bar. His passing out
of the drama on the graveyard shift was so complete that Cobb
never even came back to take a curtain call.

Anne slipped into a booth, and sat as far away from the
action as possible. A waitress brought her a cup of coffee.
She was practically an extra, having already chipped in with
her five lines, and was just trying to create an illusion of a
real Bar-B-Q and Grill by looking busy in the background.
She was young, and pretty in a lipsticky '50s way, but made
up to look sluttish and bedraggled. Up close, Anne could see
the panstick make-up and exaggerated black patches under
her eyes. The coffee was cold tea, tart and nasty, but Anne
sipped it anyway. She wanted to remain inconspicuous.

Downstage, Sam's World War Two buddy and sidekick,
played by Eli Wallach, was trying and failing to dispense
Sam-style worldly wisdom and advice to the bar-owner's
son-in-law. He, played by a young Martin Landau, was a
shell-shocked, psychologically impotent Korean war veteran
who had just discovered that his wife (Kim Hunter) had been
shacked up with Maish (Marlon Brando) while he was in a
prisoner-of-war camp. In an earlier scene, he had showed off
the automatic he had brought home with him from the army,
lovingly unwrapping it from its oily cloth, caressing it like
the woman who was lost, seeking a response from its cold

metal that he could never get from his flesh. Without Sam to calm him down, the Landau character was going to shoot someone. He was already working himself up to the boil.

Landau had his back to the black space that replaced the fourth wall of the bar, and was taking a rest. His face had gone blank, while Wallach did the acting for both of them. Anne wondered whether Stella Adler would have approved.

'It ain't so bad, Johnny,' said Wallach. 'Broads. Who can figure 'em? Maish ain't such a bad guy.'

'He wuz draft-exempted. Me an' my brudder goes to Korea, an' get tortured by the slants, an' good ol' Maish sits on his ass in a gas station.'

In the movie, Maish had sat on his 'setter' in a gas station.

'Only 'cause of his leg, Johnny,' said Wallach. 'Maish got a bum leg from when he was a kid. You don't notice it so much 'cause he got a special kind of way of walking that covers up, but he couldn't pass no army physical. You want a shot?'

'Yeah. A shot.'

Anne's father had written several different endings. She had seen the manuscripts. Landau could shoot Maish, his wife Angie, Wallach by mistake or himself. In the out-of-town try-outs, he shot Maish; on Broadway, he shot Angie; and in the movie, he shot Wallach and himself. The movie ending was a compromise. The Breen Office and the Catholic Legion of Decency had not really wanted Landau to shoot anyone: they liked Bing Crosby films about singing priests, not modern American tragedies. Warner Brothers had stood up to the censors, forcing them to back down by waving a fistful of Broadway reviews in their faces, and then told Dad he could not shoot the girl at the end. Therese Colt, the politically acceptable substitute for Kim Hunter, had to be alive to go off with Brando at the fade-out.

A stage manager put a cool jazz record on the juke box, and everyone settled down to wait for Brando to come on again. Maish had good news; he had just sold his first story to *Atlantic Monthly* and quit his grease monkey job.

Everyone else had bad news; Sam, Maish's surrogate father
and everybody's favourite wailing post, was in the hospital
with his third heart attack. He had not bothered to mention
the first two to anyone; he had been too busy serving up
advice and worldly wisdom between his steak specials and
famous salads. This was the big scene, Brando's big scene,
the one she had heard about all her life.

The jazz was a slow, sexy trumpet solo, high and piercing.
Betty, the waitress with higher billing, began to dance alone,
trying to distract everyone from their worries in her own
way. She had been hired by Sam in the first act, even
though he knew all about her backstreet abortion (jailbird ex-
husband, in the film). Betty was played with a wobbly New
York accent, from Rottingdean to the Bronx via Beverly
Hills, by Victoria Page.

Anne had not seen her mother in three years; and she had
only seen her as she was here in old movies and photographs.
She was the Hollywood Star going legitimate on Broadway,
with a terminated contract back at Paramount and an egghead
boyfriend. She was married to the Mayor of some Californian
retirement colony these days, and still occasionally did guest
appearances on television shows about geriatric detectives.
She always played the private eye's old flame who was in
trouble, and she still paused for applause everytime she made
an entrance.

But here was Vicky, her mother, younger than she was.
She looked a lot like Judi. Under the arc lights, she was even
made up like Judi. She moved sensuously, showing off her
dance training, carried away by the music, caressing herself
in way that would have to be toned down for the movie.
She started to hum – the critics had been ready to pounce,
but Dad had not written a song in for his then-fiancée
– muttering under the tune. Anne was close enough to
realise that she was just counting time, 'one-two-three-four,
one-two-three-four', but to someone in the auditorium, she
seemed to be expressing the inexpressible, summing up the
hopeless yearnings of all the night people . . .

Then Brando came on.

He had worked himself up in the wings. One night, he had got himself into such a state while thinking through the offstage bit where he quit his dead-end job that he had laid out a stagehand who had spoken to him. It was just the sort of thing Maish Johnson would have done. He shouldered his way through the door, and almost danced across the stage, giving the impression of a limp but also covering it up. Every part of his body was in motion. He never just stood still on the stage. He was a pinball, bouncing off the fixed actors, lighting up the beacons in Dad's text. Anne was astonished. She forgot herself, and felt, for the first time, the full power of her father at the height of his talent. She wished she could talk to him again, tell him that he had not lived pointlessly, that he had set down something which would last . . .

Brando grabbed Anne's mother by the waist from behind, and waltzed with her as the solo peaked and died. Then, she was dismissed from centre stage and the star was left to his scene. From the elation of his entrance he segued into puzzlement, as Maish was unable to believe that Sam was not at his usual spot behind the bar. Wallach tried to tell him about Sam, but Brando would not listen. He had to tell his news to someone. He hopped from stool to stool (Anne could see the legendary sweat pouring off him) and finally settled next to Landau.

'I guess old Sam meant a lot to all of us,' said Wallach deliberately, aware that no one was watching him. 'More than we ever counted on.'

'Yeah,' said Landau, back still to the darkness, 'I hope he pulls through.'

'Oh sure he'll pull through, Johnny. Whaddya say, Maish? Sam, he's indestructible. Like Superman. Back there at Anzio . . .'

'Can it,' snapped Brando, slipping into his big speech like Glenn Miller going into a trombone solo, 'Sam was just a guy like the rest of us. He hadda take a shit . . .' (it had been a 'crap' in the movie, and that had been a Hollywood first) '. . . he hadda wash his face. He drank cups of coffee like Brazil was goin' outta business. He was . . .'

. . . and so it went on. One critic had compared the speech to Mark Antony's eulogy, but even Dad thought that was too strong. The extra waitress, unnoticed, broke into tears as she did every night. She lost her part completely, but everyone was focused on Brando. He was talking about Sam, but he was also talking about God. Her father was talking about gods and leaders and heroes and politicians, sermonising on their greatness but saying that he did not need them anymore. Brooks Atkinson, the *New York Times* drama critic, wrote that it was about Franklin D. Roosevelt. Arthur Miller said it was about Eugene O'Neill, whose bar was just down the street from Sam's. The Farnham Commission had called it the 'throw away your crutches' speech, and suggested that it was about Lenin or Trotsky (they were not sure which). Anne found it easy to forget the missing wall, the cold tea, the painted faces. This was reality. More real than anything that had happened to her since Nina fell asleep on her shoulder in the taxi on the way to St John's Wood.

A jangle cut through Brando's tirade, and he left off. There was a pause. Audiences were too awed even to applaud. The ringing was not at all like a real telephone. It was just a sound effect. Wallach, also in tears but concealing them like a professional, scooped up the receiver from behind the bar.

'Sam's Bar-B-Q and Grill,' he said. Then, he nodded and 'uh-huhed' for 30 seconds. Brando stepped back into a shadow, forcibly diverting audience attention to the other actor.

Wallach put the phone down. He looked at everybody. It could have been the longest pause in American theatrical history. People who saw the play on its first run remembered it as lasting for a full minute. No one ever managed to wrest enough attention off the stage to time it. No one breathed

'It's Sam,' said Wallach. 'He just bought the farm'

Anne's mother started sobbing uncontrollably, and had to be comforted by Jed (Howard Da Silva), the stammering vacuum cleaner salesman. It was a fine display of histrionic hysteria, but Brando topped it, stepped on it, destroyed it, by knocking back the shot Wallach had poured for Landau and pulling apart a stale doughnut.

Anne realised that she had misheard Wallach's line. He had not said that Sam had just bought the farm, he had said that *Cam* had just bought the farm.

Cam? He would have been only two years old. In the '50s, Cam had been her father's name.

'He made this place, I guess,' said Wallach. 'It won't seem the same going on without him. I guess I'll sell up. I could move to Florida.'

'No,' shouted Brando, hitting the bar so hard that all the props on it shook. 'No. When a guy gets a Nobel Prize, it means something. There ain't no committee that can take that away from him.'

Landau got up. Everybody had forgotten him. He had been working himself back into his part. His eyes gleamed with Satanic fury, his slicked hair was mussed into horn shapes. Cuckold's horns, Devil's horns. It was a neat trick. He had his gun out.

Mother screamed again – the Betty role really was a drag, Anne realised – and Da Silva hugged her.

'Yeah,' sneered Landau, 'and nobody's takin' Angie away from me. 'Specially not you, Mr Draft-Exempt-Gas-Jockey Hemingway!'

Wallach leaned over the bar, trying to dampen Landau's anger, but it was no good. He was spitting his lines out, his still-sharp Brooklyn accent cutting into Brando's tortured presence. He waved the gun wildly.

'You and Angie thought you were God-damned smart, huh? Poor old Johnny Boy was havin' his toenails pulled by the slants, an' you had it real easy. You gotta way with words, Maish, but you don't know what dyin' is like. You seen it in the movies, you read it in books. Well, here it is happenin' to you. Dyin'. Cam died. He was a fink and a squealer, and he died. Now, you . . .'

It was time for Kim Hunter's spectacularly unfortunate entrance. Landau's safety catch was off. The door Anne had

come through opened. She leaned out of her booth to see
Angie come in. There was no one.

'Angie!'

She turned back to the action. Landau was talking to her.

'Get outta here, Angie,' shouted Brando, 'he's drunk.'

She was standing up, alone in her part of the stage. She did
not have any lines. Everyone else had got out of the way. She
looked at Landau's gun – it was not a prop – and then at his
face. He had turned into Skinner.

'Angie,' he said in Landau's voice. 'This is what dyin' is
like.'

Then he fired.

eight

IT HAD BEEN a long night for Maish. A lifetime ago, he had shambled into Sam's for a cup of mocha java and a cruller. He had been newly-born then, but with a set of memories as deceitful as Eve's belly button. He had talked, many times, about a previous life, but he had no pictures in his head to go with the words in his mouth. His stories about Angie and the gas station owner and his ambitions as a writer could have been second-hand, alibis learned by rote to cover up someone else's crimes. He thought he might have lived before, he kept being haunted by that queer sensation Sam called *déjà vu*, but he was aware that his previous lives were identical, or almost identical, to his current experiences. It was a whole lot weirder than flying saucers or the search for Bridey Murphy.

He was supposed to be a gas station attendant, but he could not imagine what a gas pump or even an automobile looked like. He was a writer, but his vocabulary was limited to the comparatively few words he had been given to speak. In his mind, he felt uncomfortable even using the phrases he could pick up from the others in the bar. He knew that he was supposed to have badly broken his leg when he was a kid, to have made love to Angie and Betty and many other nameless girls, to have written an as-yet unpublished autobiographical novel about his time with a streetgang. He knew these things, but only as simple facts. The mass of tiny details he could recall about the bar and the people he met there accounted for the only rounded, complete, satisfying experiences he had ever had.

It was just like Jed's speech. Sam's was the only real place in the world, the only place where anything counted.

Everything else was a shadowland where life was dreamed not lived. 'Th-th-this is where you puh-pay for your sins,' Jed always said, 'not in church, in Sam's Bar-B-Q and Grill.'

A minute or so ago he had said that even Sam had to take a shit. So how come he had eaten doughnuts and drank coffee all evening without having to use the Men's Room? Deep down, Maish knew there was something wrong with his life.

He had been caught in this place forever, only coming to life in the well-lit arena of the Bar-B-Q and Grill. Everything else was dark and skeletal, like an unremembered dream. Everything that had happened this evening, that would happen in the next few minutes, was familiar, planned, tedious. He knew that this world had been abandoned by its Creator, but he was still following the vagrant god's orders.

Somehow, it was different this time. The old man was dead, really dead. He had not just been carried out of the door into the darkness never to be seen again. Somewhere outside the bar, outside the world, the man had really died.

When he had been talking about Sam, he had not been thinking about what he was saying, the words came automatically. But he had been thinking, sensing how different it was this time. There was no more *déjà vu*. He was free. He did not know what freedom meant yet, but it was marvellous and frightening. Maybe being free was the same as being dead.

It was clear now. He had seen Johnny shoot Angie many times, an impossible number of times. He had taken the still-hot gun away from the man, had cradled the dying woman, had spoken the speech given him, had paused for the darkness to fall on them all. There had been variations – slight differences of placing, of phrasing, of feeling – but each time the actions had been basically identical.

This time it was different. There was no tyrant god to make him stand by and watch Angie, the woman he loved but had never really met, be killed. Things could be changed.

'Angie,' said Johnny, taking a shaky aim, 'this is what dyin' is like.'

As Johnny pulled the trigger, Maish heaved himself forwards. His bum leg gave out, but he fell into the line of fire. He felt the push of the bullet going into his chest before he heard the amazingly loud crack of the gunshot. His shin hurt more than his broken ribs, his punctured heart.

There was no one to overpower Johnny, to take the gun away from him, but the young man seized up as soon as he had fired, falling into a statue state rather than go against the script. On his knees, real blood soaking his shirt, Maish looked up at Angie. It was not Angie, it was some other woman, but that did not matter. He did not know what to say. He opened his mouth, but only blood came out.

Never again.

Never again would he limp, dance, dream aloud, drink, eat, hit Jed, lean on the bar, listen to Sam's advice, play with his switchblade, try to get a game of cards together, burst out his good news, be shattered by the bad news, watch Angie get shot, talk to the darkness, start all over again.

This was what dying was like.

nine

FOR ANGELA BUONFIGLIA, the next five years started badly. But things got better.

The homicide lieutenant, Joe Hollis, took an immediate dislike to Johnny. He had been in Korea too, and knew that Johnny was one of the GIs who had admitted under torture that the United Nations forces had been involved in war crimes. He dug up the spurious confession that Johnny had put his name to. Hollis pursued the case with a ferocity that surprised his jaded colleages and unearthed a witness – a patron of Sam's who had gone unnoticed that evening – who testified against Johnny. He had overheard the young veteran swear to get even with Maish Johnson, and claimed to have seen Johnny take a deliberate aim before gunning the man down.

Angela managed to get her divorce through before Johnny's execution, but felt obliged to visit her ex-husband on Death Row. He just sat grinning from behind the bars, playing solitaire but never winning. She went to too many funerals. Her father's brought out the whole neighbourhood for an extravagant Italian-Irish-Jewish wake that went on for days, while Johnny and Maish were laid to rest in scarily similar, sparsely attended grey-day ceremonies, one inside a prison, one outside. Aside from her, the only person at all three ceremonies was Joe Hollis, who shook her hand at Johnny's burial and vanished from her life.

Angela made enough out of the sale of Sam's Bar-B-Q and Grill to set herself up in a small business in the garment centre. At first, she simply busied herself with the accounting and retail side and bought in stock from Europe, but gradually she discovered a talent for designing patterned scarves and blouses. Her signature became a brand name, and she was able to put her prices up. 'Design by Angela' began to mean as much as 'Gowns by Ariadne'. Audrey Hepburn wore 'Angela' clothes, and Princess Grace, Peggy Lee and Jacqueline Bouvier Sinatra. When Elvis Presley and John Wayne turned up on *The Tonight Show* with identical 'Angela' ties, male adornment suddenly ceased to be considered unmanly.

She opened an 'Angela's' in Washington DC, then San Francisco, then Chicago, then everywhere. Her designs were featured in *Vogue*, exhibited at art galleries, imitated by others. She had a small love affair, with C.D. Broome – a college graduate who thought he wanted to be a novelist – but it ended messily. Tired of New York and its ghosts, and buoyed by a ridiculously large fee from a Hollywood studio that had used her designs under the titles of a glossy romantic comedy, she took a year off to travel around the United States. At the end of that, she settled in New Orleans.

She did a quarter as many designs, and sold them for four times as much. During Mardi Gras, she had a cliché meeting cute with a French-speaking aristocrat, the owner of a prestigious but popular restaurant. On the night that they made love for the first time, she told him about Johnny and Maish, and he told her about the homosexual experiences he had had as a younger man. She understood about him, he understood about her, and, three weeks later, they agreed to marry. . . .

nine

FOR ANGELA BUONFIGLIA, the next five years started badly. And things got worse.

The homicide lieutenant, Barry Erskine, took an immediate liking to Johnny. He had been in Korea too, and while he was overseas his own wife had divorced him to marry her piano teacher. He had often thought of shooting them and trying to get away with it. Erskine pursued the case with a ferocity that surprised his jaded colleagues, and unearthed a witness – a patron of Sam's who had gone unnoticed that evening – who testified for Johnny. He had overheard Maish threaten the young veteran, and claimed to have seen the dead man pull out a switchblade before Johnny drew his gun.

Johnny stayed in jail for three weeks. No charges against him were ever brought. He was even given his gun back, with a note to remind him that he would have to renew his permit in the next few months. Angela went alone to Maish's pauper's funeral, and with Johnny to Sam's. She was surprised how few of her father's friends and patrons bothered to turn out for that dismal day. Fortunately, she was able to wear a thick veil. When Johnny had found out she had been to Maish's funeral, he had worked her face over. Erskine turned up at the wake and exchanged nasty jokes with Johnny. He looked her over, grinning like a fiend, before leaving, and warned her to stay out of trouble.

It turned out that Sam's habitual generosity had got him into debt, and the Bar-B-Q and Grill had to be sold off to settle up with his many creditors. The first night that Angela spent with Johnny in their walk-up apartment after he got out of jail ended up with him breaking three of her ribs. She was

grateful that he was unable to rape her, but knew he would
think of something to do to make her sorry. Eventually, he
found out how sickened she was by his nailless toes, and
started forcing her to massage his feet. He liked to reminisce
about his time as a POW, and made up ever more elaborate
stories of torture and degradation.

The couple could not get by on Johnny's disability pension,
and Angela had to get a job as a waitress. Of course, the owner
of the diner that had replaced Sam's took her on, and she put
up with ridiculous hours, sweatshop wages, groping patrons,
and an infernally filthy kitchen with all the resignation of the
justifiably damned. She had a nasty little affair with Nino
Kenyon, one of the cooks, that broke up when someone told
him about what Johnny had done to Maish. After a while, the
patrons did not even bother to grope her.

Johnny's feet got worse, and she suspected him of opening
old wounds with broken beer bottles while she was at work.
He cultivated new scabs and scars, and had to hobble around
the apartment on crutches. He rarely went out, but followed
the televised HUAC hearings avidly. Korea had not been
enough for him. He often talked about how much he would
like to go out to Hollywood and shoot some Commies.
When the news came through that Orson Welles had hanged
himself rather than name names for Hugh Farnham, Johnny
celebrated with a three bottle binge. He wrote to newspapers
and politicians, naming prominent and obscure citizens as
card-carrying Reds. He received a thank you letter from the
desk of Hugh Farnham, but eventually Detective Erskine
came round and told him to lay off.

Erskine told Angela that Johnny was becoming an embarrassment, and ought to get some sort of psychoanalysis.
Angela barely made enough to feed the both of them and pay
the rent, and federal subsidies for veterans' medical care had
just been slashed by the McCarran administration, so she had
to ignore the advice. Often, she wondered what her father
would have said. One morning, after work, she came home
and found that Johnny had taken his gun out of its drawer
and shot off three of his toes.

ten

A NGELA DREAMED. Even tucked in comfortably next to Didier in the big old safe bed in the big old safe house she could only think of as a mansion, Angela dreamed. In the morning, she could never remember where her night thoughts had taken her. Didier could extemporise forever his dreams, their amusing quirkiness, their disorientating surrealism, but she suffered from instant amnesia. But she knew that she did dream, of Something, of Somewhere, of Someone . . .

'Perhaps, Angel,' Didier said one morning, 'it is you who are dreamed of . . .'

That kind of pseudo-insight was not at all like Didier. It was the sort of thing she would expect from one of Rod Serling's *Twilight Zone* introductions. Immediately, her husband slipped back into character, and started pressing exactly the right buttons. She was won over, and, their elaborate breakfast forgotten, they decided that Didier did have an hour or two to spare before he was needed in his office . . . .

Later, alone in the newly-unmade bed, Angela thought again about her dreams. Several of her friends were in analysis, and she knew from them that dreams could be important as a key to your character. Of course, she did not need analysis. Everybody she knew would cite her as an absolute model of fulfilment and balance. Perhaps, she thought, she was not very good at being happy. Perhaps that was why she needed to dream, to fulfil a deep-seated and perfectly natural desire to have some misery in her life.

Her husband, former homosexual or not, was as flawless a part of her world as a robot designed to act like Rossano

Brazzi or Gregory Peck. He accorded her all the reverence due
to a Victorian angel in the kitchen, and never disapproved of
her need to have compartments of her life separate from him.
Her career was important to her, and she had kept it going
after the marriage. And yet, it did seem strange that doodles
which came out of her unconscious when her mind was at
its emptiest magically turned into unimaginable amounts of
money.

In her sunken marble bath – a marvellously stupid luxury
she was almost ashamed of – she thought about the sym-
metries of her life. She was entering middle-age with the
body she had had as a 20-year-old. Her financial security
was assured for a lifetime. Their doctor saw no reason why
they could not have children if they did not put it off too
long, and she was tempted by the prospect of motherhood.
She was never alone, except when she wanted to be; she was
never bored, except when she wanted to be.

. . . and who could ask for anything more.

Later that summer, they started going to the movies like
teenagers. The film that made the most impression on her
was *North by Northwest*, a chocolate box-coloured romantic
thriller with Cary Grant and Eva Marie Saint. She had found
other Alfred Hitchcock films boring and cynical, but this was,
on the whole, lovely. Grant was charming, but she was also
attracted to James Mason, who was a civilised villain and had
many of the qualities she liked in Didier. In one scene, she
had a delightful buzz of recognition, realising that she had
designed one of the scarves worn by Saint. But there was a
snake in Eden, a disturbing presence among the thrills and
comedy. One actor – the man who played the villain's male
secretary (and former lover?), the man who trod on Grant's
hand as he dangled off the faces of Mount Rushmore in the
climax – frightened her more than any monster in any horror
movie she had ever seen.

If there was a cast list at the end of the film, the projectionist
closed the theatre curtains over it, and so Angela did not get
the actor's name. Didier, a film addict who often sneaked out
of his business in the afternoons to catch matinées of war films

and Westerns she did not want to see, could not remember the
name of the actor who played the secretary, but thought he
had been in *Pork Chop Hill*, playing a soldier in Korea.

Korea. Of course. That was who the actor reminded her
of. Johnny. He was older, smoother, less explosive, but the
wide, sneering lips and scarily glowing eyes were the same.

Oddly, unnervingly, the actor turned up again within a
week. On a summer re-run of the *The Twilight Zone*. Angela
did not really like the Serling show, but found it affected her,
unlike a lot of the network pap television had been churning
out since the industry switched from live television in New
York to filmed series from Hollywood. The episode was
a weird Western, 'Mr Denton on Doomsday', with Dan
Duryea as a drunk given miraculous gunslinging abilities
by a travelling salesman. The scary actor loitered around
the cramped studio barroom in sinister black leather outfits,
sadistically tormenting Duryea. In the inevitable shoot-out,
the man who frightened her was shot in the hand by the
suddenly superskilled Duryea, but she could not watch any
more and had Didier turn off their receiver. While he was
brushing his teeth, she got out the *TV Guide* and found out
the actor's name.

It was Martin Landau, and that did not mean anything to
her.

There was another face that bothered her whenever it
turned up on TV or in the newspapers. Hugh Farnham's.
But half America was frightened of Hugh Farnham. She had
signed a few petitions against HUAC once, at the prompting
of Maish Johnson, but had not really followed the hearings.
However, like everyone else, she had been shocked when the
stories about Farnham came out. The papers called him 'The
Modern Bluebeard' and were loudly asking why the FBI had
not tracked him down yet. The scandal sheets reckoned he
was in South America with all the Nazis. The father of one
of his young victims had become something of a celebrity
by devoting huge sums to the search for Hugh Farnham.
Even President Stevenson had spoken out against his former
opponent, and made an unprecedented top level intervention

in law enforcement to hurry up the capture of this vicious killer. Farnham was a Monster, everyone agreed.

Martin Landau, Hugh Farnham, and Johnny. They all had something to do with her somehow.

That night, while Didier slept, she thought of that evening in Sam's Bar-B-Q and Grill. The evening that Johnny shot Maish, the evening that her father died. It was the most vivid memory she had. Sometimes, she thought it was the only evening she had ever truly lived through. Since then, she had been only half the woman she used to be. Perhaps less than half.

As summer turned into fall, she started to remember her dreams. Johnny was in them, and Maish, and her father. And her sister. But Angela did not have a sister, much less a sister with clothes and hair like an alien princess from a cheap science fiction film. She dreamed of London, a city she could recognise but had never been to. And there was a man in her dreams who frightened her more than Martin Landau, Hugh Farnham and Johnny rolled into one. He had scaled skin, and a lizard's tongue. Inside, he was a dragon and she had to kill him before he consumed her.

Suddenly, she dropped her design career. She decided it was flimsy and insubstantial. She found herself talking less and less, even to Didier. Her husband remained attentive, and even left her alone when she was in a terminally uncommunicative mood. Sometimes, she tried to annoy him, to hurt him. But he could not be moved. He was too perfect.

One morning, alone in the mansion, she decided that living the shadow of a life was not enough. She was well into the second bottle of pills, washing them down with tasteless vodka, before sleep enveloped her.

She had not bothered to leave a note, realising that there was really no one left behind to read it.

It had been a nice dream, but only that . . . .

ten

ANGELA DREAMED. Even exhausted next to Johnny in the sick-smelling bed in the sick-smelling walk-up she could only think of as her purgatory, Angela dreamed. In the morning, she could never remember where her night thoughts had taken her. She only knew that she woke up as worn-out and tired as when she went to sleep. But she knew that she did dream, of Something, of Somewhere, of Someone . . . .

When she got out of bed, Angela felt like something the cat had sicked up. As usual after the graveyard shift, she had slept well into the afternoon. Last night had been a bad one; *another* bad one. She had a waitress' ache lodged permanently in the small of her back, and a couple of its children were budding under her shoulder blades. According to Betty, who delighted in everybody's afflictions, her knees and ankles would be next. She hated working all night, but the extra twelve cents an hour helped her keep treading water. It was less immediately strenuous than the three-to-ten shift, but a good deal more soul-eroding. Nobody happy eats after midnight.

Johnny was sleeping too, in front of the tiny television set, his ruined feet up on their special stool. She saw that he had been punishing himself again, and bled in his bandages. Orange and brown discolourations marred the linen that had been pristine white when she left for work. On the mantel over the bricked-up fireplace was the jam jar in which he kept his pickled toes. He still claimed that had been an accident. In her tatty robe, she tidied up around him, emptying ashtrays, clearing up glasses.

He had had his friend the cop over last night. They had

bitched and griped and watched television together. Johnny liked to threaten her with Barry Erskine. 'Angel,' he would say, 'if you leave, I'll have Erskine shoot you down just like I shot down your boyfriend.' The cop had tried to feel her ass a couple of times, but he did not have the balls to do anything with Johnny around. After all, everybody remembered who was the killer in this apartment.

The TV was still on, a news show. Hugh Farnham sat in a studio talking about Cuba with a fawning woman. Johnny still had a letter from his desk. When Pat McCarran stepped down and Nixon moved up, Farnham would be in line for the Vice-Presidential ticket. Nixon and Farnham. Angela did not think she would bother to vote. There was film of Havana, with US Marines on the streets, peasants in the fields and Battista waving on a balcony. The commentator talked about the hanging of Ernesto Guevara, and the trial of Fidel Castro.

'Yeah,' grunted Johnny, waking up, 'stick it to the Reds!'

After the piece on Cuba, Farnham talked about the new HUAC hearings, under the chairmanship of virgin Congressman Cohn. He would not be taking part this time, but he was lending his full support to 'those who would help our nation purify itself'. Johnny opened a bottle of beer with his teeth, and cheered as the froth bubbled over. 'Oughta be hung like dogs,' he snarled, 'goddamn pinkos!' The commentator read out a list of actors, soldiers, directors, writers, state officials and sportsmen who would be subpoenaed. One of them was Marlon Brando, whom Angela had always liked.

'Lousy commies! Oughta line 'em up outside the Kremlin an' open up on 'em with tommy guns. Lousy Ivans oughta be put down like *roaches!*'

Angela felt woozy, and nauseous. She backed away from Johnny and wrestled with the bathroom door.

'Whassamatter, Angel?'

Johnny never used to call her 'Angel'. It had been 'Angie' once. She thought of herself as 'Angela', but nobody ever called her that.

'I feel . . .'

How did she feel? Sick, but not quite. She cramped into the closet-sized bathroom, and crouched by the bath. Clothes hung around her from ropes stretched across the room. She had spasms in her stomach.

There was a Frankenstein Monster clumping about outside. Johnny had got up, and was moving around the room. Things fell over. Johnny swore.

Angela pushed aside a curtain of drying nylon hose and was sick in the bath. She heaved up what looked like orange frogspawn. It was like spitting a cloud of tiny pebbles that rattled on the backs of her teeth on the way out. They were pills. She could read an unfamiliar brand name on the less-dissolved ones.

For a moment, she thought she was going crazy. Then, she realised it was the other way around. Crazy was going Her. Her crazy was going. It was coming together in her head.

'Angel,' shouted Johnny, banging on the door with a crutch. Everything shook. 'Lemme in!'

She did not ache any more. Despite her recent vomiting spell, she did not feel empty any more.

Looking in the freckled mirror, she found herself changed. She was not younger or healthier or better-looking, but she was at least herself again.

'Angel, you wanna keep some teeth? Open up!'

The apartment was not next to the elevated railway, but it shook as if a train were going by. Bottles fell out of the cabinet over the sink. Talcum powder rose from a smashed jar like tear-gas from a cannister. Damp clothes flopped on the floor. The bathroom, always small, appeared to shrink to the size of a coffin.

She stood up and wiped her face on a towel.

'Angel?' Johnny was whining now, pathetic rather than threatening. She knew she could take him.

'Angela!' His voice was changing. It was darker, deeper, nastier.

'In a minute,' she said.

She found her clothes on a chair. Her real clothes. She got dressed. Johnny had stopped banging.

There was a frosted glass window in the bathroom. If you opened it, you could see the vacant lot next door and the building beyond it. Now, she knew, there was none of that there.

'Angela!' He was seriously annoyed.

She opened the bathroom door.

'Angela?'

'That's not my name.'

'Of course,' he said, straightening up, 'and Johnny is not mine.'

Skinner did not need the crutches.

eleven

THERE WERE still leftover bits and pieces of the walk-up
apartment dotted about the place, but it was a strip-lit
open-plan office now. On Skinner's desk was a presentation
case containing Johnny's Korean medals, and one of the GI
issue Mickey Spillane paperbacks he had got his kicks out of.
Perched on the central heating unit, Anne saw the jar with
Johnny's three missing toes floating in it, and a framed picture
of Sam and his daughter outside the Bar-B-Q and Grill. The
photograph was fading fast, like an Instamatic snapshot in
reverse. The faces had already gone. Behind her, there was
no bathroom, just a rank of filing cabinets.

The office had no windows, and the only door was fifty
yards away on the other side of the room. To reach it, she
would have to negotiate a maze of partitioned-off desks,
potted plants and photocopiers. A few of the magazines
she did work for had places like this, and she tried to avoid
spending time in them. Apart from the Monster and her, the
office was empty. There were Christmas cards hanging on a
clothesline on the wall, and a few perishing balloons huddled
in a corner.

The desk was between her and Skinner, but he was tall
enough to step over it. He looked no more dangerous than
a typical editor.

'You know what they say about werewolves,' she said,
'there's always a tree between you and it, but never a tree
between it and you.'

'I'm not a werewolf.'

'No, but you are a Monster, right?'

'I suppose so.' He smiled with his mouth, just faintly. His

face was anaesthetised. He could have been wearing a tissue paper death mask. It was like the old *Mission: Impossible* show; she expected him to peel off his face to reveal Martin Landau underneath.

'Anne,' he said, 'may I call you by your first name?'

'Sure.'

'Angela?'

The name was like a slap in the face. But she rolled with it, and came back, still sure of who she was.

'No, not Angela. A nice try, though.'

'You mustn't hold it against me.' He sat down in a swivel chair, and pushed himself back from the desk. He knitted his fingers behind his neck, and looked up at her. He was totally relaxed, which she knew was supposed to make her nervous. She looked down at him, not flinching.

'Don't you feel bad about Angela?'

'How do you mean?'

'Well, in a very real sense, you are responsible for wasting her. You took the pills.'

'Oh, *that* Angela. Well, it wasn't real. . . .'

'I doubt if that argument would go down very well with her. She had a great deal of self-determination, you know. She was independent of you.'

'What about the other Angela?'

'Just the same. A little less aware, perhaps, but just as valid a personality. Incidentally, what makes you think that were only two Angelas?'

'Skinner, there wasn't even one. We both know that. My Dad made her up. And he didn't give her that much. A big scene in the first act, a walk-on in the second, and getting shot in the end. She's supposed to be having this big affair with Maish, but they're only on stage together when she's being killed. All the rest comes from you. . . .'

'And you. Don't underestimate yourself. I've never been to New Orleans.'

'Okay, and me too. A bit of Dad, a bit of you, a bit of me, a bit of Kim Hunter, a bit of Therese Colt, a bit of Angela Pleasence. That doesn't make a real person.'

'Why not?'

'Because they don't, that's why. They should have kept Kim Hunter for the movie, though. But she was blacklisted by then.'

'What's that got to do with anything?'

'You're the blacklist expert aren't you?'

The skin around his eyes crinkled, and set in little folds. She knew he had not expected her to figure it out.

'You don't change that much, Skinner.'

'You're sharp.'

'And you were Hugh Farnham?'

'Once.'

'Before that?'

'Oh, you don't really want to know. Lots of names. I can't be expected to remember all of them.'

'Any famous ones?'

'A few.'

'Going back a long way?'

'That's right.'

'You're a vampire?'

'No,' he chuckled to himself. 'Well, not very often.'

She was fed up with hanging around exchanging small talk with an inhuman mass murderer. But Skinner was enjoying himself.

'Do sit down,' he said. 'Would you like some coffee?'

'Sure. If there's any going.'

She sat in a chair and wheeled it up to the desk. It was not really comfortable, and she experimented, sitting with her legs crossed, uncrossed, sprawled apart. The backrest and the arms were too low. She settled for a relatively painless perching position.

'Black with sugar?'

'Do you know everything?'

'Not everything. Just enough to get by. Judi has a good memory. She knows how you drink your coffee.'

'She did. I've cut out sugar for the last two years.'

'Okay, so I look like an idiot. I won't try that kind of Win Friends and Influence People trick again.'

He pressed a buzzer on his desk, leaned forwards, and said something in an unrecognisable, sibilant language into the intercom. Seconds later, a bell like a microwave oven went off behind Anne. She turned in her seat, and saw a blinking red light above a cupboard door.

'It's a dumb waiter.'

She opened the door, and reached in to bring out a paper cup of coffee. It was instant, but hot and tasty. The first swallow scalded her tongue, and she was careful after that.

'It's been a long time, Anne. A long time since I came across anyone as self-possessed as you are. You've held out much longer than I expected.'

'Thank you.'

'I don't pay compliments, I make statements of fact. You are a most capable young woman.'

'I know how to fix a plug.'

'I don't doubt it. Judi was good too. Not as good as you, but way above average. Still, in the long run, she wasn't good enough. Which is why she is where she is today.'

'Which is, exactly, where?'

'That's a good question. She's with me. Always.'

'*All* of her?'

'No, not all. But enough of her, Anne. Enough.'

'You bastard.'

'Judi wasn't good enough to walk away from me. And you aren't good enough, Anne. Don't feel insulted. Maybe once, twice in a thousand years does someone like that turn up. I'm old. Maybe I'll never meet anyone that good again. You have no idea how depressing I find that thought, how boring my life can get. . . .'

He was doling his words out carefully now, putting an actorish emphasis on them. If a politician talked to her like this, she would campaign vigorously against him.

Skinner trailed off, his face a mask of wistful resignation. He reached below the horizon of the desktop, and she heard a drawer being pulled open. He dipped a hand into it like a smooth gangster reaching for a concealed gun. He held up a purple lizard, gripping its tail in his fingers but letting it settle in his palm. The little reptile looked around, blinking spirally.

'Pretty, isn't he?'

'Oh sure, he's adorable.'

He held the lizard up to his eyeline, and examined it. He kissed it on its minutely horned snout, then bit its head off. He dropped the cleanly decapitated thing on the desk blotter. It bled very little, but twisted and thrashed like a loose power cable. Skinner chewed for a few seconds, then spat over his shoulder. Anne heard the pulped skull plop into an 1880s barbershop spittoon.

Skinner produced another lizard, smaller and greener, with a frilly collar.

'Want one?'

'No thanks.'

'I thought not.'

He bit again, spat again. Anne sat, hands idle in her lap, coffee abandoned, watching this polite Monster indulge his vice. Kicking bodies wound down like clockwork toys on the blotter.

'Well, Anne, here we are . . .'

'So?'

'So what are you going to do about it?'

'You tell me.'

'Um, well, the natural course of things would involve me pinning you down – and you know I could do that – and feeding off you. Everything up till now had just been an entertainment, like silly Amelia's party games. Feeding is serious. You don't understand what that means, but you must have some idea by now.'

'And if you feed off me?'

'You'll be with Judi. You'll be just like Judi, in fact. Not that that is entirely a bad thing, but I think it might be wasteful . . . .'

He leaned forwards, shading his kills, supporting his head on a bridge of his interlaced fingers. He had mismatched cufflinks.

'You have qualities, Anne. I could make you like me.'

She was annoyed. 'You could never make me like you.'

'No, not like, *like*. You could be one of the Kind.'

'You mean I could live forever, see the world, torture people and bite the heads off lizards? That's an awfully tempting offer, but . . .'

He raised a little finger and silenced her.

'Yes,' he said, 'you have qualities. You're not actually that witty, but very few people would even try to make jokes in a situation like this. Irony is a much underrated attitude.'

'And how do people get to be like you, Skinner?'

'I've always been one of the Kind. You can never have that, of course, but I can teach you things, do things for you. It's not common, but it's not unprecedented either . . . .'

'Would I be right in assuming that there aren't any lady monsters running around these years?'

He paused after that one, thinking carefully. He was slower than he used to be.

'You are very perceptive,' he said, finally. 'To answer your implied rather than your actual question, yes. I would welcome the company of an equal. Not that you could be my equal without a substantial investment of time and effort. As for whether there are others of the Kind left . . . well . . . as far as I know, there are not . . .'

Suddenly, with a squirt of creepy excitement, Anne realised Skinner was lying.

'I am the last,' he said.

'There ought to be a protection order out on you. You don't want to wind up like the dodo or the passenger pigeon.'

She was shaking now, not with fear but with rage. She wanted to take him apart. She tried not to explode. Skinner was crazy but calm.

'Passenger pigeons,' he mused. 'I saw them, you know. You've heard how they used to flock. They could blot out the sun for hours. Your country was a marvel until recently, and you covered it in concrete . . . .'

'Me personally?'

'Yes, you. And Judi. And people just like you.'

'So we paved paradise and put up a parking lot?'

'Ha! I hate America very much, Anne. More, even, than Egypt. I can't even go there any more. I was at Antietam, you know, in your War Between the States . . . .'

'I got through high school, thank you very much.'

'I'm sorry. During the ten years of your country's ill-advised involvement in Indochina, some 50,000 Americans were killed in action. At the Battle of Antietam, 40,000 fell in one afternoon.'

'And those were the good old days?'

There was something weird in his eyes now. '1862 isn't my old days, Anne. It's not even my yesterday. It's my this morning.'

'What put you off the States then?'

He shrugged, a ribbon of skin peeling from his cheek as his grin relaxed. 'Shall we say, a loss of vision?'

'So, if I marry you, we can't go visit with Mom and Dad?'

'I don't want to marry you.'

'What kind of a girl do you think I am?'

'A stupider one than you seem. Like your sister . . .'

His left eye had drooped shut, covered with dead skin. Skinner was tired, sleepy, worn out. He was still arguing, but she could sense that his heart was not in it any more.

She knew that she could get out of this.

'By the way,' he said spitefully, 'you'll never visit your father again. I heard on the world service news just now that . . .'

With a Bruce Lee yell, she burst out of her chair and threw herself against his desk. It turned on its side, and she grabbed hold of the two upper legs. Skinner's chair rolled backwards against the featureless wall. Her knees were bruised, and she was not really strong enough to heft the whole piece of furniture, but she pushed with her entire body. A drawer came free and crunched up like a matchbox. Lizards scampered beneath her feet, dispersing with unbelievable speed.

All she could see of Skinner was one pale hand, gripping the top edge of the desk, and his weakly kicking, grey-trousered legs. She slammed the desk against the wall. A desk leg came off. She drew back, and slammed again. Skinner grunted and ruptured. There was a burp of foul air. Inside Skinner, a gurgling started and stopped.

She heaved the desk aside. A partition fell over. Skinner was hunched up, arms over his head. She kicked him viciously about the shins, and battered his head and torso with the broken leg. She pried his arms apart, and smashed in his face. It dented easily. His hair came off in one piece like a wig. His chest fell in.

She stopped hitting him, and stepped back. There was no noise now, except the whir of a concealed extractor fan. She bent over Skinner and picked up his face. It was like a crumpled linen handkerchief. It tore and she had to wipe her hand on the wall to get the cobwebby scum off her fingers.

All that was left was an empty skin.

twelve

NAKED, he woke up. His long body had a reddish tinge, and he was tender all over. Even the soles of his feet were soft. His skin was young and tight, unshrivelled. He felt his face. The nose was a little flat, but the flesh was firm. The change had been relatively painless, and he thought he would be satisfied with the results.

Still a little light-headed, he stood up. There was a kimono hung on a hook nearby. He clothed himself. He rubbed the clear gum away from his eyes. He had not bled anywhere.

Anne was standing at the other side of the office, holding bits of his old skin. He was between her and the door.

He was not sorry she had turned him down, but, newly reborn, he was not ready to feed on her yet. He was still overnourished from his pre-change gluttony, and he had to reestablish control over the ghosts he already had before he could take on another one. Especially a ghost who was liable to be doing a lot of struggling.

'Anne,' he shouted, 'over here.' His voice had an unfamiliar, boyish sound in his ears. He liked it.

She turned to look at him, the bitch.

He grinned. His teeth were sharper now. With simian agility, he leaped on a desk. While he was in this state, he wanted to stretch himself a little. His backbone was elongating, making use of his extra ribs. His fingers developed an extra knuckle apiece. His toes turned to fingers. He flattened his hair to his almost oval skull, slicking it down with natural juices. He wanted to sing.

She was scared. Perhaps for the first time, she was really scared. He could taste it, and he was aroused.

'Keep young and beautiful,' he crooned to her, 'if you want to be *loved*. . . .'

She came for him, for the door. He twisted on himself, gripping the desk with his handclaws, and flipped his lower body around. He took a semi-orgasmic pleasure from his own muscle strength.

He was going to let her go again; for a while. She could not get far. There was only the Dream out there. He had his lines into her head. He could reel her in and land her any time he wanted. First, he had to give her a few more jolts, tire her out, take the fight out of her. . . .

He reared up on his hind legs, and sprang in front of the door. Her way was barred. He shrilled one of the old songs, in the language he never got to use these days. In the song, he boasted of his ghosts.

Then he stepped aside, opened the door, and mimed an 'after you'.

She was past him faster than one of the lizards and in the hallway. She looked at the lift doors and – clever girl! – decided to take the stairs.

Pausing in the stairwell, she turned to look back at him. Was that supposed to be a come-on? Was she enjoying the chase. In any case, he was not ready to follow yet.

She stuck her middle finger up in the empty air, and said 'suck on that salamander!'

Then she was gone.

thirteen

THE BUSINESS of getting out of the building was straight-
forward. She had been expecting everdescending stairs,
windowless walls and doorless lobbies. Exposure to Skinner's
worldview had led her to assume his office would be the only
inhabitable portion of a skyscraping concrete coffin.

She was wrong. They had not even been more than five or
six storeys above the street. And, on every floor, the stairwell
was outfitted with a picture window. The eternity lighting
made dark mirrors of the plateglass oblongs, but she could
make out the outlines of a world beyond. There were points
of light out in the night, and dark shapes, moving things,
people, ghosts . . .

All of which worried her; it meant that he was saving up
for something special. 'Snake-hearted bastard!' she spat.

The lobby was spacious, flavourlessly modernist and empty.
The stand-up ashtrays were empty, and the continent-shaped
patches of fading damp on the tiled floor testified to the
fairly recent presence of the after-hours cleaners. There was
a revolving door cylinder, but Anne chose to push against one
of the sets of conventional swing doors. That seemed less risky.
She stepped outside. The swing doors swished shut behind her,
sucking back the bubble of warmth that had been protecting
her.

Back in the night, it was bloody cold. Her breath frosted
around her in a cloud, and she pushed her ungloved hands
into her coat pockets before the chill bit into her fingers. She
was on a flat expanse of concrete twenty feet off the ground.
Wide, apparently free-floating slabs stepped downward from
either end of the terrace. Beneath her was a shallow, well-lit

pond. The dirty blue bottom was covered by yard-round scallops of coconut glacé. Ice hung off the tricorn fountains like drapes of frozen tripe.

She knew exactly where she was, for the first time since . . . Since when? New York, New Orleans, Sam's Bar-B-Q and Grill, the tube train, the station, Soho, Amelia Dorf's house, the taxi, Soho again, Nina's flat, the Club Des Esseintes, the Nellie Dean, Cam's hotel, the hospital, her flat, her bed? When this was over, where would she be? In bed, waiting to be woken up by Inspector Hollis' phone call? Or in Skinner, waiting to be conjured back into some kind of half-life?

Right now, she was on the plaza outside Centre Point. The reinforced concrete and glass erection stabbing the empty sky above her was at the intersection of Charing Cross Road, Oxford Street, Tottenham Court Road and New Oxford Street. From where she was, she could see the large yellow flag outside Foyle's, the famous bookshop where she had always found it impossible to find anything. The view was all very detailed and realistic.

She had heard that most of Centre Point was untenanted, because London W1 rents were too high for even the wealthiest businesses. There was, or perhaps had been, a hostel for the homeless on one of the floors. For her, the white elephant was one of the city's best investments. When she had first come to London, it was the first useful landmark to impress itself upon her – unlike most touristy places, it was in the middle of the area where most of her business meetings had to take place – and she still used it often as a point of reference when in the centre of town. Furthermore, it was perched on top of the tube station she had to use most often, and the 134 bus, which went right past her flat, terminated underneath it.

The familiarity was not comforting, although she knew that she had something to do with the selection and recreation of this particular plot as part of the Dream. It must be about four o'clock in the morning, after the departure of the latest of the late night people and before the arrival of the earliest of the early morning men. A single car circled the building and vanished into a side street, carefully negotiating a one-way system designed to cope with the heaviest traffic in the country even though it made incredibly complicated the process of making a simple right turn.

Everything was given a pale blue illumination by the street lighting. A few Christmas displays winked. It all looked real, but Anne knew better by now.

She looked up at the building, trying to read an expression on its long tall face. She thought she could make out a gameshow host grin, barracuda-toothed and insincere. Skinner's eyes were somewhere up there. She smiled herself as she backed away, realising the mistake. Somehow, Centre Point had wound up with the Empire State Building's dirigible mooring mast.

'When does the gorilla show up, old man?'

A venomous frost had spread like lichen across many of the upper windows. A sheet of ice the size of a large Vermeer detached itself and slid free. Anne's heart clutched like a fist as the glassy mass shattered ten feet away from her. Cracked ice spread towards her shoes like a flood of marbles. Skinner was reminding her to keep running.

She hit the steps and got off the plaza. The usually impossible intersection was easy to cross against the lights. The car, a boxy '30s model, had gone. There were no people at all in sight, which proved she was still in Skinner's wonderland. Even in the deadest of the dead hours, this place was populated. Not as thickly as nearby Soho or the West End clubland, perhaps, but these were still 24-hour streets.

So, what next?

Running had done her no good so far, but she was getting the idea that it was expected of her. Putting up a stiff resistance might not help her win, but it got her a few bonus points. However, she also knew that nothing was going to persuade Skinner to let her off the forfeits. She even got the feeling that the more she inconvenienced him in the short term, the more he would get out of feeding off her in the end.

Feeding off her? What exactly did that mean? Doubtless, something unbelievably nasty.

Of the four main avenues, she chose Oxford Street. She started to walk towards Marble Arch, then turned left, heading back into Soho. The place seemed to be in the middle of this business. It was like Skinner's secret lair. Somewhere in the vice heart of town, the Monster was waiting for her.

She had no crucifix or wooden stake or pistol-load of silver bullets or flaming torch or hammer and sickle or bell, book and candle. That stuff would have comforted her less than an M-16, or one of those skeleton-handled Uzi sub-machine guns, or an anti-personnel rocket launcher. Preferably, she would like the Air Force to lay down some pretty heavy napalm around Skinner, then send in the Green Berets led by John Wayne, Sylvester Stallone, Arnold Schwarzenegger, the Incredible Hulk and Godzilla. After that, and only after that, she would ask the President to fall back on their country's thermonuclear resources. Even then, she figured her chances at about twenty-eighty against. All she was going into Hell with was her mind. Christ, that had better be enough . . . .

Gradually, she became aware of the ghosts. Not used to them, exactly, but alert to their presence. She had them pegged as a sideshow, and did not want to expend any energy worrying about that sort of thing. She would need everything for the Main Event. They were in shadows, behind shop windows, in pedestrian subways, congregated in car parks. She did not want to look too closely, half-aware that concentrating on them would give them more substance. Then, they might get in her way. So far, they were not bothering her like the things on the train had, but they could easily be provoked.

In a lamp halo, standing at a shelterless bus stop, she found a man from the past, dressed in a white tropical suit and panama hat out of *A Night in Casablanca*. He had spats, and a wing collar, knife-edge trouser pleats, and no face. The cigarette in his holder was burning to ash without any help from him. He had no mouth, so there was no point to his habit. Otherwise, he was placid and unfrightening.

Likewise, the gaggle of gypsies in Soho Square, huddled under the eaves of the gardener's hut, nursing their wind-whipped fires, quaking with superstitious fear. Their horses whinnied and shifted between the shafts of their gingerbread-decorated caravans. They made signs at her like Transylvanian peasants in a Dracula movie, warning her not to go to Borgo Pass on Walpurgis Night. Were they trying to help her? Grandfather Nastase, dead long before her birth, had been from the Carpathians. Or was she being misled? She waved to them, trying to be jaunty, and kept on walking.

The next apparitions, which she encountered in a passage between Dean Street and Wardour Street, were a little more hostile. She was only a few doors away from the place where Nina's flat had been when two men in vaguely piratical costumes stepped out. Had they been visiting Tina – Teenage Model One Flight Up – or just waiting to ambush her? They had headscarves, baggy pants and cutlasses. One of them touched a cigarette lighter's flame to the oiled and pleated ends of his beard and moustache, setting them to burn slowly. They snarled and showed their claws like threatened cats, but stayed away from her.

The samurai in Wardour Street was not so timid, and his sword was definitely nor ornamental. He waved the three-foot razor within an inch of her face, slicing loudly through the cold-thickened air. He yelled, and made a series of dazzling passes in front of her, like Sergeant Troy in *Far From the Madding Crowd*. She had no doubt that he could have chopped her thin like salami if he had been allowed to. She stood still as a mannequin, flinching only when the flashing light from the sword got in her eyes. He was a dirty, pockmarked man with bad teeth and an elaborate topknot. Like the other ghosts, he was a bit faint; not see-through exactly, but a little lighter than a living person ought to be.

'Tell me, Toshiro, how much of your life can you call your own?'

He seized up in mid-slice, stared into her face as if pondering the question, and relaxed out of his stance. His sword drooped, and became a bow handle as its point pressed the ground. In a fluid move, he sheathed his weapon, saluted her, and was running off. His sandals flapped against the sidewalk. He turned right at the end of the passage, and was gone. Behind him, he had left a perfect white camellia. She picked it up and found that it was a paper thing that came apart in her hands. He really had looked like Toshiro Mifune.

'I suppose that was supposed to be a warning, old man,' she said aloud, as if addressing a God who was hard-of-hearing. 'Go no further, right? Well, I think you're bluffing. I figure all this shit is putting a strain on you. I reckon you're slipping. . . .'

She walked Southwards, deeper into Soho, towards the lights.

'. . . those last couple were pathetic, Skinner. Not your standard at all. If you watch too many old movies, you cripple your imagination. Yours is gone, old man, atrophied. You're hobbling right now. . .'

A sign above a closed sex shop on the other side of the street came on: YOU WISH, ANNE, YOU WISH.

She turned to the storefront – a modest expanse of crushed red velvet littered with lacy corsets and studded leather – and talked back to the sign.

'. . . and wishing makes it so, right? Piss on that, old man. This is my dream too, and I can wish you out of it.'

The bulbs darked and came on again in a different pattern, in different colours. I WON'T BE A BEDPOST FOR YOU, ANNE.

She got it at once.

'Very seasonal, old man. But that doesn't win you any gold stars. Even I've read *A Christmas Carol*. Here's one for you: you're nothing but a piece of undigested beef!'

A pause, then: ANGELA, WHERE'S JOHNNY?

'You still playing that game? I'm out of that forever, and you know it. You haven't got one tenth the creativity my Dad has, you can't do a sequel to *On the Graveyard Shift*. That's like Harold Robbins writing *The Brothers Karamazov Ride Again*.'

ANGELA.

'There is no Angela any more. Just me, Anne. . . .'

ANGELA, SAM'S DEAD.

'Dead and in a play, Skinner. That doesn't count.'

ANNE, YOUR FATHER IS DEAD.

She did not let him hear the sob in the back of her throat. She swallowed it, and went on. 'I know. I suppose you want the credit, old man. It wasn't you. It was just old age. You ought to know something about that. How are the arteries, then? Hardening nicely? How many more skins can you get rid of before there's nothing left of you?'

ANNE, I'M FOREVER.

'Like Hell . . .'

YES, LIKE HELL.

He took her from behind, like they had trained him to take North Korean soldiers. Armlock around the neck, punch to the kidney. She turned in his grip, so the blow thumped into her spine. It hurt, but did not make her crumple like a Raggedy Ann doll. She tried to get a knee round to slam into his groin, but she could not turn that far. Hot breath condensed on the back of her neck and in her hair.

It was Johnny, of course. He did not look like the Martin Landau of *On the Graveyard Shift*. This was a post-*Mission: Impossible* caricature, with an overemphasized satanic cast to its features. Landau was made up as Johnny turning into a demon. He had reptile eyes, several rows of tiny teeth and a lashing adder's fork. He nuzzled her, licking her cheek with the wet, sandpapery tongue.

'Angel, Angel,' he slobbered, 'never leave me again . . .'

She pincered her elbows behind her, as if doing the Turkey Trot, and slammed into his ribs. It did not do much good. He did not have a proper hold on her anymore, but she was not free either. He let go her neck and grabbed her elbows.

'Angel, let's get back together . . .'

'No way, Skinner. That's all over!'

She knew what to do now. She brought her knee up towards her stomach, tensed her thigh and belly, and smashed her heel down on the thing's instep. It yowled in agony and let go of her. She whirled away from him, turning to face him. The rubbery thing was hopping comically, holding its throbbing foot like Deputy Dawg (*'oh my toe bone!'*) and spitting wildly. Maliciously, she stepped forwards and stamped on the other foot. It took a few tries, as the thing dodged her shoes, but she got it in the end. It screamed again, and went down on its knees. Johnny was a liquid image for a moment, held together by a soap-bubble skin. Then, it collapsed on the pavement, and ran through the cracks between the paving stones. Not even clothes were left. Only a set of Korean War issue US Army dogtags.

Breathless, laughing, hurting inside, Anne shouted, 'hah! That wasn't even a nice *try*, Skinner. Give up and go home!'

The next one was just *sick*. It was Clive, dead, hanging in an old-fashioned red telephone box. Up close, she realised he was not suspended, he was floating. The box was full of something as thick as milk, but as transparent as water. An eerie light filtered down through the liquid. The body gently shifted. The jacket was spread out like folds of skin and muscle during open-heart surgery. By Clive's ankles, the telephone receiver floated like a too-light anchor.

His neck was ripped open, as it had been the last time she saw him alive, and there was a dark stain on his torn shirt. The liquid and the distilled light rendered him in black and white, but she could tell it was blood on Clive's shirt. His face had shrunken onto his skull, and then been bloated by the water. The result was not normality.

Clive opened his dead-as-coins eyes, and tried to outstare her. Like Johnny, he was horribly funny. She would have left him to pickle, but she wanted to see what came next. After all, in his position, what could he *do* to hurt her? He was moving now. It must have been an effort to bring those arms down, fighting against the thick liquid and clogged clothes, especially considering that he was dead in the first place. His mouth was like a goldfish's, opening and closing. The wound in his neck pulsed like a sphincter. It was either a makeshift gill or a revolutionary new design for an asshole.

His swollen palms flattened against glass panels, and his back wedged against the other side of the box. He looked angry, although his lips had been soaked too long to be able to recede over his teeth in a snarl. It was not funny any more. A shoe scrabbled against one of the lower panels. Then, he started to exert some pressure, bending and straightening his body as best he could. He was still quite strong.

She got out of the way. The door came open. For an instant, the mass of liquid retained the shape of the telephone box. Surface tension or something, she supposed. But even in this world, there was no miniscus that could do the job of a plate glass fishtank. The level of water fell, and a torrent emerged from the lower quarter of the box. It spread into the street. The Clive Thing came out in a sitting position, and landed on his ass. He did not flap like a fish. Words and water spouted from his mouth and neck.

'You cunt, you cunt, you cunt, you're going to die, you . . .'

He pushed against the paving stones and launched himself upright, then stumbled for her, arms outstretched. His sleeves were splitting at the seams as his arms pulsed and grew. She backed away from him. His fingers were winding together, making a point, the nails fusing into a needle-barb. His hands were becoming obscene organic syringes.

'You cunt, you cuntface bitch, you know you want it, you know you neeeeed it. . . .'

His jacket burst at the armpits, and swelling sacs, rough-skinned with sparse hairs, descended. His arms were transparent now, a spiral tracery of clear plastic veins laid around the white bones, bunching together at the wrists.

He was frothing purple at the mouth. His underarm testicles pulsated, spurting fluid into his arm-tubes.

Anne knew what it would be. Nina had shot him fully of it. It would probably be high-grade, unpolluted heroin. The best death money could buy.

'The first jab,' he said, his words distorted by his misshapen mouth, 'is free.'

A pearl of smoky white liquid grew at the tip of his right syringe, and dribbled down the glans-like swelling that had been his hand.

'The rest, you have to pay for.'

She ducked under his thrust, and punched away his second, left-handed, attack.

'Hey, cunt, want to go to a club,' he said, 'and see some damage done. . . .'

He was awkward, finding it difficult to move. He was full of heroin now, bursting to get rid of it. He shot a jet in an arc, and it splattered against the window of a stylish fashion shop, dripping like soapy water. The veins in his neck were throbbing purple, and water was still pouring out of his clothes.

She wrenched a waste-bin off a lamp-post, and held it in front of her, blocking his darting syringe stabs.

She threw the bin at him, and dented his forehead. He slipped, his heels working against the wet sidewalk, making scuffmarks. Overbalanced, he went down again. His left arm shattered like a dropped glass, and he screamed as brown-streaked fluid exploded out of him.

She took a careful, malicious, aim and kicked the sac under his right arm, feeling the satisfying give of weak flesh under her toepoint. The Clive Thing's screech cut through the cold night and filled her ears with his pain. He writhed, falling apart in the slippery mess. She got her foot under the thing, and easily rolled it over onto its stomach. He moved as if attempting the breast stroke, his ruined left arm flapping. She brought one of her killer feet down on his spine, snapping it in several places. The crack was like a rifle shot.

She walked away. The Clive Thing tried to swim/crawl after her, dragging its sodden lower limbs. It gave up quickly. When she looked back, it was just a man-shaped smear on the road, kicking feebly.

She was in Old Compton Street now, but not the Old Compton Street she had been in that afternoon. And she knew she was hurting him.

The city was less realistic now. The sky above was solid black, like a tent canopy, and the street was closed off at either end like a film set. Most of the buildings were probably false fronts or backdrops. Patisserie Valerie was painted on loose-hanging canvas, not very well, as if it were supposed to register as realistic from the back of the Royal Circle rather than up close. It had been painted for the daytime, with frozen patrons clogging the place and white and red pastries in the windows, and looked wrong in this night scene. The dream was fraying around the edges.

She brushed by a pillar box, and stopped to examine it. The thing had not felt right. The slot for letters was a strip of black pasted onto the red. There was a poster for a rock gig slapped on the side of the box, but it did not have real writing on it, just a series of squiggles. The whole thing was as soft as a pencil eraser. Soon it would be foam rubber, then gelatine, then ice cream, then candyfloss. Then, just a smudge.

'I think you're spread too thin, Skinner. You're rushing things, getting careless. It's time to turn in, old man, time to go to sleep. . . .'

Another set of lights came on, above an amusement arcade this time.

I'LL GET YOU YET, MY PRETTY.

'Uh huh? You wish, old man, you wish!'

fourteen

IN HER DREAM, Judi was being neglected.
   She did not know where she was exactly, but it looked mainly like her father's house in New Hampshire, although her room was like the bedroom of the flat she shared with Coral in the Elephant and Castle. Looking at the walls, covered with pinned-up pictures and news items from magazines and papers, she saw a collage of her entire life. There were a few posters from her brief infatuation – now a shameful, much-suppressed memory – with John Travolta in the era of *Saturday Night Fever*, and an overlapping series of book-covers, neatly torn from paperbacks like hunter's trophies, marking her absorption of the matter that had been in the volume. Then, there were magazine illustrations that had caught her fancy at some time in her life – the craggy face of W.H. Auden in black and white, socialites in bow ties grinning in nightclubs, a *Spitting Image* Ronald Reagan as Rambo, a pleasure boat sunk in the Thames, a poster for *Blue Velvet*. There was Cam at a concert, Clive shaking hands with the Prime Minister, Anne trying to get an answer out of a police constable who did not want to be interviewed, her mother and William Conrad in a TV movie, her father in Stockholm accepting his damned prize.
   There were other people in the house, but they did not see it as she did. They had their own Dreams. Some of the other ghosts she had known in life. Jeane Russell, who had been a professional swimmer, came in wearing a navy blue one-piece bathing suit, her dark hair dripping. She was friendly, but offhand, refusing to acknowledge that this was not normal. She had a gymnasium somewhere, and was

obsessively working on her body. In her father's study, among the comforting books and signed photographs, she found Coral, one arm stiff at her side, her free hand clamped over her eyes. Judi could not communicate with her either. In the music room, she found Cam, whistling tunelessly. Clive had drifted past once or twice, and tried to catch her attention, but he was strangely shrunken – perfectly-proportioned but only three feet tall, wearing a miniature version of one of his usual smart suits. She was tempted to hit him, but let it go.

On the front lawn, where the children had been allowed to play croquet only if they promised not to argue and always ended up in tearful fights, Judi found Amelia Dorf, a used-up husk in a line of similar remains, some of them dressed in the style of remote historical periods.

There was one ghost who frightened Judi, and who would occasionally loiter around. She was called Giselle and seemed to be a lost little girl, but her face was ancient. She could usually be found on the lawn, playing with the remnants, crooning madly to herself. She was spiteful, and could pinch and nip if she got close enough. Feelings were deadened in the Dream, but there was still pain.

The Dream did not extend far beyond the boundaries of the Nielson property. Judi would sometimes sit in the driveway and look out into the white mists that hung immobile just a few yards down the drive. The road disappeared into them, and the hedges just faded out. Nothing came out of the limbo, and no one ever ventured into it. But Judi knew that, just beyond sight, there was someone. A woman, young and strong, with nearly white hair. She was not in the Dream, but she could tune into the dead channel if she chose. A name formed in her mind: Ariadne. It was a seductive name. She rolled its syllables around her mouth, imagining the name's owner.

Judi tried to remember the village as it had been when she had been living at home. She and Anne, blessed and cursed with the sophistication due to the offspring of the smart and famous, had never had much to do with the local kids. They had had a private name for them, the stupids.

There had been a point in her life when Judi would have done anything to be a stupid. But you cannot unlearn anything, cannot regurgitate knowledge, experience and aptitudes like an undigested meal. Still, she had tried hard.

She wondered what had happened to Trey, the 19-year-old bar-helper she had gone with when she was fourteen. He had been a major stupid. His idea of success was becoming a cop or a rock singer. His first ambition had been out because of his string of juvie beefs, and he had dumped her, after a beating, when she had told him he could never make it in music because he was too white.

Most of the time, it was just boring. She tried the television and the radio, but could only get dead static. The appliances all worked, but the records in their perfect sleeves were all smooth and uncut. She realised that she had read all the books in the house, and wondered if this was hell . . . .

Sometimes, she was let out. Skinner put her to sleep and woke her up somewhere else, to have her appear to some-one . . . .

She could still remember the subway train, and Anne.

But most of the time she was left on her own, to her own devices. She lay in her bed, and tried to practise total recall, seeing how much of her life she could put together in perspective.

She thought a lot about Anne. She wished she had tried harder to get on with her sister, had tried harder not to disrupt the already shaky peace of the family. With a father who was a walking open wound, a mother who flitted by on occasional whims and a half-brother who wandered about like an army officer in a POW camp, thinking only of his hidden escape tunnel and an eventual release, the Nielsons had not been anything like the families she remembered on television, *The Brady Bunch, The Partridge Family, The Waltons* . . . .

She had never had a chance with Cam, but she could have had a real relationship with Anne. But now, it was too late . . . .

At first, she had been sure she was dead. Now, she knew better. Her body was dead, but she was still around, as part of the Dream. The Dream was somewhere out of space and time, carried around in Skinner and yet immeasurably vaster than him. It was possible to die out of the Dream – Amelia and the corpses proved that – and she sometimes wondered whether she should try to finish herself off and get it over with.

There were already enough zombies in her family.

She could not do it, though. Even at her lowest, she had never wanted just to die.

Remembering, she found more lows than she would have liked. There was a temptation to dwell only on the better moments, but the lows were as much a part of the pattern, and she felt obliged to summon them up.

She did not know whether she had been conscious when Skinner killed Coral, but she saw it replayed over and again as if she had been. Of course, Coral had been there, and Amelia and Clive had been involved. Perhaps Judi could now sample the memories of everyone in the Dream. It had been upstairs in Amelia's house, in one of the old bedrooms, with the two-way mirror on the wall. Even Amelia had been shocked, and had run for her cocaine stash as a way of handling it. After Coral, came Judi. She remembered the Monster feeding off her, remembered the bursting of her own heart, remembered the struggle that had come afterwards. Skinner had called in Clive to handle the bodies, and from him Judi could see herself propped up in a Soho alley in the early hours, swiftly dumped like a bundle of newspapers for collection. Coral was buried deeper, on a rubbish dump in some to-be-redeveloped wasteland.

Eventually, she went out onto the croquet lawn and found what was left of Coral, her arm separate from her, lying with Amelia and the others. Giselle was sitting next to her, breaking her fingers, trying to feed off the girl but tasting only dry ashes which made her sick. Giselle coughed up grey matter, and crawled away, disgusted. Judi touched Coral, and the remains fell apart completely. The girl was gone. So, it was possible to die more. She wondered if she would miss Coral.

The girl had been fun. Once, giggly drunk in the flat and surprised at themselves, they had made love. It had been pleasant, but they had never repeated the experiment. Very few of Judi's good memories had to do with sex or love, and so that once was precious. She had never really enjoyed hurting or giving hurt, but that was the way it had all too often worked out.

She slept and ate, or at least pretended to, and changed her clothes regularly. She had a lot of clothes. Everything she had ever owned was in the house, and it all, back to her smallest baby-dresses, still fitted her.

She learned the names of some of the other ghosts. She had long conversations with an Irishman named Niall Baum who thought he was in a Dublin boarding house in the 1870s, and learned from him a little more about the Monster. From him she learned that Giselle was of the Monster's kind, and that she had been his wife – a thing beyond imagining – until an end was put to her. Too many of the others spoke and thought only in languages she had no way of understanding.

Bored, she tried to kiss Niall, and he disappeared. She felt strange after that, and could remember Shanghai, a series of explosions, and a bloody struggle in a temple in the hills. She felt some of her fuzziness disappear, and was not sure what had happened.

The ghosts were becoming fewer in number, and she was feeling more solid. It took her a while to realise that she was taking them all into herself. It was bizarre, not entirely comfortable, and – she suspected – dangerous.

How could she hope to stay Judi if she were taking all these others on board?

She could understand Mandarin now, and Turkish and mediaeval French, and other useless tongues. She had died in battles from before the time of Christ down to Khe Sanh, and in numberless squalid, fundamentally unchanging, beds down through the centuries. She felt especially close to Macha Igescu, who had died for the first time in Istanbul in 1938; they had both been whores, both been wasted in a city across the sea from the land of their birth, had both excited and

touched the Monster. . . . Digging deep, she was surprised to
discover a thinned relationship: Macha's cousin in Bucharest
had been married to a Nastase whose uncle had emigrated to
America and changed his name to Nielson.

Judi had seen the Clive ghost with a similarly shrunken
young man, whose perfumed curls and thin greased moustache made him a childish dandy, and learned from Macha that
this was Demetrios, who had been her pimp and protector.
After feeding off her, the Monster had killed Demetrios as a
favour. It was one of his many capricious gestures.

Eventually, Nina Kenyon turned up. She was wearing torn
clothes, and her make-up had streaked. Judi was glad to see
her, and they hugged.

'Judi,' the other girl said, 'I'm so tired.'

'Sleep, then.'

'I will.'

Judi stroked Nina's hair, and the frail ghost became faint
in her embrace. Macha joined them, more hair, more hands,
and Judi felt the Roumanian girl's cheek sinking through her
own.

Suddenly, she was alone, remembering Coral smoking at
school and a boat trip across the Bosphorus.

She was still Judi, but she was Nina and Macha too.

She saw Clive and Demetrios, but they were the size of
housecats, and scurried away.

She remembered shaving her head, surrounded by religious
relics, and vowing to bring down the King of the Cats.

Then, she knew that was Niall Baum's memory.

As an experiment, she seduced a ghost. A tiny Indian girl
with an elaborate pearl ornament shaped like a snail's shell in
one nostril. Judi took her, and absorbed her. There was a rush
of unfamiliar experience, and a sense of gratitude at being no
longer alone. Kanchi was by far the oldest of the ghosts she
had come across, and Judi was startled by the vividness of her
memories.

The Monster, whom she thought of as Guillaume of
Oswestry, had accepted her in marriage as a gift, and fed
off her a little at a time over a period of months. There was

nothing in Kanchi's experience which jibed with any history Judi knew, and so she could not even guess how long the girl had been a ghost.

The house changed with each of her absorptions. She found new rooms, fabulously unfamiliar and yet homely. She lived memories, fantasies and illusions. The Dream expanded, the mists receding, and the New Hampshire house became a higgledy-piggledy palace.

She collected ghosts, absorbed and became them all. She swam with Jeane Russell, and was exhilarated by the self-image of a healthy, perfectly-tuned body. She fought with Stefan Snieszawski, and was astounded by her sword-wielding courage in battle. She crept up on Cam and finally put things right between them, absorbing him gently. She was surprised at what she found within her half-brother, and a little shamed by his turbulent depths.

From Nina, Judi learned about Anne. She saw, and was delighted by, her sister in the Club Des Esseintes, hitting Eric Wardle with a chair. It was strange, as Anne threaded herself into pictures Judi knew intimately but could not associate with her sister. Here was Anne in the Club, in Nina's flat, at one of Amelia's 'entertainments' . . . .

She found a dried-up doll on the lawn, and knew that it was both Clive and Demetrios Malacou, gone forever. They resembled a pickled set of Siamese twins in a freak show. She tried to suck them in, but there was nothing left.

She was almost alone in the Dream. She was all the ghosts in one. She remembered being Niall Baum, Kanchi, Nina, Macha Igescu, Cam, and the others, but she was still herself, still Judi.

Giselle hid from her, but she saw her handiwork everywhere. Rooms were vandalised, and the remains violated.

Finally, on the lawn, she caught the ancient little girl and, shutting her ears to the shrieked pleas, ate her all up.

As Giselle gave up the struggle, Judi felt a sudden vertigo. The palace, the lawn, the mists beyond. They all collapsed, leaving only a limitless darkness.

Judi was the Dream.

fifteen

THE CLUB DES ESSEINTES was not hidden now. A fiery, twisted sign burned above the window of the nostalgia shop, casting a hellish glow on the display of comics. All the covers stuck to a formula – the superhero in trouble. There was Superman OD'd on Kryptonite, Iron Man rusting away to nothing, Swamp Thing falling victim to a Deep South drainage and reclamation scheme, the X-Men Xed out by the League of Evil Mutants. Anne knew that, in the end, these super-guys would win. She was not super, but she was in trouble, and she thought that she could win too. She had to think that. She had to.

The amusement arcade next door was a joke, with clanking, clattering and bleeping sound effects but no moving parts. Crude tailor's dummies posed over the pinball tables and video games, their stiff hands unfit for the tasks they were supposed to be performing. The music was wrong too – big band jazz, not hip-hop loudness. Skinner was giving up on the street.

He was in the Club Des Esseintes, and he wanted her to come for him. Fair enough. Then, he would not have to bother dreaming the city properly. They would have it out, and one of them could go home to sleep. Anne was tired, but she would be okay for the big finale. She was sure.

The nostalgia shop was locked up, the sign on the door said 'open'. So in she went, knowing the way now. The shop was empty of people, but there was a whirring and clicking in one corner. The collection of Japanese warrior robots was swinging into action. Eyes flicked on and off, mighty plastic arms lifted, jet planes became miniature android colossi, death rays warmed up. She took a light sabre from a *Star Wars* display and swept the robots off their stand. Designed to take the aggressive play of even the most creatively destructive child, the robots were unharmed and dangerous.

She stamped on a hawk-faced humanoid with buzz-saw bracelets. She had been doing a lot of damage with her feet recently. This time, all she did was hurt her ankle. One of the little bastards pinched her calf with blunt metal claws. She kicked it away. The plastic light sabre was proving useless, so she exchanged it for the centrepiece of a display promoting a video-only splatter movie, *The Cincinatti Flamethrower Holocaust*.

She wished it were for real, and so it was. She adjusted the nozzle like the one on the weedkiller spray back home in New Hampshire, and turned the flames on. A spurt of fire came out of the hose attachment. She swept the flame in a scythe-swath in front of her, aiming low. The robots went up instantly, and fell aside. They became little mounds of bubbling plastic and twisted tin. The stench was ghastly. The fire spread to some early *Howard the Duck*s, and died out suddenly. She dropped the toy on the floor, and stepped over the burned patch.

The spiral staircase was still there. The burning smells were stronger, and some were coming up from below. She had never come across brimstone, but this was what she would have guessed it was like. Also, there were waves of heat coming up from the Club.

She went downstairs.

The corridor was the same as it had been this morning, but the portrait frames on the wall were untenanted, containing either sheets of blank coloured canvas or meticulously dull paintings of chairs and curtains. She expected that the Marquis de Sade and his intimate friends were wandering around.

There was no execioner-suited bouncer guarding the doors. Eric must only work the day shift. She was glad of that. He would have been sure to remember her and hold a grudge. This time, the musak was reworking an old Everly Brothers song, 'Love Hurts'.

Again, she went into the Inferno Lounge. Inside, it was Hell.

sixteen

IN THE PLACE that had been the Inferno Lounge, but was now simply an Inferno, he waited for her. He had put her image up on the television monitors, and watched her coming for him. In his freshly-stolen youth, he was impatient for it all to be over. The expectation of pleasure coursed through his body. There was an electric tingling in his venom glands, in the flesh under his fingernails and in the tip of his penis. All the self-control he had learned was needed now. His mind kept his body on straining leashes.

The change had made him himself again, but he would have to discharge some of his surplus energy before the build-up literally tore him apart. He watched Anne on the monitors. The ghosts he had sent after her, to signpost the way to his lair, were pussycats compared with the ghosts forming in the red shadows of this room. He cheered and hooted as she overcame the weaklings he put in her way. He was glad to lose them. Once out of Anne's sight, he knew they would cease clinging to existence. They were gone forever. He sensed her growing confidence in her ability to survive this game, and the muscles in his arms spasmed in delight. She would be a feast, an unparalleled feast.

Although he was paying most attention to the monitors, he had other things to take care of. With a splurge of raw thought, he reshaped his environment, tearing down and building upon the banal Dante-and-Bosch conception of Hell that had been fostered by the decorators of the Club Des Esseintes. In the murals, damned souls began to wriggle in their torment, snake-tongued devils prodded them with tridents, vats of blood and excrement came to the boil, the

Vices cavorted in a sinful jubilee. Every scream he had ever heard was replayed in a choral symphony of terror that Anne's brother would have sold his soul to have written. At the bar, a former Pope of the Black Church set up a line of fire and ice cocktails.

The best of his ghosts were with still him, the ones who had been as vital as Anne, the ones who had kept him alive well into his third millennium. Judi was there, and the three from China, and those who had come against him earlier. They had given him a hard time once, but they were his now, his utterly, to do with as he wished.

He called Judi out of the Dream, and bound her with fire. Surprised at the strength he still sensed in her, he threaded iron through the fire to make sure. She rattled her manacles, but was held fast.

Manacles would have many memories for her, he was sure.

He fashioned a throne of twisted corpses from the mural, and sat regally upon it. His ghosts stood like attendants. On the screens, Anne burned a horde of dolls. He liked playing the Devil, but it was just a game.

'I'm just a thing of nature, like you,' he told his unlistening ghosts. 'I'm no more the Devil than an alligator or a trap-door spider is. All this . . .' he gestured to the fiery lakes and the infernal landscapes '. . . is your Dream. I'm only borrowing it for a while.'

Anne was outside now, in the corridor. Her television image flickered with its soon-to-be-released ghost. How sad, he thought, that she would never appreciate how special she was. At least, not until she had lost the qualities that made her so.

Anne came into the Inferno Lounge. The doors banged behind her, and became a part of the gargoyle-sprouting rock wall.

'Gotcha!' he shouted.

seventeen

A T THE CENTRE of his Pit, he was sprawled casually in a high-backed chair wrought from a tangle of living limbs and torsos. Bones had been broken and reset during its manufacture, and the component people still suffered the pains. A face stared out from between his elegant ankles, silently screaming. Its eyeballs burst like lanced boils, spattering the backs of his trousers with steaming humours. Skinner did not mind. He could walk through a downpour of burning filth and stay as well-turned out as Fred Astaire. To her surprise, he had some of Astaire's loose-limbed vitality. Even as he relaxed, she could see the agility and expertise of his movements. He was younger than she had ever seen him, but the youth of his body was coupled with the skills and experience of an immortal genius. The ridges of his multiply-healed scars lit up like orange neon veins under his skin. He was laughing at her. It was the least human sound she had ever heard. In this light, his hundreds of teeth were ruby-red and shark-sharp.

She did not believe in the Devil, she did not believe in the Devil, she did not believe in the Devil . . .

'My world, and welcome to it, Anne.'

. . . but the Devil believed in her.

'You look like a dream,' he purred.

Standing behind his throne like Satan's lady-in-waiting was Judi. She was whole again, and wholly his creature, wrapped in chains. He held out a hand, palm up. She took it, and stroked it, the links of her handcuffs polished and shining. Her studs and chains and zippers held a million reflected fires. Her face was as dead and beautiful as that of a make-up-masked magazine model.

As usual, Anne could expect no help from her sister.

She stepped towards him, fingers hooked into claws. She was going to open his face like a pair of thick curtains. She did not get very far.

She could not see them, but they came from everywhere – out of the walls, swimming up through a floor that was solid to her but liquid to them, from under the Club Des Esseintes' bolted-down tables, out from their perches on ceiling fans and light fixtures. Horny hands grabbed her, and held her like leather straps. Her elbows, hands, knees, feet, hips, neck and head were held fast. She was forced to look ahead, at Skinner. Something with damp fingers was pulling her hair. Something with fingertips that stung like nettles had a hand in her clothes, and was painfully tickling her stomach, circling her navel with mosquito bites. Barely audible obscenities were cooed into her ear.

This, she knew, was nothing.

Skinner got out of his throne, and strolled towards her. He did not dance, but his walk had the pantherlike litheness of the very best professional golfers. He put his huge face near hers. Clamped down, unable to look anywhere but into his eyes, at his teeth or up his nose, she felt like the victim of skilfully sadistic dentist. If she looked to her extreme left, rolling her eyes so far that her optic muscles ached, she could see a black and red blur. Judi was standing back, watching the operation without interest, like a dental assistant who has seen all the bridgework she ever wants to but knows that she has a better job than all her friends who are waitresses.

He did not need a drill or a probe or a hammer and chisel. He extended an impossibly long finger and began to trace lines on her face. When the tip came near her mouth, she clenched her teeth, determined to resist any oral rape. Even when the sheathed but sharp nail caressed the soft swell of her eyelids, she kept her eyes open, looking fixedly up at him. His breath was sweet, like cinnamon. There was something about him that reminded her of every lover she had ever had.

He unconsciously licked his lips, and kept on touching her face. She knew he was getting off on it somehow. Unusual little muscles in his throat, cheeks and temples were twitching slightly. He had closed his eyes, and was transported with pleasure. She felt the fight going out of her, as if it were draining into him through pinprick pores that opened wherever his fingernail pressed.

Not pinned down, but embraced. Not dying, but living. She wanted to go to sleep.

Her face cooled as he massaged it. She relaxed, became absurdly comfortable. The stinging on her stomach faded away. All sensations went away . . .

. . . she dreamed she was floating in a warm sea, endowed with a painless buoyancy. Only her face was above water, and gentle waves broke on her chin. Anemones brushed her heels as she drifted away from the shore with the tide. There were clouds high above her, and circling seabirds. She knew she would have to make one last effort, take one last breath, and then propel herself downwards, through fathoms of clear, sun-filtering water. Only at the bottom of the sea could she sleep.

Then Skinner took a fold of skin under the hinge of her jaw between his thumb and forefinger. He pinched hard, twisting the flesh deftly, and a network of painways came alive in the lower left quarter of her face. Nerves in her cheek flared and died like fuse wire. Half her teeth became explosions of pain.

. . . she dreamed that the Monster who was always coming after her, coming to get her, had at last caught up with her and was at last getting her. *Getting* was something worse than she had ever dreamed.

'. . . and that was just a playful touch, dear. Nothing special. There's more.'

Next, he sliced through her sleeve and pressed somewhere in the socket of her shoulder. Her arm jumped like a galvanised frog's leg, twisting free of the hands that held it down. She tried to make a fist, but could not. The arm hung limp, put out of action by an instant's agony.

'This is foreplay?'

'Oh no,'said Skinner, 'this is an aperitif.'

She would have spat in his face, but there was no water in her mouth, no strength in her lips.

'You don't know how much you mean to me, Anne, how much you're going to give me.'

He kissed her on the mouth. She felt the outlines of his teeth behind the press of his thin lips.

He was holding her all by himself now. The other presences were gone, drawn back into their master. She felt a cool, slim hand take her own, the hand that still flapped like a skewered starfish from Skinner's nerve press.

It was Judi.

'Now I've got you here,' he was saying 'I almost wish I could prolong the moment indefinitely. It's my favourite part, you know . . .'

'Ah,' she said, 'but you can't have your cake . . .'

'. . . and eat it. I know, Anne. I know.'

Her hand was gripped tightly, sending a new charge of pain up her arm. Skinner was wrapped up in his own personal rituals.

'You're going to be my banquet, Anne. I wish I could make you understand how old and important what I am going to do to you is. Perhaps afterwards. If anything in this world is sacred . . . .'

She was weak now, dulled almost to a swoon, but when he started to do it to her, she found she still had the strength to scream.

He began to feed off her.

From deflating lungs, through a dry and shrieking throat, out of a pain-throbbing mouth, she screamed and screamed. . . .

eighteen

AT THE MONSTER'S right hand, Judi felt him feeding off her sister as he had once fed off her. She remembered her own death, and those of all the other ghosts. Innumerable times, she died, feeling life flow from a broken body, from a thousand broken bodies, into the eternally renewed substance of the Kind. It was an everlasting agony.

The Kind thought of their prey as food, sometimes as submissive lovers. But the ghosts knew different. Bleeding their life out in lumps, they were all their murderers' mothers, their screaming deaths violent and protracted labour pains. The cycle of rebirth left all the parents shadows in the Monster's Dream, but it also gave Judi a strength she found surprising.

She was more real than she had been since her death. When the Monster was feeding, he was unaware of everything else, like a man caught up in the throes of a protracted orgasm. No man can come and think of something else, Judi knew, and the Monster was at his most manlike this very moment. And while he was a lover, he was also a baby, demanding life, tearing through flesh to reach the air, suckling, sapping Anne's whole being. For the Kind, there must be deaths with each birth, with each rebirth.

There was no blood yet, but there would be soon. Anne's screams seized up in the back of her throat as she felt the monster's tendrils fixing like hooks into her mind.

Judi looked at Skinner's broad back as his head dipped towards Anne's chest, and met her sister's eyes. Anne was rigid, refusing to tremble, fighting him inside her head.

Judi remembered. They all remembered.

Judi felt Anne's mind pressing in upon her own, the sisters overlaid upon each other. Anne's ghost was forming around her as Skinner sucked her dry. Instamatic fragments of Anne's memory fell into Judi's consciousness. Amid the confusion of faces and feelings, Judi saw herself made different by an unfamiliar personality prism.

She loved her sister, and her sister loved her. At last, she knew their father had loved them both with an equal distance, an equal dread of losing them as he had lost so much else. Things between them were right, at last.

There was a streak of white zig-zagging from Anne's temple into her hair. Her eyes opened wide while her pupils contracted.

Judi and Anne met in the Dream, and found themselves handcuffed. They melted together. Their communion triangulated the Monster. He was a white hot presence, the apex of their triangle.

Judi was able to latch onto Skinner.

Skinner was enjoying his meal, relishing his fuck, exulting in his escape from the womb of womankind. Later, he might even get sentimental about his ghosts, about the empty meat he left behind. But now he was naked need, all the lusts wrapped up in a forever body.

He was in control, but he was caught between the sisters.

It would end now, they decided. The Monster was not forever. Everyone died. No matter how long it was put off, death must come.

Judi laid her insubstantial hands on the Monster's shoulders as he killed Anne, testing her ability to feed off him.

Then came the sunbursts from the deeps of the Monster's mind. The pressure of his prodigious weight of memory drove Judi near to madness. He had had to repudiate nine tenths of his past in order to remain sane, but he had not really forgotten anything. Thousands of years of dreams swept through Judi. Beautiful dreams, dangerous dreams,

altruistic dreams, depraved dreams, monomaniacal dreams.
Suddenly, she knew his true name, his original name. Even
he thought he had forgotten that.

She knew things she could not continue to live with, even
live this Phantom Zone version of life with. Death should
really be forever. And, as she wanted to die, she wanted her
sister to live.

She took her hands away from the Monster's shoulders and
put them into his skull. The ectoplasmic wisps sank easily
through his hair, into his brain. She made fists, and then
opened them, stretching her fingers as widely as she could.
Then, catching all the weight she had just taken on and adding
it to what little reality she had had, she hurled herself down the
funnels of her arms, through the bottlenecks of her wrists, and
into her solid hands.

The ghosts swarmed inside her, and were channeled
through her almost-real form. They slammed into Skinner
like ectoplasmic bullets, and exploded inside him.

Her legs, her body and her head became truly ghostly, but
her hands filled out like welder's gloves full of lead shot. She
had her bony hooks in the Monster's brain. He let Anne go
as she yanked him backwards. He was too tall, but she could
float off the floor as he stood up straight, flying from the
fixed points in his head like a girl-shaped flag. He grabbed
for his head, trying to force the fingertubes sticking out of
his forehead back into him.

Inside his head, she could feel a Hiroshima firestorm.
All that was his was leaking into her hands. It hurt
her.

There was a name. Ariadne. Who was Ariadne? An answer,
or just a sledge thrown into a fire? Under the circumstances,
Judi did not care.

He was ruptured. This, after everything, was the last
night of his life. Judi felt his incredulity for a moment . . .

. . . then something flooded into her wispy body with the
force of a hundred gallons of boiling lead squirting into an
inflatable sex doll. What was left of her flesh exploded, and

was spread throughout the Dream like the components of a new universe after a new big bang.

Just before her mind went out like a spent firework, for an eternal moment, Judi thought that *she* was the Monster now . . .

And then there was light.

nineteen

IN THEIR DREAM, Judi and Anne were Siamese twins, connected by the hind-parts of their brains. Each had a separate personality and a different face, but they shared an unconscious mind. Each loved her sister, although each could never really know what the other's face looked like. When they were born, they were holding hands, and they grew up to make their parents and friends proud. Judi became a famous actress and talk-show personality, noted especially for her Ibsen women; and Anne became a best-selling author of fairy tales and fables. A doctor once thought they could be separated, but Judi and Anne were happy just as they were. They never did die, and there were no such things as Monsters. The End.

twenty

H E FELL INTO her arms this time. His face was still young, but it might just as well have been drawn on a paper bag. He was senile. Anne could feel nearly naked bones inside his clothes. She heaved him away. It was as easy as tossing a bin-liner full of screwed-up envelopes over a table. Skinner bounced on the bar, and only just managed to stay standing up. He turned, looking for her. She wondered if he were blind.

'Anne,' he said, his face starting to curl around the edges, 'Angel . . .'

The fires were out, but the tawdry inferno lighting was still on. The Club Des Esseintes was pathetic again. An early Beatles track burbled tinnily on the p.a. 'Chains'.

He was not much of a Monster any more, but he was still coming to get her.

'Don't think I'm dead, dear. With your help, I can start all over again. Easy.'

He lurched forwards, a badly-made scarecrow with a rancid pumpkin head, and made it halfway across the floor. She backed away from him.

'I've been in worse shape than this. Plenty of times. It'll be you and me, Angel . . .'

'I've told you before, Skinner,' she said, *'that's not my name!'*

Her shout cut through the music, and struck him like a well-aimed blow. He reeled, and staggered forwards, arms out before him, hands hanging from his wrists like dead leaves.

The wall behind her was cold. The mural was flat and unmoving. There was a rack next to her. She flicked a glance

at it and saw a selection of leather whips and bludgeons.
S and M tools. Weapons.

The thing she reached for turned out to be a leather-
sheathed stick, jointed in the middle, about two feet long.
At one end was a contoured grip; at the other a cluster of short
tails. Their undersides were lined with sharp little hooks. It felt
heavy in her hands, and dangerous.

Putting her whole strength into the swing, she hit Skinner
across the face. It cracked open. The stick came out of her
hands and somersaulted away from them.

Skinner shrank, and she fell on him, shrieking, tearing at
his split face. The skin flaked under her clawing fingers
and came off like an onion skin. Beneath was an older,
greener mask. And beneath that, another, and another,
and another. Progressively older, progressively less human-
seeming, progressively deader. The layers were dry and
crinkly. He seemed to have no moisture in him at all.

Long before she exposed the curiously shaped skull, the
Monster was still. His ghosts had gone with Judi, and he was
dead.

Ding-dong, the witch is dead!

She spat on him now, and kicked his tenantless body. It
felt good. Skinner came apart like a man-sized breadstick.
She pulled off his arms and legs and twisted them like wet
towels. She trampled his ribs underfoot, squashing his internal
organs as they were exposed. Dust rose from the many rips
in his skin. With the stick, which she reclaimed, she thrashed
the whole mess until it was unidentifiable. His clothes tore as
easily as his desiccated flesh.

His pocket watch shone among the rotting fragments. She
picked it out, and gripped it in a painful fist. It was too large to
be contained completely by her hand. But it was real. Solid. It
ticked. Real seconds passed. The past ate up the future.

'That's forever, Skinner!'

Suddenly, she was tired. She had been awake around the
clock.

Dawn

———————

L ATER, but not much, Anne escaped from the Club Des Esseintes. All the doors were locked now, so she had to use a crowbar-like instrument of torture on them. There was no fire damage in the nostalgia shop. It had a secure-looking grille over its window and front door, so she had to force her way out of a side door.

She came out roughly where she expected to be, next to the already-open amusement arcade. No one bothered her. She binned the implement, and walked away.

There was a pale woman outside Patisserie Valerie, almost an albino. Anne could not help noticing her. She wore heavy dark glasses. She needed to tell someone, so she told the woman.

'Dead,' she said, 'it's dead.'

The woman nodded, a ripple running through her silk-white hair. She did not answer, but she leaned forwards and placed a cold kiss on Anne's cheek. It was like a mild electric shock.

The woman was walking away, slipping into the crowd. Anne dropped Skinner's watch into her coat pocket, and felt the cold.

There was a closed newspaper stall on the corner, with a poster of yesterday's *Evening Standard* headlines. AZIZ VERDICT RETURNED. POLICE CONSTABLE CHARGED. Anne felt waking life calling her back.

She looked around for the woman who was the last of the Dream, but she was gone.

It was nearly dawn now, and the streets were busy. Her breath frosted as she walked, and she felt all sorts of aches and bruises. She wanted to get home and take a bath, but she did not feel sleepy any more. She was wide-awake.

The pre-work traffic made crossing streets difficult. She did not feel ready for the underground yet, so she walked to the bus stop under Centre Point. It was just a building. The buses were already running, but there were none waiting. As she stood around, stamping her feet against the cold, the skies lightened and the streetlamps went out.